# WHITE ROSE, DARK SUMMER

ELEANOR FAIRBURN

# WHITE ROSE, DARK SUMMER

*Dublin, Ireland, 1449*

Sent to virtual exile in Ireland, Richard Plantagenet, Duke of York and his beautiful Duchess, Cecily Neville, remain loyal to their pious Lancastrian King Henry VI. Yet it is Henry's Queen, the passionate Margaret of Anjou, who makes an enemy of the House of York, stirring the animosity into an explosive confrontation: York vs Lancaster.

In this much-anticipated sequel to *The Rose in Spring*, Cecily Neville – matriarch of the House of York – remains at the heart of the conflict, as she fights to protect her children and for her family's rightful place: England's throne…

# White Rose, Dark Summer

BOOK 2: 1449-1461

ELEANOR FAIRBURN

First published in 1972 by Robert Hale, London

All rights reserved
© Eleanor Fairburn 1972

This paperback edition first published in 2022
by the Fairburn Estate

Produced by KB Conversions, Norwich, United Kingdom

Cover Illustration & Design copyright Patrick Knowles 2022

The right of Eleanor Fairburn to be identified as author of this work has been asserted in accordance with Section 77 of the Copyright, Designs and Patents act 1988 This e-book is copyright material and must not be copied, reproduced, transferred, leased, licensed or publicly performed or used in any way except as specifically permitted in writing by the publishers, as allowed under the terms and conditions under which it was purchased or as strictly permitted by applicable copyright law. Any unauthorised distribution or use of this text may be a direct infringement of the author's and publisher's rights, and those responsible may be liable in law accordingly.

ELEANOR Fairburn (1928 – 2015) was born in Westport, Co. Mayo, Ireland. She was educated at St. Louis Convent, Balla and went on to train in Fashion, Art and Design in Dublin. After moving to England, she supplemented her income by writing articles and stories for newspapers, as well as producing knitwear designs for Vogue and Harper's Bazaar.

She settled in North Yorkshire with her husband and daughter, and began her career as a novelist in earnest. Her first book, 'The Green Popinjays' was published in 1962, followed by her most successful book 'The White Seahorse' (1964) about the infamous pirate queen Grace O'Malley.

In all, she wrote 17 works of historical fiction as well as crime thrillers under various pseudonyms, including Emma Gayle, Catherine Carfax, Elena Lyons, and Anna Neville. Alongside her work as a novelist, she taught a writing course sponsored by the University of Leeds, and was also a founding member of the Middlesbrough Writers' Group.

After the death of her husband Brian in 2011, she moved to Norfolk to be closer to her daughter, Anne-Marie. Eleanor Fairburn died peacefully in Norwich on 2nd January, 2015 at the age of 86.

With sincere thanks to Mr A. Swann
Custodian of Middleham Castle,
for help during research in Wensleydale, Yorkshire

# 1

'La-a-and. Land to starboard…' The cry from the crow's nest floated down through summer morning mist to stir the press of armed men on the flagship's deck.

Excitement leapt like a flame in the high, cramped vessel as pennants were shaken out, blue and murrey liveries slapped free of creases, trumpets given a final polishing on leather sleeves. At the same time, all eyes were straining for a first glimpse of the Irish coast.

'There it is,' cried an old priest, 'the headland of Howth. That's the north tip of Dublin Bay. The bay curves in from there towards the city. I mind it well from fifty years back when I was here with King Richard—'

'Arms!' bawled the master-sergeants, and their commands could be heard echoing from vessel to vessel of the fleet strung out astern of the flagship – phantom hulks rearing up out of the sea mist that had eerily quilted the Isle of Man as they'd sailed past it on this voyage from Wales.

There was barely enough wind to fill sail canvas. The fleet glided towards Howth on a moon-coloured sea. But the east light was strengthening now. It picked out the crimson and gold of the ensign that flapped at the flagship's masthead: the Royal Ensign, as statement that the vessel was carrying the King of England's Lieutenant into Ireland this July morning of 1449.

Richard, Duke of York, came out onto the fo'castle deck with his young sons, the Earls of March and Rutland. Laying a muscular arm about their shoulders, he bent down to speak to them. The brown of his hair matched that of his younger son, Edmund, who was six, and strongly resembled him: stocky, broad-backed. But there was no physical likeness between the Duke and the heir of York – seven-year-old Edward, Earl of March, who was tall and gold fair. Friends of York maintained that March was a balanced mixture of Neville-Plantagenet, his parents' blood. Enemies were equally emphatic that he was a bastard, sired by a Captain of Archers in Normandy.

Patting both boys' shoulders with affection, the Duke strode to the fo'castle rail, pressed his hard soldier's hands against it and leaned forward to watch the ranks of his men forming below. He knew each one of them by name; many had served under him in France during his time as Governor there; or he'd fought alongside their fathers before that, in the turbulent days of Joan of Arc. Today, these men formed a picked force. Not numerous, but loyal, disciplined, sensitive to his command. The sight of them down there gave him hope of some success in Ireland.

For he *had* to succeed where so many had failed. He, Richard Plantagenet, had to enforce the King's law and collect the King's taxes more efficiently than any Lieutenant had ever done before in this ungovernable island, if only to prove his own loyalty to King Henry the Sixth – a loyalty that had always been in doubt because of his own royal blood. He was being sent here into virtual exile from the King's favour.

'God, let me not fail...' At thirty-eight years of age, his hard-won experience and authority demanded a man's success. For himself. For his children. For his beautiful wife, Cecily Neville.

He took his hands off the rail and stood upright as the great banner of York was broken out beneath the Royal Ensign. On a field of blue, the Falcon and Fetterlock gleamed silver around the five-petalled White Rose... Then he left the fo'castle and went below to join his officers and captains.

'We're coming into the north channel, Your Grace.'

'Aye. Good.' Richard could see the height of Howth clearly now but the rest of the coastline was still undefined except as a shadow hiding its city. For an instant, his confidence faltered before this alien land which he must subdue and govern in the name of a feeble King – a King who could not even be relied upon to reinforce him if the need arose. Hunching his short, powerful neck into his shoulders, he growled at a hovering squire who'd come with the Yorkshire levies:

'Hastings, see if Her Grace be near ready.'

With Cecily beside him he'd feel better at once – *cokke's bones, did she need to take so long attiring and ornamenting herself?* Yet he had to concede that he'd never known his wife be late for any public occasion.

The space below deck was a confusion of busy women-folk. Robust north-country servants moved purposefully in their grey kerseys and white linens. Fine-bred and fine-dressed damsels flitting like bright birds. Formidable matrons of wealth and title stalked about, supervising everyone.

Squire William Hastings, fourteen years old, stood

irresolutely amid the bustling throng. This all-female world unnerved him; his entire service – as page, and latterly as squire – had been passed in austere Middleham Castle in Wensleydale, Yorkshire, with the hard Neville Earls of Salisbury and of Warwick, father and son. True, there'd been plenty of women there but they never gave themselves such proprietary airs as the Duchess of York's entourage was flaunting at this moment.

'I crave your pardon—' He tried to stop a young lady dashing past but the whip of her skirts cut him off. 'I crave —' Now it was a bunch of keys in a plump female fist that silenced him. 'I—' Buffeted on every side he looked wildly around. 'Where can I find Her Grace?' he asked desperately of no one in particular.

'Up yonder, lad. I' the pavilion.' The old dame, who'd abruptly halted to tell him this, fairly drenched him with a bowl of water she was carrying.

'Thanks.' Dripping, he fought his way towards the circle of blue silk curtains which, he could now see, was the centre of all the to-ing and fro-ing. In there, Her Grace would have bathed and dressed and put on her jewels. Debating on how to penetrate the silken fortress, young Hastings recognised Mistress Fletcher, chief woman in waiting to the Duchess Cecily, as she emerged from it.

'Madame,' he panted, 'my lord wishes to know how soon Her Grace may be ready to join him above. We're nearly into Dublin Bay.'

Mistress Fletcher gave him a look of amused maternal tolerance, from cap askew to sodden hose, then said with the slight French accent which she still retained: 'You may ask Her Grace personally. Come.' And she held aside the blue silk for him to step into another world...

It was an enclosed world, white-lined like a shell. He felt the softness of rugs under his feet and smelt the single sharpness of herb essence. And there was an ordered serenity here – that total lack of fuss associated with a calm, central authority which contrasted utterly with the chaos outside the pavilion. Then he was looking into a polished mirror and meeting the clear blue eyes of Cecily Neville, Duchess of York. For an instant, her beauty struck him dumb; he'd never seen her at close quarters before.

'Yes?' she said – her fine eyebrows lifting as she caught sigh of his untidiness behind her in the mirror. Mortified, he felt she'd have turned on him in outrage had not her servants been arranging her high, V-rolled headdress for her at that moment. Instead, she remained marble-still while the point of the V was rested on her smooth forehead, covering the parting in her thick fair hair.

William Hastings pitched forward onto his knees and stammered his lord's message. At the same time, he was aware of the long slim line of the Duchess's legs, sculpted by her gown; and of an intense excitement he'd felt several times within himself these past few months (especially when he looked at young Katherine Neville of Middleham Castle) but never so sharply defined as now. In this instant, he knew himself a lover of all beautiful women.

'I shall be up directly,' the Duchess was saying, unhurried. She was critical of her own reflection in the mirror as her attendants arranged a gold crespin from the headdress point, to flow forward across shoulder and throat. Then she stood up, a tall regal woman. And the still-kneeling squire, gazing at her in awe, saw how the fitted, black-laced gown accentuated the curve of her six-month pregnancy.

That the next child of York would be born in Dublin, in October, was common knowledge.

WITHIN CLEAR SIGHT OF LAND, Richard ordered the third of the great banners he'd brought with him to be unfurled.

The scarlet silk tossed out its folds, displaying the Black Lion and the Dragon of Ulster: those badges he had of Elisabeth de Burgho, his great-grandmother, from whom the March and Mortimer inheritances had come to him (and, thereby, his unmade claim to England's throne). He wanted the Irish to note these cognisances: a reminder that the new Lieutenant was Earl of Ulster might make them more biddable to English rule than they'd been these fifty years past. It was just fifty years since King Richard the Second had hurried home from Dublin to find his crown usurped by Henry of Lancaster and his own tomb awaiting him. Henry – anointed as the Fourth of his name – had immediately become too occupied holding his position in England to bother much about the western island. And, since then, the French wars had caused Ireland to be neglected almost entirely. With money and troops scarce, and colonists slipping away whenever they had the chance, territories had shrunk until only in the eastern province of Leinster now did the King's writ run. Richard must bring the north to obedience so that the south might follow and eventually – if it could be reached with troops – the west, where he also had hereditary lands: he was lord of Connaught.

The stony height of Howth was growing clearer. He visualised the crowds who'd be gathered there; flags waving; trumpets and ceremonial armour glinting. None of these people would be native Irish, he knew. Except for the inevitable spies of the chieftains, they'd all be classed as English born – colonists, or descendants of the old Norman-Welsh invaders – because the real Irish lived tribally outside the King's 'land of peace', known as the Pale, and were allowed no part in Crown-loyal government.

With these natives Richard intended to talk (or to fight, if they preferred it that way) in order to bring them all to allegiance to King Henry, and to make them pay the taxes on which his own administration would depend. But let the spies first note the mighty banner of Ulster and report upon it to their chieftains. That way, not as strangers would he and Cecily be received in this land but as Earl and Countess of the old northern province.

Turning, he saw his wife come towards him with their two small daughters, Elisabeth and Margaret. The girls were five and three years of age respectively but Margaret looked the older because of her strong, handsome face which favoured her maternal granddame, the Countess Joan Beaufort. Two male babies had been born, after Margaret, to himself and Cecily but both had died. And they had another, eldest daughter, Anne, now ten, who'd been betrothed last year to young Henry Holland, Exeter's heir, and had been left behind to grow accustomed to her new family state. Anne hadn't wept nor shown the least emotion at parting from her parents. And Richard knew that Cecily worried sorely about this strange, hard firstborn of theirs who would be Duchess of Exeter one day. Watching his wife approach regally through the ranks of the men-at-arms, Richard marvelled how neither private sorrows nor worries ever scarred Cecily's public face. At thirty-four, she was lovelier than she'd ever been.

He held out an arm for the familiar comfort of this strong, proud woman's presence. His hand tightened on hers within the rich folds of her trailing sleeves. On her fingers he could feel the jewels which matched those on her gown and about her throat; those flashing gems of York and Neville that had all been in pawn at one time or another to pay troops in the King's service. People always trusted the House of York to pay not only its own debts but the King's. With gentle irony, Richard Plantagenet smiled as the majestic height of Howth came suddenly clear in the morning light and a decorated barge pulled out from the shore.

'Here comes the Irish Sword of State,' he muttered to his wife. 'I wonder how heavy it will lay upon me?'

CECILY WAS glad there was no wind to buffet her high headdress. But she'd thought it wise to have the train of her gown looped up – the great hanging oversleeves, furred and gem-encrusted and embroidered, would be hazard enough while disembarking.

As they waited for the barge to come within hailing distance, she remarked to Richard: 'How quiet it is...' leaving the inner thought unspoken: *how little like Calais or Harfleur in the old days*. One hadn't to recall those times when the Duke of York had been Governor of Normandy. They were gone. Just as surely as the King's French empire was gone; disintegrated; lost by incompetent men. She knew enough of Richard's bitterness on this subject not to remind him of it. He'd given years of his life and a royal ransom of his own revenues to save Normandy. But the Dukes of Suffolk and of Somerset had now lost all of France for England except Guienne, Calais and the city of Rouen. It was gall to a soldier like York to have had to stand aside for four humiliating years and watch the conquests of Henry the Fifth fall back into Valois hands. In the end, he'd been almost happy setting out on this Irish assignment, leaving unquiet England and lost France behind him.

'It's only the mist that silences everything,' he told her.

'Once we're ashore there'll be clamour enough even for our sons' tastes!'

'Oh, I expect there will be.' Laughing, she glanced over to where the young Earls of March and Rutland were running about among the members of their father's guard. They were both wearing very short côte-hardies that displayed their sturdy thighs above turn-over knee boots, and they each had a new hunting knife proudly thrust through the leather loops of their gipsires, and new metal-plated belts with all manner of gadgets dangling from them. Looking at these two robust sons, their mother could almost forget the three who had died in infancy. But she had determined to think not at all about the child she was carrying – not to make any plans nor even formulate a name for the unborn. So many dreams had shattered on the tombs of little William and John – as on that of Henry at Hatfield nine years ago.

She concentrated instead on the nearing coastline and tried to remember all that she and Richard had learnt about Ireland in the nineteen months since his appointment. Conditions here were far more complex than they'd been in France and she doubted if she'd ever have more than a surface grasp of them – certainly never the instinctive understanding which Richard seemed to have. But the main thing to be borne in mind, it appeared, was that there were three distinct classes of people on this island. There were natives, who spoke and dressed in the Irish manner and lived in tribes under the chieftains as they'd done since the dawn of time. There were the 'old English', descended from the Norman-Welsh conquerors of near three hundred years ago. And there were the English, the modern administrators of the Pale. There was no difficulty, it seemed in recognising the first and the third classes: they were hostile opposites in all things. It was the class in between – a sort of middle nation – that was the shifting puzzle. The 'old English' were powerful, wealthy, cultured and proud of their ancient Earldoms; but they were moving closer to the real Irish, despite laws forbidding intermarriage and fosterage, and further from the English King with every generation. They were 'loyal rebels' demanding independence for the land of their adoption. They were the Butler and the Geraldine Earls: Ormonde, Desmonde, Kildare…

Ormonde – James Butler, the fourth and often called 'the White' Earl – was an old friend of the Yorks. They'd known him in Rouen; a witty, much-travelled man whose compassionate intelligence had once altered the course of Cecily's life. It was he who had warned her about her obviously growing affection for Captain John Blaeburn; and who had stayed by her side during the terrible days after she'd sent the Captain away and learned of his death. Gossip had then promptly made Ormonde her lover ('the White Rose for the White Earl' was a tavern toast for a while) but Richard's trust in him had silenced the tongues eventually.

Cecily recognised Ormonde now, standing erect in the approaching barge; the magnificent figure almost as imposing as ever, though aged and a little shrunk. Deliberately, she looked away from him, cutting off the associated memory of that other man to whom death had denied old age…

With Ormonde was the Baron Devlin – whom last year Richard had appointed as Lieutenant's Deputy – carrying the Sword of State; and flanking the Baron and the White Earl were two other men, their badges proudly displayed. These were the badges of the House of Fitzgerald in its two mighty branches of Kildare and Desmond. Desmond was a young and handsome man, black haired, fair skinned. He had alert blue-grey eyes which fastened on Cecily in undisguised appraisal, as though he had to give an exact account of her to all his absent friends.

'We bid Your Graces welcome to Ireland,' Ormonde called as the barge came alongside and the Sword of State was handed up to Richard.

Sunshine was pricking the last of the mist with silver as the barge turned to escort the flagship into Howth harbour.

## 2

A vast throng of officials and their wives, backed by ranks of armed men, crowded the northern shoreline of Dublin Bay. As Richard helped Cecily to disembark, and the trumpets sounded, everyone bowed low. Then, immediately, the full battery of eyes was upon them both as they walked forward onto Irish soil to be met by the Archbishop and the Lord Provost of Dublin.

After taking refreshment with the St Lawrence family in their Castle of Howth, the Yorks with the Earl of Ormonde led the long processional ride into the city, keeping close to the curving shore of the Bay.

Mist had vanished now and the water sparkled silver on blue. Inland, there was a profusion of wild flowers and trees in heavy leaf. It was a very fair country, rich and spacious; and Cecily's heart lifted with a lark overhead. Everyone seemed so genuinely *glad* to have Richard and herself and the children here…

As they passed through Clontarf, Ormonde held the boys spellbound with the story of Brian Boru's victory over the Danes there in 1014. They knew, of course, that their father was descended from this Irish King by the Ulster connections of his lineage; but seeing the battle plain where a country's enemies had been vanquished and a royal life lost, excited them as no mere lesson in pedigrees had ever done.

'Your sons are becoming more Irish every minute,' Ormond smiled, resuming his place between Cecily and Richard. Then he went on to talk of the city whose distant towers showed behind the inner curve of the Bay. 'Dublin is said to have been founded by the Danes on an old Irish settlement, and called by them "the town of the hurdle ford on the black water". True enough, the soil there is still oozy after rain—'

'Is the Castle damp?' Cecily asked sharply, thinking of her children and the unborn infant.

'Only the dungeons near the River Liffey.'

'Oh...' She should have become used to the presence of prisoners in Rouen's Bouvreuil Keep but she'd never done so. Loss of freedom and light had always been to her the greatest human tragedy, the ultimate cruelty. She turned to Richard: 'Dickon, you won't use the dungeons more than can be helped while we live in Dublin Castle?'

He gave her a curious smile. 'My love,' he replied, 'I've already made plans for any prisoners I may have to take. Those plans don't include use of the dungeons. Nor of the execution block either, come to that. So rest easy.'

'I shall certainly not rest until I know what you have in mind.'

'Very well then. I intend to treat all prisoners as guests. They will stay with us, comfortably, until they see reason and sign the necessary treaties. No Irish chieftain will be shorn of his dignity by me.'

She looked in astonishment from her husband's face to that of Ormonde and saw where the revolutionary idea had been borne. Ormonde knew the native Irish. Generations of his ancestors had known how to bind Irish loyalties to the House of Butler. Now the ageing Earl was passing on this knowledge to Richard Plantagenet for a reason which, she sensed, was beyond friendship; beyond a simple desire for present peace. An old unease edged back into her mind and stayed with her until Kilmainham Priory was reached...

There, aldermen and justices and churchmen swelled the procession. Then the heralds rode to the city's north gate and proclaimed the Viceroy's arrival to the crowds within.

Cecily had never taken part in such a tumultuous entry. By comparison, Rouen's welcome to Queen Margaret four years earlier had been a restrained affair. The mighty bells of Christ Church and St Patrick's Cathedral boomed among what sounded like hundreds and hundreds of other bells. People near the edges of the thronged thoroughfares shouted their comments, above the general uproar, to those behind who could not see:

'The White Earl is coming.'

'God bless Ormonde – God bless Ormonde!' Was the many-throated response from the rear.

Then: 'His Grace our Archbishop follows.'

Ah—' roared the crowd with one voice '—hell roast all Talbots.' The Archbishop's warrior-brother, John, Earl of Shrewsbury, had not been a popular Lieutenant here, especially during his last term which had ended two years ago, by which time the Talbot's persecution of Ormonde had rubbed many feelings raw. Though Ormonde himself seemed to have forgotten the whole business and had lately married his daughter Elisabeth to Shrewsbury's son.

'*Now here come Their Graces of York!*'

The volume of cheering increased deafeningly. There

was a forward urge of the crowd. The escorting men-at-arms tried to keep the way clear but Cecily and Richard's mounts were soon pressed flank to flank, with enthusiastic citizens hanging onto their trappings.

People who hadn't been able to get close enough wanted to know: 'How do they look? Tell us how they look—'

'The Duke is a fine man. Very broad and strong. He rides like a soldier.'

'But his lady? Tell us of the White Rose Duchess.'

Cecily hid a smile behind her draped crespin. It was extraordinary how widely known that little badge of Richard's had become, the simple five-petalled White Rose. And yet its recognition always surprised and pleased her.

Suddenly a giant of a man grabbed the snaffle-ring of her horse, almost halting the animal. The man looked up earnestly into her face. Then—

'She's beautiful,' he announced to the crowd in a bellow. 'She's gold fair and—' his eye travelled the length of her body '—tall and—' The eye came back to the pregnant curve of her gown front and he immediately swept everyone out of the way with a scything motion of the arms. 'She carries a child into this city,' he concluded, backing away.

Now a wave of mass emotion engulfed herself and Richard, and their two sons who'd managed to catch up with them again. Cecily had never expected a welcome like this, even though Ormonde had told her how the news of Richard's appointment had been delightedly received in Dublin: 'You understand, he's the first royal Duke to be Viceroy within anyone's memory, and certainly the first heir to the throne. It gives Ireland a vast new importance after years of being ignored on almost all accounts.'

She looked ahead now, past the ranks of the clergy

forming the Archbishop's retinue. The way was sloping down towards the river which divided the city into north and south. Across a bridge, the way sloped up again, and she could see the towers of a mighty castle rising above the roofs of houses and churches.

On the bridge – whose northern end was commanded by the Dominican monastery of St Saviour on King's Inn Quay – the stench of the river was overpowering. Its level had dropped with the ebbing tide so that seaweed and black mud was exposed on either bank; and the remaining water, forming only a channel in the centre, stank of sewage over which gulls screamed and quarrelled… Fighting a sudden attack of nausea, Cecily kept her head lowered and her gaze fixed on the timbers which her mount cautiously trod. She forced her mind to think of matters other than the present until the wave of pregnancy sickness would pass. And a vision came to her of another bridge, that over the Tees at Winston on the Yorkshire-Durham border… For all that her father had left money in his Will for the completion of that structure, it had not yet been finalised in stone: the river kept sweeping it away despite all labours, and the careful legality of dead men's wishes. Last time she'd inquired about it, she'd been told that it was still as temporary a wooden erection as on her betrothal eve, 22 and a half years previously…

The booming of a mighty bell from the south shore announced that Christ Church cathedral awaited the Viceroy. Before its High Altar, he would be formally presented with the Irish State Sword, and would take his oath as Lieutenant of King Henry the Sixth.

THE GREAT HALL of Dublin Castle was very large, and no pains had been spared to hide its shabbiness and neglect from the new occupants and their banquet guests. The smell of beeswax, fresh rushes and herbs overlay the stench of old damp-fungus, incarcerated men and rat droppings. Tapestries hid areas of running wetness on the riverside walls. And the carved panelling put up behind the dais for King Richard had had its rottenness mended with plaster under the new gilt paint.

Keeping her gaze determinedly fixed on the still-lovely windows, Cecily moved towards the dais to receive the civic dignitaries who were trooping in, with their wives dressed in fashions of a generation ago: immensely wide, rail-veiled head-dresses, and gowns tucked up at the front to show their kirtles. She realised how revolutionary her own high, narrow headdress must look here; and her plain fitted bodice, cascading into a depth of folds below the hip with never a trace of kirtle showing anywhere, must be foreign indeed. Ah well, the seamstresses of Dublin would soon profit from her introduction of a new fashion!

Near the dais, she paused in astonishment. It was impossible not to notice the incongruous presence of a huge cannon. 'What on earth is it doing here?' she asked the Earl of Ormonde.

The White Earl replied smiling: 'King Richard left it, with instructions for its shipping back to the Tower. But no one has ever decided whose property it is since his death.' He put his head on one side and regarded the gun thoughtfully, then added: 'Now, however, His Grace of York may lawfully claim it for he carries the inheritance of King Richard's heir.'

'I doubt he wants a fifty-year-old cannon,' Cecily said obliquely as she stepped up onto the dais. She knew quite well that Ormonde's meaning ran much deeper than appeared – a swift, dark river of meaning that struck fear to her heart.

The procession of people bowing before the chairs of herself and Richard seemed interminable after a while. Tired, though not admitting it by one muscle-quiver, she adopted a practised rhythm of nods and smiles to coincide with each new face, and then retired into her own thoughts.

They were still entirely centred in England, where civil strife had been breaking out everywhere before they left, and going unchecked by a heedless government. Suffolk, the leader of that government, was too powerful to be dislodged. He now held every key office in the realm, he was immensely wealthy; and, with the feeble King under his thumb and Queen Margaret approving everything he did, he could ignore the rage of a people oppressed by his exactions – he had debased the coinage, flouted Customs' laws, terrorised his own tenants – all in the interests of personal money-making which was, increasingly, his obsession. He seemed indifferent to the hatred he had sparked. The blame for all manner of disasters was being stored up to his name. For bringing an impoverished, haughty Queen to England. For causing Humphrey of Gloucester's death. And – most bitter accusation of all – for giving away Maine and Anjou.

Yet it was Beaufort, the present Governor of Normandy, whose bad faith and bad leadership were responsible for new troubles in France. Edmund Beaufort, Duke of Somerset, had failed to maintain the vital truce so that the Valois King Charles of France had declared the war open again.

God alone knew where it would all end. Another war had broken out with Scotland, which meant that good men like Cecily's brother of Salisbury were too occupied in the north to attend to anything else. Salisbury had told herself and Richard, when they'd last visited him at Middleham, to collect the men he was loaning them for Ireland: 'There's no justice at Westminster any more. North-country men ceased bringing their lawsuits south long ago. Now they come to Percy or myself for redress – or else they settle their disputes with Carlisle axes! Increasingly the latter since this new trouble with the Scots. And you know that widespread disturbances in the realm have always begun in the north. I tell you, I'm uneasy. Especially about your leaving for Ireland, York—'

'I daren't delay any longer. But I'll see the King once more before I go.'

'Much good it'll do you, brother-in-law! Henry has no power; no *will*, even, to govern. Suffolk is the real king. And he holds the Queen…' On which dark note, they'd all gone to their apartments inside the mighty walls of Middleham Castle. Next morning, Salisbury had ridden off to the Marches, taking his growing sons with him and an escort of Dacres, Scropes and FitzHughs, while Cecily and Richard went south to Nottingham where the King then was.

At Nottingham, Richard had made a final attempt to demonstrate to Henry the chaos of his realm. But Henry had merely said helplessly, while looking down at the quaint, round-toed shoes he always wore:

'Forsooth, dear cousin of York, I am sure the Queen and Duke William are doing their best to right injustice and keep order. Now, I pray you, hasten to Ireland and perform as good service there…'

Reporting this dismissal to his wife, Richard had said broodingly:

'Henry is a pious man. There is no evil in him. But I fear he's lost the confidence of the people. They've always preferred soldier kings to monkish kings – they feel more secure under a good general, even though he demands their lifeblood.'

'Well,' Cecily had replied, 'it looks as though they'll have to endure a saint for a long while yet: Henry is only twenty-seven.'

'I know. And I, his heir, ten years older and much worn... Ah, I think it unlikely I shall ever wear the Crown of England, Cis. Which is a pity—' smiling, he'd kissed her '—for you'd make a more popular Queen than Margaret.'

'A more sensible one, in any case. I wouldn't involve myself with factions—'

'*Wouldn't* you? Ho, I think we'd have an all-Neville government if you had your way, pet. First, you'd bring your brother Robert down from the Rock of Durham to Canterbury. Then you'd pack the Court with red-headed nephews from Middleham—'

'They're *not* redheaded. They're all deep auburn. Except George, who's nondescript...' She was aware of changing the subject. But even jokes about Richard's nearness to the throne filled her with an indefinable unease. It was danger, she sensed, both to him and to their sons.

Yet his position had never been formally recognised; and, of late, Edmund Beaufort had challenged even the latent claim. Edmund contended that, when the original Beauforts had been declared legitimate by King Richard, they had been admitted to 'all honours and dignities' by the document which the King had signed. It was only a cautious and insecure Henry the Fourth who had inserted the clause, ten years later, '*except to the royal dignity*'. Without that fatal clause (which the present King could easily be persuaded to remove) the surviving son of the eldest Beaufort was nearest in blood to the throne – although King

Henry's Tudor half-brothers were closest personal kin to the reigning monarch.

Thought of the Tudor boys absorbed Cecily during the next three presentations of Dublin wives... She'd seen these young half-brothers of the King a few times – always in attendance upon Queen Margaret. The elder one, Edmund, Earl of Richmond, was very like his royal mother, the late Catherine de Valois: fine-boned and fragile looking, with blue-veined skin. But he lacked her lovely length of neck. Like King Henry, he was rather round-shouldered and he often hunched himself up still further in the coughing bouts to which he was prone. Poor boy, he seemed very delicate. Though marriage might make him more robust: he'd recently betrothed the late John Beaufort's heiress, Margaret, whom Suffolk had taken in ward after her father's death. Strange that Suffolk hadn't grabbed her marriage and inheritance for his own son, John de la Pole. But probably the King had insisted on his half-brother's getting the heiress. Henry could be obstinate when he chose.

The younger Tudor brother, Jasper, Earl of Pembroke, was stocky and fresh complexioned. Taking after his father, people who'd known Owen Tudor said. No one was certain what had become of that amorous Welshman since his release from Newgate gaol, where he'd been held on a charge of treason after Queen Catherine's death because he'd wedded (or at least bedded) the royal widow without anyone's approval but the lady's own—

Cecily smiled at the last plump Dublin matron to curtsey before her. Then she and Richard gratefully withdrew to their private apartments for a short rest before the banquet.

By the time that meal was over, it would be a marathon day, and Richard was anxious about his wife. But he consoled himself with the recollection that Cecily had always taken everything in her stride – outwardly, at least: for when she reached the dregs of her energy, the devil's staying-power of the Neville's took over! He sometimes wondered how their children would be in maturity: Plantagenet-Nevilles, an unknown breed.

## 3

The new Viceroy began his reign with decisive action. By mid-July he had summoned the Archbishop of Armagh and many other loyal English lords and clerics to attend him with fighting-men and provisions. By early August he was riding northward at the head of a considerable force.

Watching him go – an imposing figure in full travelling armour, and with all his great banners carried before him – Cecily tenderly remembered the young officer who had stumbled from the rout of Orléans; the harassed young Constable of England who had policed Paris during the Coronation; the young Governor who had taken over from mighty Bedford... Then she recalled the maturing ruler of Normandy; and the man who'd come home to fight for justice in an England that had wasted his talents for four years... What had now emerged, like ripe fruit from all these seasons of living, was a complete commander: firm, confident, purposeful, with no need of bluster or display. His orders were quiet and concise: they were obeyed. His claim to authority was deep: it was respected.

*Ah, Dickon,* she thought as the last supply wagon trundled out of sight, *if King Henry were only more like you, there would be order and justice in England.* Then she took the children to Christ Church, to pray for their father's success with the Irish chieftains.

The boys were far too excited from the morning's doings to be able to kneel quietly in the old Danish cathedral so, after a while, she gave them leave to go and look at Strongbow's tomb – access to which was always open from the nave because it was upon the tomb that Church tenants paid their rents. This last resting-place of one of the original Norman-Welsh invaders had fascinated Edward and Edmund from the start, and they'd plied the Earl of Ormonde with questions about its occupant: why was he nicknamed 'Strongbow'? – what part of Wales had he come from? – had he been kin to the other invaders, the Carews, FitzGeralds, FitzMaurices, FitzHenrys, Fitz-Stephens? – already the boys were well versed in 'old English' genealogies. Ormonde had had to spend an entire hour telling them the whole 300-year-old story, which began:

'One upon a time, when William Rufus was King of England, a beautiful golden-haired Welsh princess named Nesta married one Sir Gerald de Windsor, Captain of Pembroke Castle…'

Cecily had lost track of the tale after a while – it was very complicated although this hadn't seemed to worry her listening sons and their sister Elisabeth – but she'd been aware throughout of Ormonde's thoughtful gaze upon herself as he'd traced the descendants (who'd been Strongbow's companions-in-arms) of the Princess Nesta, '… a golden woman whom many men loved.'

'Are you implying, my lord,' Cecily had asked quietly, 'that this one woman started a war?'

'No, Your Grace. It was her sons and her kinsfolk who did that. But hers was the metal which bound them…'

Now, keeping her small daughters kneeling beside her while the boys examined the tomb, Cecily struggled on with her prayers; seeing again, before the massive High Altar, the husband for whom she implored God's help receiving the Irish State Sword and being clothed with the ermine-trimmed mantle which proclaimed his office. How majestic he'd looked, this mature, solid lord of many titles! A beauty transcending his plain-faced soldier's exterior had shone around him; and the crowds packing this splendid richly-dark cathedral, with its huge nave and choir and transept, had shouted 'York – York – God bless the White Rose!' as he'd left for the adjoining Commons' Hall. That day and ever since, Cecily's heart had been filled with joyous pride. And it seemed to her today, despite her bleak feeling after Richard's departure, that the High Altar of Christ Church kept a kind of glory, as from a coronation witnessed there—

Her unborn child, lively these several weeks, moved convulsively. She was already bigger with it than she'd been at full term with the last two babies, who'd lain small and quiet. Maybe this one would be healthy and would live. But she hadn't included it in her prayers.

As the month of August blazed on, Richard's letters provided a diary of his progress – wedged in between loving greetings to himself and the children, and descriptions of the places on the northward march from Dublin: Swords, Balbriggan, Drogheda—

*'August 22$^{nd}$, from the city of Drogheda… We have been a week now in this strong town. At first, only the lesser chieftains came in to*

*swear their oaths of fealty to King Henry. But today I received the MacGuiness, the MacMahon, the MacQuillan and both the O'Reillys. Between them they brought near 3,000 men, horse and foot. I now await the submission of the O'Neill. He may come without trouble, if only because he recognised my title to the Earldom of Ulster years ago, and I hear he is a man of his word; but if he does not come, I must march upon him through Dundalk and Armagh; for there must be no lack of decision apparent in my progress.'*

Cecily waited a tense week for the next letter. When it came, she was relieved to see that it was still headed 'Drogheda'.

*'Henry O'Neill came in today. He is son and heir of Eoghan O'Neill, the Captain of his Nation, and he has full power to treat with me for his father, his brothers, and all their subjects. He has undertaken to restore the de Burgho lands, to pay the taxes anciently due to the Earl of Ulster, and to provide me with 1,000 men. This as well as keeping peace in the north at his own expense. For my part, I have sworn to protect all the O'Neills and to cause justice to be done them in the event of any injury to their person, property or lieges. I think we are both well pleased with this agreement. It was solemnly made on the Gospels, and on a certain golden cross here containing a portion of the Holy Wood.'*

A postscript to this letter stated triumphantly:

*'The O'Neill's example has now been followed by a number of the O'Hanlons, and also the Berminghams of Carbury. I have drawn up formal indentures with them all and heard their loyal oath to King Henry. But if any more chieftains bring me tributes of cattle, I will need a separate army of drovers for my return to Dublin.'*

Laughing, Cecily read the letter over again before sharing its contents with her household. Then she went to the Castle chapel to give thanks.

The news of such success was overwhelming. No bloodshed. No prisoners. Just dignified agreements between chieftains and a Viceroy whom they accepted unconditionally because he was Earl of Ulster. It was almost a miracle in this land that had so fiercely resisted other royal lieutenants.

Yet she knew that the greatest test of Richard's strength lay south of Dublin, where the ferocious O'Byrnes held the Wicklow mountains, and Donal MacMurrough Kavanagh signed himself 'Rex Lagenie'... Richard had no hereditary title in the south except the weak lordship of Cork. The terrain was difficult. And he now had a very mixed force of English and Irishmen to wed into one army.

That army – including the tribute cattle – passed through Dublin on September 5$^{th}$. It was as orderly as the Governor's Guard in Rouen had been, and it drew not one complaint of outrage or pillage from the admiring citizens. It was a model army under a general who now inspired awe.

The few minutes she could spare from admiring her husband, Cecily spent in looking at the Irish levies. She'd never seen tribal fighting-men before, and their physical magnificence excited her admiration. Lightly clad in short-sleeved tunics that barely reached their knees, they looked like tough Roman soldiers; bronzed, muscular and indefatigable. They laughed and sang far more than their English counterparts did. And, instead of entrusting their belongings to the sumpter-wagons, they carried them rolled up in the rough cloaks that were pinned to their tunic-shoulders with barbaric-looking ornaments. Their leather belts held knives and darts. And they wore only thonged sandals on their feet.

The babble of an incomprehensible language reached her as they passed: it was the first time she'd heard Irish spoken.

Richard was anxious to complete his campaign before autumn rains and storms turned the deep valleys of the

Wicklow mountains into death traps; so he spent only one night in Dublin Castle while his troops bivouacked along the south shore of the Bay. At dawn he was armed and mounted again.

With a blurred vision of her own parents long ago at Raby, Cecily handed him up his stirrup-cup and remembered, nostalgically, the mazer they used to call Bulmer... Bulmer had been taken to Middleham Castle after her mother's death.

'Don't look so sad, love,' Richard murmured, handing the emptied cup back to her. 'I'll be home before the infant is born.'

She smiled and nodded, though she didn't believe that he could be home in time: her delivery was due the third week in October...

Yet, again, the miracle of success attended York's progress. After only a rattling of swords in Wicklow, the O'Byrne submitted – swearing to become a loyal follower of King Henry, to pay tribute, to give up the wreck of the sea which he was accustomed to keeping. Further, he promised to learn English, with his children and all his retainers; and to have English clothing worn in his household. As earnest of his goodwill, he sent Cecily a pair of hunting hawks.

O'Byrne's peaceable submission brought in other Irish leaders of the south-east and, finally, the great MacMurrough himself – he who had never bowed the knee to anyone in his bellicose life, he came to Richard; greeted him gravely, in Latin, as 'Earl of Ulster and lord of Trim, Leix and Cork and Connaught'; and announced his willingness to treat 'with this Viceroy but with no other.'

At Kiltimon, in Wicklow, the indentures were drawn up and signed on September 21$^{st}$. By Michaelmas, Richard was back in Dublin, where he called a meeting of the

Great Council for October 17th. There was a mass of legislation to be attended to, and the administrative work would occupy him all winter.

He was pleased, but not intoxicated, by his success so far. He knew that there were vast tracts of country yet to be penetrated – hundreds and hundreds of chieftains to be persuaded to an oath of fealty, and then kept to their promises. Promises were easily broken – especially if the Viceroy ran short of the money necessary to maintain a show of strength and royal backing.

No money had come from England so far for this first quarter; no viceregal salary, and no troop wages. The old Normandy problems were rearing their heads again.

Richard wrote to King Henry, asking permission to sell or mortgage part of his own lands held in chief of the Crown, so that he could meet the expenses of his office. But he kept this letter secret from Cecily: there was no point in worrying her when her confinement was almost due.

It was an old wives' tale, Cecily reflected bitterly between pains, that labour became easier with each child. This was her ninth confinement, and the longest and most difficult. It seemed that the infant fought against being born.

'Her Grace will grow weak from exhaustion,' one of the women whispered. 'A whole night and a day now.'

'Aye. An awkward child. Big, too, and laid crosswise, God preserve us; only Mistress Fletcher saw to that in time—'

'Will you be silent?' Anne Fletcher hissed, pushing them away from the bed. She was exasperated by the press of women in the rooms of the Duchess's suite, and by the air which grew staler every hour behind the sealed windows. But there was nothing she could do to alter the traditions of noble birth: every woman in the Duchess's entourage had the right to be present, and all fresh air had to be excluded from the fire-heated rooms. Sighing, she bent over Cecily: 'Is my lady well?'

'Drowning in her own sweat,' Cecily said through her teeth. 'How long more before this lazy infant comes into the world?'

The Frenchwoman drew back the sheet that covered her mistress's nakedness and looked attentively for the signs. 'Not long now, Your Grace,' she said with relief – motioning to those attendants who stood with towels and bowls.

'Not long...' Cecily felt she'd been hearing that same meaningless phrase for hours, while the familiar enemy of the pains crushed her swollen body until she could hardly breathe.

How stupid, once, to have felt sorry for a little girl in a novice's dress and veil... Such a long time ago. One snowy morning at Raby Castle—

She tried to grasp the sensation of snow, to pack it against her fevered skin, but all she could feel was the fire's heat.

There had always been a winter fire in her mother's apartment at Raby. Never had it burned with such clear, crackling brightness as on that February morning when Cecily had run into the room to put on her betrothal gown. Yet a little corner of her joyous mind had remained, pityingly, back in her own cold bedchamber. For there her sister Jane, who was to be a nun, was still kneeling in prayer. *Poor Jane, poor Jane,* she'd thought; never to wed; never to have babies.

'Jane chose the better part,' she groaned now, aloud, as

the pains came like anvil blows. Yet she knew she'd alter that opinion the very next time she saw her husband and her children...

The infant was born late that evening, October 21$^{st}$. He was a healthy, fair-haired boy. Every bell in the city rang for him and, before he was twelve hours old, the Great Hall of Dublin Castle was heaped with gifts of all descriptions for him – including such unlikely offerings as weapons, horse-gear and a litter of wolf-hound puppies; these latter from the black-haired Earl of Desmond whose city house was near the Castle, and who was as frequent a visitor as was Ormonde and Kildare.

'This baby is going to be spoilt, I know it!' Cecily said – realising that she herself would be more like to coddle him than anyone else, for terror that he join his dead infant brothers. Already little Margaret, his nearest in age, was taking an intense interest in him, while the less forward Elisabeth and Edmund worshipped from afar.

It was only Edward, the York heir, who remained uncharacteristically aloof from all the rejoicings. Normally he was the foremost to whoop and revel in whatever was going on, and he was the most outwardly affectionate of all the York children. But this event seemed to have put his handsome nose out of joint.

Understanding that jealousy was probably at the root of her eldest son's withdrawal, Cecily called him to her bedside and assured him of her unwavering love. Whereupon he flung his uncomfortably powerful young arms around her neck and vowed to marry '... a lady just like you, *Maman*.' He hadn't called her *maman* since they'd left France, and she was surprised that he remembered.

'What kind of lady will that be, my son?'

'Fair. Like the Queen in the Mortimer tapestry.'

'Oh, I see...' She'd always thought the woven figure in

this old tapestry bequeathed by Richard's uncle rather supercilious in expression. But maybe she herself looked like that during the strain of public occasions – certainly she had the reputation of being able to quell familiarity at a glance! '... Well, never mind about your future wife just now, Edward,' she said, hugging him. 'Your father and I would like you to choose a name for your new little brother. Because you're the heir of York and will need to guide him in many matters later on. Therefore it is right he should bear a name you approve.'

Pride and confidence surged back into the summer-blue eyes of the boy. His mouth smiled its most winning and gracious smile, lighting up his whole handsome face in its frame of yellow hair.

'*George*,' Edward shouted then.

'George?' Cecily feigned surprise. Actually, she knew that Richard had put it into his head after they themselves had decided on the name (a kind of exiles' gesture, they'd laughingly admitted to one another, to christen their new son after the patron saint of England). 'Oh, well, George it is then, Edward. And you shall accompany him to Christ Church for his christening and shall protect him from all harm on the way.'

'With my knife?'

'*No*.'

'What then?'

'With – with your dignity, my son. Learn to bear yourself like your noble sire; that way, you shall come to all honour and be able to do great things for your brothers and sisters. Because you're the heir, and they will always look to you when they're grown.'

'I have no tutors then?' Edward hated the short leash of authority. 'No one to order me to do this, do that?'

'Everyone has a master, son.'

'Except the King.'

'Well…' For a moment, she was at a loss whether or not to discuss King Henry with him but decided on changing the subject altogether: 'It's time for you to go and have your new clothes fitted for the christening ceremony. Run along.'

Clothes were one of Edward's many passions: he went with alacrity. Only then did his mother ask for the new baby to be put into her arms for cuddling and kissing.

'George – George,' she repeated tenderly, learning to fit the name to the placidly sleeping face against her breast.

## 4

*The thirteenth day of November,* Cecily thought before she even opened her eyes, *the anniversary of my mother's death. I must be at Christ Church for her special Mass...*

Trying to gauge what time it was from the now familiar sounds of Dublin city – river traffic, and carts along the quays, and church bells – she lay unmoving by Richard's side. Everything seemed unnaturally muted this morning. She parted the bed curtains and sniffed the cold air. It had a bitter smell which she recognised: the smell of a walled town on which snow was falling, forcing downward the smoke of a thousand chimneys. Paris had smelt like that during the icy December of King Henry's Coronation. And Rouen during the bitter winter that had followed Edward's birth... Cecily dozed, to dream of France.

One of her serving women, using a bellows on the bedchamber fire, wakened her again.

'I'll give it a minute to warm up,' she decided. Dublin Castle was the coldest, dampest, draughtiest place on earth; but at least its upper apartments were fairly small so that they heated quickly from a good fire. She snuggled close to Richard and reflected contentedly that snow would keep him city bound. He'd cherished the theory that Irish winters were mild, and that he'd be able to lead a force westward as soon as present work in law court and council was done. Now he might have to wait until the spring to bring the western chieftains to allegiance.

This possibility pleased her, though she knew it wouldn't please Richard. A demon of energy possessed him nowadays. Sometimes she hardly recognised the quiet, rather slow-moving man she'd married. He was like someone who'd smashed a shell of routine and caution, accumulated over the years, to let his true self become apparent to the world: the challenging world of Irish government where he was virtually a king.

She stroked his hair in the curtained darkness. Only a few days ago she'd noticed the first grey ribs in the brown lock over his forehead. Sometimes, the ever-quickening rush of the years frightened her although it seemed to leave no mark upon herself; only on Richard... Yet she'd always valued a mature man. Magisterial, as her father had been. Mentally and physically strong as she remembered Captain John Blaeburn. Now Richard had outstripped the adult qualities of both. He was near his prime and she found more cause every day to admire him. He'd overcome his natural reserve to make himself a forceful speaker: the October Parliament had given him everything he'd asked for. He'd buried his contempt for display: the Ulster banner had brought him bloodless victories. And he was giving rein to a long-suppressed warmth and wit which was getting him a reputation for rare judicial talent.

Cecily had attended a few sessions of the Dublin Law Court recently. She remembered one case in particular: a petty Irish chieftain – who spoke English – was suing his neighbour for stealing his cattle.

'A hundred head he took off my lands, your Grace, to the utter destruction of me and all my dependants!'

'But I understood,' Richard said mildly, 'that you and this John O'More were friends, and that you often went hunting and – er – raiding together?'

'So we did,' bellowed the plaintiff. 'And all things *my* house shared with *his* house since time out of mind.'

'Did that sharing include a herd of cattle from the nearby MacDermott territory on All Saints' Day last?'

'Indeed it did. We divided the beasts to the last-born calf. *And 'twas those O'More stole off me.*'

'I see. Then both you and O'More will each return your spoils – *to the MacDermott*. This settles two cases in one except for the matter of your fines, which will be considerable.'

'But, Your Grace – listen – listen to me—' The protesting Irishman was led away and Cecily had waited tensely for sounds of strife between him and his guards. After a minute, however, he could be heard laughing uproariously from the passage outside the courtroom – shouting that he'd had his vengeance on that devil's limb, O'More, and may God bless the Duke of York for such heart-warming satisfaction!

By such unpredictable logic was Richard's fame spreading among the Irish. He handled more complex cases with equal ease; displaying a knowledge of tribal customs, ancient history and current events which often combined to lead him to the truth. Also, he understood the wide differences between native Irish and official English minds (nurtured, as they were, on two totally opposite forms of law) and between the positions of Marcher lords and old English settlers... Cecily found all this a truly awesome display of wisdom and insight into men's temperaments.

Generally, Richard avoided holding prisoners. But if a proud chieftain had to be kept in custody until he'd paid his taxes or taken his oath of fealty, he never lodged in the dungeons. He became the Yorks' guest – just as Agincourt prisoners had once been guests at Raby – and was allowed to quit his apartment and share meals with them at the High Table. The chieftain's grudge against England seldom lasted more than a few days in the face of such honourable treatment from the King's Lieutenant: he swore his oath, he paid his tax-debt, and he went back to his people with no loss of dignity.

'Never diminish a man,' was a lesson that Richard had always taught his children while, at the same time, warning them against the use of flattery. Now, in example, the lesson was working with the Irish who had been diminished too often in the past. Frequently, ex-guests returned to Dublin Castle, laden with gifts, and bringing their wives to meet Cecily...

These women were a surprise after the rough chieftains. They were gentle – often beautiful – women, who spoke a little Latin or French if they did not know English. Cecily got along splendidly with them; learned from them several haunting new melodies for her gittern; and accepted gifts of embroidered cloths and illuminated parchments in the strange, interwoven designs of a culture that had burned brightly, she knew, during Europe's darkest ages. Some of the city ladies who visited her disparaged these things as 'worthless barbarities'; but the Countesses of Ormonde, Desmond and Kildare assured her that her growing collection was priceless and unique.

'You'll display it in your London house one day,' the ageing Elisabeth Butler smiled, 'and everyone will envy you the possession of it!'

*Yes, maybe*, Cecily thought, fighting an absurd attack of

homesickness for the old manor out by Pimlico. One day. But how many years from now? *How long before they could all go home?*

Resolutely she got out of bed – fastening her fur-lined robe tightly while a little maid helped her with her slippers. The fire was crackling busily. She crossed to the prie-dieu and said her morning prayers, with a special remembrance for her mother who was nine years dead today...

More than an hour later, as she came out of Christ Church, snow was still whirling dizzily from a leaden sky and there were few people about in Castle Street. But as she neared the west gate, a band of wretched-looking men staggered out of a lane leading from Wood Quay. They walked stiffly, like men who'd been a long time at sea, and they didn't appear to have any belongings expect their swords. She assumed they'd just disembarked from a vessel down there on the tide-swollen river.

The castle sentries were challenging their leader as she herself reached the gate. The leader drew aside to let her pass and she saw his face.

'Sir David Hall!' she gasped. He was a knight who'd gone over to France with Richard in '41.

'Your Grace.' He could hardly speak but he made a brave attempt at a bow.

She put her hand on his sodden sleeve and nodded to the guards to let him and his companions pass into the courtyard with her. As in a dream, she recognised other faces now; Sir John Bedford, bastard son of the late Duke John; old Sir Robert Waterton, who'd first brought her husband to Raby as a four-year-old orphan; one of the de Veres of the star-badged House of Oxford... What these men were doing here in Dublin, in such condition, she couldn't even guess; but they were in no state to answer questions so she hurried them through the busy Great Hall and into the solar behind – ordering servants to bring food and drink there and to find His Grace of York at once. There was certainly a crisis when knights like these left Somerset's army in France.

Richard arrived at the same time as the food and wine. Waiting only for the servants to withdraw, he went from one near-fainting man to the next, greeting him by name and drawing him towards the table. 'Eat and drink first; we'll have your news later—'

'No, Your Grace,' old Waterton said stiffly. 'Deserters have no rights to hospitality. Only to questioning and fetters.'

'If deserters are also my friends,' Richard replied, 'I prefer that they should be conscious before we talk. Sit. Eat and drink, all of you.'

John Bedford was the first to lower his cup. He said: 'Thank God my noble father died before Normandy was lost!' and that brought the whole incredible story tumbling from the others...

Numbed, Cecily listened to the account; of towns fallen before French artillery; of an English army beaten back on Rouen, the last citadel—

'Then,' Davey Hall choked, 'three weeks ago, Governor Somerset surrendered Rouen to – to Charles de Valois.'

In the sudden silence Richard's voice came sharply: 'He *surrendered*? After how long a siege? Great God, the walls of that city are unbreachable. I know. I had every foot of them strengthened myself.'

'Your walls held, my lord.' De Vere looked up for the first time so that his terribly eye-scar, received at Pontoise, was fully visible. 'And your storerooms were still packed with provisions. But—' a shrug, 'Somerset lost his nerve: the Bretons were coming at us from the west, the French from the south and the Burgundians from the east — our men had enraged them all, you see, by their looting and indiscipline ever since Le Mans was handed over in March.'

'Somerset hadn't kept his troops in check?'

De Vere sighed: 'My lord, nobody has kept *anything* in check since you left in '45. It was the chaos of hell — even during the royal marriage truce at its sweetest! Soldiers went unpaid. Ships' masters took to piracy. Commanders' orders never penetrated the walls of some garrisons—'

'But what, in God's name, was the Governor of Normandy doing during all this?' Richard thundered.

'Nothing, Your Grace. Except drawing his salary.'

'He was paid? From England?'

'Yes, Somerset was always paid. I can vouch for that.'

'I see. His idleness and incompetence rewarded while I — But go on, go on.'

'Well, they say that a stray French cannon ball entered the window of the chamber where the Governor's wife and children were. Whatever, he suddenly gave up. Ordered us all to fight no more. Then he went out and sold the city to an astonished Charles, who'd been prepared for a six-month siege at least… Ah, truly the Maid of Orléans is still with her Dauphin!'

Cecily watched Richard's clenched hands as Bedford said: 'Aye. The Maid. Just twenty years ago since we brought her from Burgundy. And now we know she spoke truth—'

'Do we?' Richard asked. 'We still have Calais. And Guienne… Well, *haven't* we?'

'Calais, yes,' old Waterton admitted with his mouth full. 'But Guienne's been under pressure for a long while now and reinforcements can't reach the south like they can reach Calais.'

'How about Normandy? Were reinforcements sent there?'

'Not latterly, Your Grace. We heard an army was collecting at Southampton but it never crossed the Channel. Anyhow, what use are men when they're not allowed to fight? That's why we got out: Somerset had agreed to leave all the King's guns in Rouen on condition he could take his own goods away unharmed. So we left while we still had our swords—'

'You mean to tell me that Somerset abandoned the King's possessions while taking care of his own? And that he allowed guns to fall into enemy hands – *guns in working order?*'

'Best cannons we ever had were in Rouen, as Your Grace well knows. No, they weren't destroyed before we marched out.'

'Blood of God, something will have to be done about Somerset. Where is he now, d'you know? Is he going to be brought home for trial?'

*Trial?*' de Vere's scarred eye puckered more horribly. 'A friend of mighty Merchant Suffolk and Queen Margaret to stand for trial for aiding the French? Nay, Your Grace. He got a Dukedom for doing nothing at all. Now Queen Margaret will embrace him for laying down arms before her noble father and brother who were both with the Valois outside Rouen— Though maybe,' he added on a mumbled breath, 'I shouldn't speak so harshly about your lady's cousin. Maybe he only inherited a defeat that began long ago.'

'There's no need to make excuses for Edmund Beaufort, Sir Robert,' Cecily said quietly. 'I did not choose my kin. But my husband's enemies are mine; likewise his friends.'

'Then it seems, ma'am,' Davey Hall cut in heartily,

'that you might have further hospitality to dispense before very long. Because more and more men of the old Normandy garrisons will be making their way here—'

'*No.*' Richard brought his fist down on the table. 'Even you must return to England within a few days. I cannot employ you.'

There was an embarrassed pause. Then John Bedford nodded sympathetically. 'Your Grace is right. We cannot ask you to run the risk of being branded traitor by turning your capital into a refuge for deserters. 'Twould soon be made to sound ill at home were Suffolk to get hold of the news.'

'Do you imagine that fear of William de la Pole would make me cast out my friends? No; it is only that I cannot support any of you.'

'Dickon,' Cecily asked, 'what do you mean?'

'I mean, my love, that we haven't had as much as a pinch of salt from England since we came here. And now, with the revenues of Normandy lost, the King will be bankrupt, and Ireland the least pressing of his debts. We are on our own here. In a depressed and isolated city which is cut off from the land whose capital she's supposed to be. The boundaries of the Pale strangle Dublin. The chieftains pay their taxes in cattle – can we run this vast administration on beef alone? Of course not. Even for our household we must have flour, oats, salt, spices, cloth – ah, I would see merchants instead of soldiers on this city's quays! Yet the House of York could not buy supplies from them for even another dozen men, let alone a hundred. So I take no soldiers from France...'

His words chilled her to silence. And the men around the table, too, became very quiet, ceasing even to eat. Clearly, they'd hoped to serve again under their old commander: their disappointment was palpable...

But de Vere recovered quickly. 'Well, we have a ship,' he said. 'The old *Marianne* is entirely ours; we bought her honestly with our combined savings. So, since neither France, Ireland nor England can support us, we'll keep to the sea, just as Suffolk's pirate-admiral Bob Winnington does! But instead of attacking the Hanse fleet and thus enraging Burgundy, we'll simply divert unwelcome visitors away from these shores. And if there's news worth carrying to Dublin – why, we'll carry it and ask no recompense but friendship. Agreed, comrades-in-arms?'

'Aye, agreed,' said the others, brightening visibly.

Richard leaned forward on his fists over the table. 'What will you live on during this service to me?' he demanded.

'Fish, my lord,' Davey Hall replied innocently. 'Fish of all kinds and from all depths. We're not particular.'

Two days later, after the *Marianne* had sailed for secret harbours in England, Richard said to Cecily,

'May God forgive me for turning a band of deserters into spies.'

But he was lighter of mood than she'd known him for a long while because he was in contact with the familiar world again. So she kept her fear for him close to her heart: a fear that he had already put one foot into the quicksand of intrigue that surrounded the childless King, whose true heir he was no matter what Edmund Beaufort, Duke of Somerset, might maintain to the contrary.

# 5

During the next six months, the reports which the *Marianne* carried from England to Ireland formed a chronicle of mounting chaos.

Sir John Bedford told Richard and Cecily just before Christmas: 'Your good friend, Lord Cromwell, has been set upon and almost murdered by Suffolk's henchmen for bringing charges in Parliament against their master.'

'Did the charges stick?' Richard asked hopefully – after being assured that Cromwell would recover.

'Unfortunately no, my lord. But they've had some effect nevertheless: the party rats are running. Bishop Lumley has retired from the Treasury and Bishop Moleyns has resigned the Privy Seal.'

Richard smiled tightly. 'It'll need an anvil to straighten the Seal out after Adam Moleyns has held it.' He could never forgive the Bishop's lying campaign against himself following his return from Normandy.

'Ay, Moleyns is as crooked as a crab's walk. Yet the latest thing I heard before we sailed was that he'd just been entrusted with the wages for Kyrielle's army at Portsmouth.'

'You mean to say,' Cecily asked incredulously, 'that those troops *still* haven't gone out to France?'

'No, ma'am. They've been rioting and looting all over Hampshire since last October but no sign of them sailing yet. My own guess is that Suffolk is keeping them in England in case he needs them for his own defence. And that'll be the reason he gave their command to a scoundrel like Kyrielle (one of his own creatures) instead of to Your Grace's kinsmen of Buckingham or Norfolk. Ah, there's trouble coming, make no mistake. You can tell by the songs in the taverns. The latest one begins: "God keep our King aye and guide him by grace; save him from Suffolk and from his foes all—"'

John Bedford finished his Advent fare of bread and salt herrings. Then he returned to the *Marianne* with the promise that she'd be back in the Liffey by the end of January.

IT WAS Sir David Hall this time who came up to the Castle; and his news was of violence and bloodshed.

'Bishop Adam Moleyns,' Sir David related, 'went down to Portsmouth with the troop wages. No one knows exactly what happened there on January the ninth except that there was an argument about the sum involved, and the Bishop was accused of keeping certain moneys for himself. Anyway, he was set upon by Kyrielle's men. And those who saw the body afterwards said it was unrecognisable – torn to pieces... A few days later there was a riot in Dowgate Ward, with the crowd chanting: "By the town, by the town, for this array the King shall lose his Crown." '

When she'd found her breath, Cecily whispered: 'A man of the Church murdered by Englishmen. Now the King threatened. Oh Dickon, what are matters coming to?' But Richard was already firing questions at Davey Hall who was doing his lumbering best to answer them fully.

'Aye, Your Grace, Parliament met on the 23$^{rd}$, and new charges were brought against Suffolk then. Something to do with "treasonable actions in relation to France" though nothing very clear-cut I hear, and he talked his way out easily enough. Just like before, he blamed Somerset – blamed the King's poverty even! 'Tis said there's £3,000 owing now to the royal household servants alone, and £400 to the King's private chapel.'

Richard groaned. Henry's financial affairs were in an even worse state than he'd feared. There was no hope of Irish officials' salaries being paid this year, let alone any of the huge debt owing to the House of York... He was becoming seriously worried. Ireland was a bottomless well where money was concerned, and he himself had been footing the administrative bill for the entire country since the previous July although even his five-year-old tallies for Normandy were still unredeemed.

'One last item,' Davey Hall was saying. 'Archbishop Stafford has given up the Great Seal to Kemp; and you know Kemp is no friend of Suffolk's so it looks as if the tide is beginning to run strong against the merchant-Duke at last—'

IT WAS. In March, formal charges were brought against William de la Pole, alleging serious offences inside the realm of England. The French treason charge had been rejected by the King as being too dangerous in the country's existing temper: the last thing Henry wanted was to have to execute his chief minister, his Queen's favourite. On the new count however, the most that could be demanded was banishment for a time until matters simmered down. So, early in March, Suffolk was committed to the Tower to await his High Court Trial on the English charges.

'I must hand it to the Queen,' John Bedford quietly told Richard and Cecily afterwards, 'she stood by William de la Pole four square. Even after the entire Council had slunk off, fearful for its own neck, Margaret fought on, tooth and claw. D'you know, she even wanted to bring Kyrielle's murderous band up from Southampton to London to defend him by armed threat? But London had no mind to be ravaged like Hampshire. The authorities saw to it that those troops went out, at last, to harass France instead of England. And on March 17th, Suffolk's sentence was pronounced in the High Court: he's been condemned to five years' banishment and has to be clear of the country by Mayday.'

'Well, I hope he doesn't choose Ireland for his retirement,' Richard sighed. 'We have troubles enough here as it is: general discontent about money and some of the chieftains throwing off their allegiance; burning and looting on the Marches. I've had to summon a Parliament to Drogheda for next month. But we'll cross our bridges when we come to them. Tell me one more thing, Bedford, about Suffolk's trial: was he found guilty on *all* the English charges?'

'No, one was dropped: that was that he'd once tried to wed his son to young Margaret Beaufort, in order to see the pair of them ascend the steps to the throne one day.'

Cecily stared. 'What an absurd accusation to bring in the first place,' she said. 'I'm not surprised it was thrown out. Suffolk wouldn't be stupid enough to imagine, would he, that my late cousin John Beaufort's heiress carries any hereditary right to the throne?'

'Well—' John Bedford rubbed the large nose that was a replica of his dead father's '—your other cousin, Edmund Beaufort, had been doing a deal of talking before he went to France.'

'Talking? What about?' Cecily asked sharply; though she already knew.

'About the famous legitimation document of the Beauforts, ma'am, with its added clause... Anyhow, at that time his niece Margaret was still Suffolk's ward. So maybe Suffolk lent a willing ear to what Edmund was saying and decided that the child in his care would make not only a rich, daughter-in-law when she came of age but a pawn in the royal game as well. However, as we know, King Henry put an end to the whole affair by betrothing her to his own half-brother of Richmond. So I suppose it makes no difference *what* Suffolk had in mind at one time.'

'No, I suppose not...' Yet Cecily had an uneasy awareness that Suffolk's trial must have brought the succession question very much to the fore. It would have been discussed in every alehouse in the land. And the doubts which Edmund Beaufort had raised, about whether John of Gaunt's children by Katherine Swynford had been legally barred from the royal dignity or not, would now be magnified by the new publicity. Englishmen might well take sides: Beaufort – or Plantagenet—

She looked at Richard. He was frowning thoughtfully as if his mind were engaged on some mounting problem... The Beauforts had always dogged his steps although their blood ran in his own children; what if hostile Edmund of Somerset should now champion his nine-year-old girl, Margaret Beaufort? – made her the figurehead of a new party with himself as leader? With Suffolk in exile, Edmund could draw ever closer to the childless Queen who'd be seeking a substitute for her banished favourite. And the Queen would certainly favour Edmund of Somerset (of whom she was rumoured to be rather more than fond already) far above Richard of York. Her patronage could be decisive...

To break the heavy silence Cecily asked Bedford:

'Do you think, John, that the Duchess of Suffolk will go into exile with her lord?' She was interested to know if Alice Chaucer, who had shared William de la Pole's rise to wealth and power, would now be willing to share his temporary obscurity.

Bedford smiled. 'I doubt it, ma'am. The lady Alice is an astute woman – they say she's been the force behind her husband all along. Now she's well entrenched in his lands and castles. The tenants fear her. And she's still a close friend of the Queen's, remember... No, I believe she'll stay in England with her son – and with the band of cutthroats she keeps around her for protection! When Duke William returns after five years, he'll find the seat of power still kept comfortably warm for him.'

BUT ALICE CHAUCER was never to see William de la Pole again. On April 30th, the ship carrying him to exile was intercepted in the Channel by a renegade vessel of the royal fleet. As he was being dragged aboard, Suffolk asked what the ship's name was; and, upon being told that it was called the *Saint Nicholas of the Tower*, he went white and muttered to himself: 'There was a prophecy made by the Wizard Stacy long ago – my wife told me of it – that I should be safe until I entered a place of that name upon the water.' Afterwards, he put up no defence when the ship's master sentenced him to death.

He was beheaded with a rusty sword which took half a dozen strokes to sever his strong neck. Next morning, his body was cast upon the sands of Dover.

RICHARD WAS STILL IN DROGHEDA – after presiding over the Irish Parliament where he'd refused to tax the poorer people although his own financial position was now desperate – when details of Suffolk's murder reached him.

'My God,' he muttered to old Waterton who'd brought the news, 'that's the second public figure to be butchered this year.'

There was to be a third. On June 29th, Bishop Ayscough of Salisbury was dragged from the altar of Edington Church in Wiltshire and was stoned to death on the porch steps by a crowd of six hundred people. Then his palace in Salisbury was sacked and more money found there than any man of God should own. Some maintained afterwards that his killing was the result of a long quarrel with tenants of Church lands; but others said that he'd been to blame for the Queen's childlessness when, as Henry's spiritual adviser, he'd urged marital chastity upon the obedient and simple-minded King.

Ayscough's murder, however, was only one more wave of violence in a demented ocean. Two other bishops – Booth of Lichfield and Lyhart of Norwich – were threatened by angry mobs after their belated flights from Court to their neglected dioceses; and the people of Gloucester plundered Abbot Boulers' country. The men of Essex were fashioning farm implements into weapons of war. And rumour was running wild because nothing was now

too horrific for credence: when it was noised about that
'all Kent was to be turned desolate' as reprisal for
Suffolk's murder, the great highway from Dover to
London became crammed with men making for Blackheath where a mysterious leader called Jack Cade had set
up his camp.

Cade was demanding, among other things, the recall of
the Duke of York from Ireland to take control of a
distracted country.

Richard was kept informed by the crew of the *Marianne*
about Jack Cade's movements and demands. Yet, refusing
to heed the reports, he concentrated doggedly on Irish
affairs.

'My place is here,' he told Davey Hall who was urging
him to return. 'If the King wants me, he will send for me.'

Yet Henry had answered none of his letters, and
Richard doubted that any of his pleas for help had ever
even been read. No money had come in any case. The
plate and jewels of the York household were again in pawn
to pay troops. And Richard was now borrowing money
from his friends, a thing he had never done before in his
life.

By June, in final desperation, he was writing to his
brother-in-law Richard Neville, Earl of Salisbury, telling
him of the position on the Irish Marches and begging him
to exert his influence within the royal Council:

'...*The chieftain MacGeorghegan, who submitted in the autumn,
has now risen again with other Irish captains and a great fellowship
of English rebels. They have burnt Rathmore and other villages in
Meath. They have murdered the inhabitants, and they be yet assembled in woods and forts waiting to do hurt to the King's subjects. If
my payments do not come in haste, my power cannot stretch to the
defence of this land and very necessity will compel me to return home.
For I had liefer be dead than that any loss should occur through my*

*default. It shall never be chronicled, by the Grace of God, that Ireland was lost by my negligence.'*

This sincere and passionate letter he entrusted to the young squire, William Hastings, to carry to the north of England for him; though he was aware that it might be weeks before Salisbury even received it, let alone acted upon it, because the Earl and his sons were defending the vast Marches towards Scotland and were seldom in the Castle of Middleham these times.

Weeks! Great God, he couldn't survive that long. For eleven months his country and his King had ignored him. He who had always been so loyal, so faithful in his work for the Crown, was cast off – forgotten; his wife and children reduced to shameful poverty.

As the desperate days went by, more and more ominous news of Cade's rebellion was brought to his military camp in Meath.

'Cade now says,' de Vere reported, 'that his true name is John Mortimer, that he is a bastard cousin of yours, and that he is fighting for your rights.'

'Robert, I never asked him to fight. I don't even know who he is.'

'Well—' an odd look came into de Vere's puckered eye '—be that as it may, people are flocking to his camp at Blackheath because he uses the name of Mortimer. If such a host can be raised to one of your inherited names, my lord, what couldn't be achieved by your appearing *in person?*'

'You'd have me lead rebels – against my King?' Richard was very quiet.

'Your Grace, they're *not* against the King. They merely demand the reform of government, with you as first minister.'

'And I have told you, Robert: when Henry asks me to

assume such office, I will at once obey him. Until then, I stay in the Irish Lieutenancy to which he has appointed me...' But the question hammered in his brain: how long *can* I stay? Many of the men were sick from Irish fever; many more had been wounded, and the rest were suffering from malnutrition. He had to have replacements for these men if he were to continue the campaign. He had to have food for them; ships to carry the gravely ill home; cloth for winter apparel. But he had nothing else left to sell. Cecily's personal jewellery was all gone. She was even having some of her gowns cut up now to clothe the growing children—

His wife's magnificent spirit had never been more apparent to Richard than in this crisis. Somehow, Cecily was managing not only to cope with the Castle household and its many visitors, but even to continue giving an impression of affluence and serenity. Only her most trusted servants and her closest friends knew the truth: that the discipline of good management which she enforced had its springs in necessity rather than in choice.

Like himself, she had many friends. Yet, for how long could they both continue to borrow from those friends—?

De Vere was leaning towards him. 'My lord, listen to me. Since nothing else will move you, I must tell you the truth: *Queen Margaret has accused you of Suffolk's murder.*'

He stared at de Vere. 'You must have misheard.'

'No. And that's not all. The Cade rebellion is also being laid to your charge. When the Queen learned that Cade was Irish-born, she got the fixed idea you'd sent him over from here – having first trained him in how to conduct himself. For, before God, he handles an army on your own principles: discipline, justice, clear objectives – 'tis no rabble at Blackheath: there are near a hundred gentlemen and priests amid the merchants and the craftsmen there, the farmers and the fishermen. If Cade were a common upstart, would they follow him? No, they *believe* he's a Mortimer – a cousin of yours sent to test the ground for your own arrival. Richard, this army is an act of faith in you!'

'I tell you I do not know its leader and I had nothing to do with his appearance.'

'All right. Though it makes no odds now: your names are linked so that yours is as black-dyed in treason as Cade's is. Because, by this, he must have reached London from Blackheath—'

ON JULY 4<sup>TH</sup>, the personable man who called himself John Mortimer rode into the city at the head of his troops. Pausing at the ancient London Stone, he struck it with his sword and cried: 'Now is Mortimer lord of London!'

In his gipsire he had the well-drawn-up Complaints of the Commons of Kent. This document demanded, among other reforms, the removal of corrupt servants from about the King's person and the restoration of true lords to the country's government. York's name headed the list of such lords.

By the night of July 5<sup>th</sup>, a fierce battle was in progress amid the blazing timbers of London Bridge. Cade had lost control of his troops after he'd sanctioned the executions of the Lords Saye and Cromer, two Crown officials hated in Kent for their exactions; and now many private scores were being bloodily settled. Houses of unpopular magnates had been ransacked. The Tower garrison was fighting a losing battle with the rebels.

Wisely, Queen Margaret took her feeble consort and fled with him to Kenilworth. There was nothing Henry could do: he could barely support the weight of his demi-armour, what chance had he of leading royal troops against rebels? And neither must he be allowed to parley with them: Henry was too lenient. Besides, they might capture him; and whoever held the King, held the country. Margaret had no intention of letting Henry out of her sight for one moment. Let London take care of itself.

London did, by coming to terms with the men of Kent and Essex. They were promised that all their grievances would be looked into; then hundreds of free pardons were issued and the recipients urged to go home and see to their harvests.

But the pardon given to Cade was made out in the name of Mortimer – a name to which he could prove no legal right. So, still a rebel, he fought on until he was killed by royal troops on July 12$^{th}$.

No one ever discovered who he really was. Mysterious he came; and, without any last words of explanation, he died. But his brief public career was like a comet, trailing the sparks of civil war; for his death did nothing to quiet his followers – they went on agitating, demanding that 'Cade's Complaints' be investigated as had been promised. Demanding, above all, the return of the Duke of York as recognised heir-presumptive to a tottering throne.

## 6

Richard's letter to his brother-in-law brought a swifter reply than he'd dared hope for. One morning in mid-August, a ship sailed up the Liffey with the unmistakable figure of Salisbury's eldest son standing near the helmsman.

Cecily was overjoyed to see this nephew and godson of hers again. He'd long been her favourite among the children of Middleham Castle. But she hadn't met him since Rouen in '41: he'd always been away on the northern Marches when she visited Yorkshire. He'd been helping his father to patrol these Marches since he was thirteen. He was now twenty-two, and had just become Earl of Warwick through his young wife, Anne Beauchamp, whose only brother had died soon after inheriting the title. There had been a good deal of trouble about the matter of the transfer – trouble stirred up mainly by Edmund Beaufort who begrudged any advancement to his Neville cousins – but, at last, all the wealth and power, lands and castles of the Earldom of Warwick had come to Salisbury's heir.

Cecily's first impulse was to kiss her nephew when he strode into Dublin Castle but she decided against it. He was so grimly dignified, so Olympian in his slim tallness. And he looked much older than his years with his long, chiselled face and narrowed eyes. A totally adult face – cold, and yet deeply passionate, she thought, holding out her hand to him.

As he bent to kiss the White Rose ring – which was all she had left of her personal jewellery – she noted that his hair had darkened. It was now that curious shade of purplish copper which a beech-tree turns in autumn – seeming almost black in distance. She also noted the new badge displayed on his doublet-front as he straightened: the Bear and Ragged Staff of Warwick.

'You're welcome to Dublin, Richard,' she said; and reflected that no one – not even his wife – would ever call this steely young man 'Dickon' or any other pet-name. He would always be Richard Neville, Earl of Warwick.

'I thank you, my lady aunt...' As he added a brief greeting from his parents, his brothers and sisters and his wife, she could sense his impatience for the real purpose of his visit. So she didn't delay him with questions – though there were many she longed to ask about the north-country – but left him with her husband while she went to arrange refreshments.

When she returned, they were closeted together in the solar, and she knew at once, from the crackling atmosphere, that young Warwick had pushed Richard to the decision he'd been struggling against making.

'Cis – we're going back to England—'

She sat down carefully on a bench. The news was no surprise, and yet it touched her like fire after the cold fog of doubt these many weeks during which Dickon had been silent. He'd been like a stranger to her, even when he'd got her with child again recently. For the first time in their married life, he'd made love to her almost absent-mindedly; the dutiful act of a home-coming husband with no hint of the lover's passion he'd always had for her before. But now she sensed that he was himself again; that he'd rediscovered the involvement and direction of his life.

'Is it time for such action?' she asked quietly.

'It is, sweetheart. Your brother of Salisbury advises it. He says I should go straight to the King. First, to refute this charge of having been behind Jack Cade. And second, to claim leadership of the government before Beaufort does and brings the country to ruin – he's been recalled from France and made Constable of England! One could imagine him a conquering hero instead of a failed general—'

To divert him from the topic of Edmund Beaufort, she asked quickly, 'How much opposition will there be to your going home, Dickon?'

'A good deal, my love. You and the children must remain on the Welsh Marches until I send for you – at Ludlow or Wigmore, whichever you prefer. Both castles are provisioned and guarded.'

She'd never liked Wigmore: there was a darkness, a withdrawn quality about that castle in the woods.

'Ludlow,' she said. 'But where will you be?'

'Difficult to be certain for a while. You see, our nephew here has just told me that Queen Margaret has put out orders for my arrest as soon as I set foot in England.'

'*Arrest?*' She looked wildly from him to the aloof young Warwick and back again. 'But was it not a condition of your appointment that you might return whenever you wished, to consult with the King?'

'Yes, that was stated in my letters patent. But so many of their conditions have never been honoured that I dare not make formal request for this: I might wait a lifetime for the King's reply. So I shall appoint a Deputy and leave without permission. I've chosen Ormonde.'

She was glad about the White Earl. He'd been their truest friend here in Dublin... But Warwick was frowning.

'Ormonde?' he asked. 'Is he safe? I mean on account of his heir, young James Butler? Remember that James is such a favourite of the Queen's, she made him Earl of Wiltshire recently. If the father were to die while you were away, his power and the Deputyship would go to Wiltshire.' Warwick's objectivity was chilling.

'At barely turned sixty,' Richard smiled, 'I cannot accept that the White Earl has one foot in the grave just yet. He's a splendid campaigner and shows no signs of old age.' But he avoided Cecily's eye as he spoke, for they both knew that their friend's health was slowly failing. 'Now, let me see the chart your father has sent,' he said briskly to Warwick.

The younger man spread out the ink-drawn chart and ran his finger along the line which roughly represented the coast of North Wales. 'You'll be expected to land somewhere around the Dee estuary – here, my lord uncle – and to march through Chester. Then southwest for the midlands. And so on down to London. The Queen has already posted Stanley and de l'Isle along this route with strong forces to intercept you.'

'So soon?' Richard muttered.

'She thought you'd come during the height of the Cade rebellion.'

'And play straight into her hands for a treason charge?'

'I suppose so...' Warwick was detached from interest in

anything except the chart before him. He tapped it with his index finger, trying to bring his uncle's attention back to it. But Richard walked over to the window, demanding in sudden, oblique anger:

'Why does Margaret hate me so? We got along well enough at first; what's altered her? Why is she now pursuing me like this when I have done her no harm?'

A shrug from Warwick. 'She's changed these last few years, they say — since the people turned against her over the Maine and Anjou business and started calling her "the Frenchwoman". She must have taken that to heart. Then there have been the slanderous ditties lately about herself and Henry — replacing those that *used* to be sung about her and Suffolk! Of course, Suffolk's death hit her very hard.'

'And she blames me for that death? As for the Cade rebellion?'

'So they say.'

'Then her hatred may be no older than this year?'

'I know not, uncle. Except I heard that she was not overpleased when your last son was born healthy.'

Cecily went rigid. So Margaret begrudged her and Dickon the life of baby George! What a vicious, evil-minded woman she must have become.

No. Merely confirmed in her own childlessness. Margaret couldn't be blamed for envy of the three York sons. Yet such an envy, bred in barrenness, was much to be feared. And it was directed at Dickon.

Cecily looked at him where he stood over by the window — his broad back turned towards her, his neck hunched under the cropped hair where the grey ribs were multiplying, and his leather belt dragged tight across his hips by the weight of his hooked thumbs. It was a familiar stance — with the legs planted astride — and it gave an impression of immovable solidarity; of enormous strength of both body and will. She had once defined this quality as 'untoppleable'. But now she recognised that even the mightiest oak could be felled, and she feared for her husband. If anything were to happen to Dickon—

But it would be useless to plead with him: 'Don't go. Don't challenge the Court party which is still entrenched against you.' He'd been kept on a short chain all his life; this might be his one chance of slipping it. And she was the last person in the world who would deny him freedom, at whatever cost. She loved him. She believed in him…

Warwick was showing Richard the alternative route which his father had suggested should be followed: 'Land at Beaumaris in Anglesey. Go *south* through the length of Wales instead of east at Chester. Gather a force from your own lands as you go, and cross the Severn at Gloucester. Then make a dash for London. That way, you should reach the King while Stanley and de l'Isle are still looking for you in the midlands. Speed is the thing.'

Richard nodded distantly. He was reviewing all the official tidying-up he'd been doing lately, in preparation for this hour of final decision. How long ago was it since the first thought of returning home, without royal sanction, had struck him? Four weeks – six – eight? He didn't know. He remembered only the initial dismay at his own sense of violent compulsion to act – *act*. Then the growing excitement which he'd suppressed – denying its existence even to Cecily while she'd lain naked in his arms.

But now the time of self-doubt was over. In spirit, he had already left Ireland.

∾

By early September, Cecily had reached the castle at Ludlow. Nerve-racked after the secretive journey through the Welsh mountains with children, servants and packhorses, she'd tensely awaited news of Richard' progress.

The first messenger to cross the Teme bridge and ride up to the old Norman castle was an esquire named Roger Roe, freckled-faced and red-headed. Roger told her that her husband had collected many armed men on his march through Wales, to swell the skeleton force he'd brought from Ireland and the band she herself had sent out from Ludlow. He was now travelling fast for Gloucester. If he could cross the Severn, she thought, before news of his leaving Ireland reached his enemies—

But she had to hear, with sinking heart, that those enemies already knew of Richard's landing in Anglesey; and that the Treasurer of the King's household, Lord Dudley, was marching down upon him from Chester. Also, that Abbot Boulers of Gloucester — who laid the recent sacking of his own house to Yorkist agitation — had ordered his Church tenants to arms. York could be caught between the two unless he could fight both forces.

'What about his allies?' she demanded. 'Have none of them reached him yet?' Secret messages had been sent to the Nevilles and other friends.

'Alas no, Your Grace,' the kneeling squire told her. 'And — and Sir William Tresham has been killed on the way.'

Tresham; Speaker of the Commons and one of Richard's most faithful adherents. He'd agreed to act as decoy by taking the Chester route.

She crossed herself. One good friend dead already. How many more must follow? Then she asked: 'Who else will join my lord?' There hadn't been time to await replies, to estimate what help he might count upon.

'Your nephew of Norfolk, ma'am…'

Ah yes, her sister Katherine's son – though he was fighting a private war of his own in East Anglia with Alice Chaucer, she'd heard! Still, he had wide territories in Wales… 'What about my brother-in-law of Buckingham?'

'He's yet delayed in Calais, I fear. And my lord of Salisbury and his sons are hard pressed by some new trouble in the north—'

'Trouble? I thought the Scottish fighting was over?'

'Yes, Your Grace. But the Earl of Northumberland's sons have now taken up arms, it is said, against the Nevilles. Though I know no details.'

*Oh God,* she thought, *trust my sister Eleanor's brood to make strife at this time!* The second boy, Thomas, had inherited all the worst characteristics of his mother and his Percy grandsire, 'Hotspur'.

Seeing her dismay, Roger Roe said: 'Madame, the Earl of Devon will surely come to His Grace's aid from the south.'

'How can he?' she asked distractedly – getting up and walking about as she signed the lad to arise from his knees. 'Is Devon not at war with Lord Bonville and the Earl of Wiltshire?' There seemed to be more private warfare going on in England than there'd ever been in France or Ireland. She was only just learning the extent of it all from her household officers here at Ludlow.

She wished, now, that Richard had never left Ireland. There, at least, he'd had numerous friends and supporters among all classes. At the end, the volume of affection for him – even among the Irish chieftains whom he'd subdued – had been quite extraordinary. People had worn the White Rose as a badge of devotion to York and had vowed to remember him and his sons to the end of their days. But here, in his own land, he was being pursued like a felon although, as a royal Duke, he ought to be able to go unhindered to his King. And that was *all* he wanted, she told herself: to see Henry! Yet he had to put his life in danger to do it because of the Queen and Edmund Beaufort and all their treacherous adherents like Dudley and de Ruthyn, Stanley and Lord Hoo and de l'Isle.

'Your Grace,' Roger said confidently, 'the Duke of York needs no great lords to defend him when he has the commons of England at his back.'

'Aye, the commons...' Her face relaxed. Dickon had always had a way with ordinary men, be they soldiers, merchants, craftsmen or labourers. A plain blunt man himself, though his blood was royal, he spoke their language, understood their difficulties. And he had that mixture of justice and sternness which they preferred to the King's effusive mercy and disorganised generosity.

'For months,' the squire went on with enthusiasm, 'they've clamoured for his return. Think you now they'll fail to support him on his way to London? Why?—' with passionate pride in his master '—they'd hail him as King tomorrow were Henry to die!'

'*Shush*, Roger,' she whispered. 'You know 'tis treason even to *think* of the King's death! And there has never been the slightest question of our loyalty to the reigning House.' Agitatedly she walked away from him again. She thought she heard him mutter something under his breath, which sounded like: 'That's what Harry Bolingbroke said,' but, because she wasn't sure, she ignored it. Maybe the words were imagined; an echo of her own thought... Aye, Harry had come back from exile in 1399, demanding merely his rights as Duke of Lancaster, heir to John of Gaunt. But, very soon, the crown of murdered Richard the Second was on his head—

Was *that* what Queen Margaret feared from York? The deposition of Bolingbroke's feeble grandson? If so,

Margaret need not worry: Richard of York was no usurper. Though, by treating him as an enemy, she was making him one... Well, she might come to her senses before it was too late.

Cecily said to her husband's squire, 'You may rest awhile now; then return to my lord with all speed. Where did he arrange for you to meet him?'

Roger grinned, stretching his freckles. 'Beyond the Severn, Your Grace; on the way to Cirencester...' And she had to smile at the implied certainty that Richard would safely cross the tidal barrier between Wales an England.

She made the meeting of her husband with his sovereign the focal point of all her hopes.

YORK CAPTURED Lord Dudley and Abbot Boulers at Gloucester and left them prisoners in his castle of Wigmore. Then, joined by the Earl of Devon and the young Duke of Norfolk, he pressed on eastward for London. He was now leading a combined army of 4,000 men; but that was not enough, he knew, if strong royal forces came out against them. So by subtlety he must proceed – counting on the fact that neither the Queen nor Edmund of Somerset had much generalship between them. Margaret was impetuous; Somerset inefficient. They must be induced to wasting their forces.

Richard gave out that he was making for Hatfield – that he believed the King to be there. Margaret ordered Lord Hoo to concentrate his men north of the capital, and she left Stanley at Leicester, de l'Isle at Northampton. She was convinced that York would approach London from the north.

He came out of the west and stormed his way to the King...

Henry was at dinner with his household. Margaret was on the one side of him and Edmund Beaufort on the other when the royal Chamberlain flung open the doors at the end of the Hall and announced:

'His Grace the Duke of York.'

In the stupefied hush, Richard walked towards Henry and bowed low before him. 'I claim my right of audience, Sire,' he said.

Henry, alone, was unaware of the charged atmosphere in the crowded Hall. He'd been told nothing of troop movements nor of orders for arrest.

'Right, welcome you are, good cousin of York.' He smiled his perplexed smile. He was often confused by people's sudden comings and disappearances. But he was glad to see his cousin even if York *did* look excessively grim. 'You come in peace?' he inquired nervously then, suddenly remembering some odd things he'd overheard.

'That I do, my liege lord. But I would inquire who sought to prevent me.' Richard's eye raked the places at the High Table occupied by Margaret, Somerset and all their friends; the friends headed, he noted, by a glaring Alice Chaucer.

'I'm sure nobody did so,' Henry said wonderingly, his long pale face blank in its innocence. 'You're here safely, are you not, cousin? – so God be thanked. Now sit by us and tell us of our Irish realm...' The disproportionately small hands made a gesture for Somerset to move down one place.

Somerset sat unmoving while Margaret leaned towards the King and said through her teeth: 'York is a traitor. He left Ireland without your permission.'

Henry blinked at her. 'Oh no, my dear,' he corrected

apologetically, 'my permission was not needed. And Richard is always welcome by my side – but what is that noise from the courtyard?'

Somerset had already heard it and was on his feet. Now Margaret listened tensely. Hundreds of throats, it seemed, were shouting, 'York – York!' – and there was cheering and the flare of torches.

'See,' she cried to the King, 'he comes leading rebels! *Now* will you believe that he had your ministers murdered? That he sent Cade to rise against you? That he has stirred up all the people to disrespect and outrage of your person and mine?'

York had sat down calmly in Somerset's place.

'My liege lord,' he said to the trembling Henry, 'there are but a few dozen unarmed men out there, bidding me welcome home as heartily as you yourself have done. If they become unruly, Norfolk's guard will quiet them without blows. I have given orders that there is to be no fighting, no bloodshed... Now, if you have finished your meal, Sire, I would speak with you privily on a few urgent matters.'

The King's pale eyes regarded him sadly. 'I trust, cousin, these matters do not concern money? For it seems I have none; not even for my dearest project, the college and chapel at Cambridge...'

While the King spoke, Richard looked slowly and deliberately all around the table. Then he raised his voice to reply:

'I am owed £10,000 for my service in Ireland alone. But we will not talk of that. We will talk, instead, of the loss of France,' he stared at Somerset, 'and of disorder, treachery and corruption at home; of slanders and murders and misuse of power...'

His voice carried to the furthest reaches of the Hall;

authoritative, accusing. Nobody moved. All eyes were fastened on this man who might be the next King. For many, it was an uncomfortable possibility. Then they watched him rise massively to his feet and hold out his sword-arm to Henry.

Sighing, Henry left his dish of cold mutton and shuffled along by his cousin's side between the crowded benches – his shabby blue mantle trailing behind him from sagging, rounded shoulders... The royal household watched them go out together, the strong man and the weak.

'Imbeciles!' Margaret hissed at the group of captains who had gathered around her. 'I told you York was not to reach the King. He was to have been prevented, *by any means*—'

'Madame,' an elderly prince of the Church came forward to lay his hand on hers, 'the noble Duke will get no good of this action except to wear himself out. I pray you, leave things to me. A lawyer's brain can outwit a soldier's any day.'

Her great dark eyes regarded the ring on the yellowed fingers closing over her own. She hesitated to meet the hooded gaze above; for this man, Cardinal Kemp, had been the enemy of her greatest friend, William de la Pole. But she was unwilling to show her animosity towards him now, for she might have need of him; so she kept her too-expressive eyes downcast.

'Very well, my lord,' she said. 'You may conduct matters as you see fit.'

Cardinal Kemp, Archbishop of York and Chancellor of England, allowed himself a withered smile. During the late Suffolk's ministry, Queen Margaret had frozen him out; he'd spent ten years in the wilderness beyond the Court. And even last January, when he'd taken over the Chancellorship from old Archbishop Stafford, she'd continued to ignore him. But now he saw full power within his grasp at last. If he could defeat York, the Queen's gratitude would be sweet indeed!

Even at seventy years of age, the favour of a young woman as beautiful as Margaret of Anjou was warmly desirable – such excitements seldom came the way of a Canon lawyer...

# 7

London was full of armed men. As Cecily rode with Richard, Devon, Norfolk and their escorts through the wet December streets, groups of horsemen and foot soldiers wearing every badge and livery imaginable passed by. She saw the fetterlock cognisance of York being displayed in many places, and citizens wearing white roses on their sleeves. She heard people cheering Richard as their deliverer from misgovernment.

But Richard, riding alongside her from Westminster, was unresponsive to London's enthusiasm. He knew now as well as she did that it was over-optimistic...

Cardinal Kemp had tutored the King in evasive replies to all his demands. There would be no dismissal of royal officers. Henry 'saw no reason not to keep virtuous servants' by him. There would be no treason charge brought against Somerset for the loss of Normandy; instead, Somerset was to become head of the royal household. And, as for the Commons' plea that York be recognised as heir to the throne – the answer to *that* was the imprisonment of Thomas Young, the member for Bristol who'd voiced the petition.

'Yet,' people were arguing, 'should the King die childless without appointing an heir, will there not be strife between the followers of York and of Somerset?' These followers were now riding about in full armour so that the capital looked like a city invaded.

Reaching Blackfriars, Cecily saw Richard look with nostalgia to where Gloucester's old mansion, Baynard's Castle, towered above Puddle Dock. He'd once considered buying the huge place whose owner had been his friend but she'd advised him against doing so because Gloucester had died under a treason charge and with the Queen's enmity pointed at his throat. Cecily hadn't wanted Richard's friendship with the dead Duke to be remembered. Nor had she herself wanted to live in the same castle where Eleanor of Gloucester had practised witchcraft against the King. Henry's half-brother, Edmund Tudor, lived there now. She'd heard he'd already begun preparing it for his child-bride, Margaret Beaufort, who must be about eleven years of age by this time... Determinedly not looking at Baynard's Castle, Cecily rode on; but, in her mind's eye, she could still see the Hamolake Tower, its stones much older than any other part of the building, rising from the courtyard wall, and hear her dead cousin of Gloucester's voice proudly proclaiming its history: 'That tower was given to Sir William de Ros of Hamolake in Yorkshire by my grandsire, King Edward the Third, for the yearly rent of one rose—' Ah, poor Gloucester, such romantic details had always fascinated him.

A commotion outside a house that lay just ahead brought her attention back sharply to the present. Voices were chanting, 'Justice – justice – vengeance – vengeance!'

and a great rabble of murderous-looking men was converging upon the house.

Richard motioned his body-squire to get Cecily out of harm's way down a side street. Then he himself, backed by Devon and Norfolk, charged the crowd and fought his way around to the back of the building.

'What is it? – what's afoot?' Cecily cried to the squire who was dragging her nervous horse towards an archway.

'Aw, just a bunch of mutinous soldiers back from Normandy, ma'am,' he panted. 'They've nowt to do these times except brawl.'

'But the house – *who lives in there?*' It was the focal point of hostility.

He backed her mount under the arch.

'Edmund Beaufort, Duke of Somerset,' he muttered.

Beaufort's house. Lord God! Richard had gone around back to gain entry: he could kill Somerset and blame it on the mob. Only yesterday, he'd vowed to have the ex-Governor of Normandy's life—

Shivering, she watched the heaving, cursing band break down the gates, then surge towards the house entrance. Now they were smashing windows, climbing through with weapons and torches, and shouting: 'Beaufort – Beaufort – come forth to answer for Normandy!'

She closed her eyes and swayed against the esquire's arm: her advancing pregnancy often made her feel sick lately...

The journey from Ireland and all the worry since then about Richard's position had exhausted her. Yet she'd insisted on being in London for this Parliament, to hear for herself how things went for him, because he always tried to keep the worst news from her. Now she knew he'd gained nothing by seeing the King at Michaelmas. Kemp had thwarted him. And the Queen had joined with Somerset in an implacable hostility to all his aims. Only the commons were with him. The majority of the lords were against, in fear, suspicion and jealousy.

The crackle of flames was growing louder than the shouting. She opened her eyes to see orange sparks flying – blood and sweat gleamed on the soldiers' faces—

Oh, it would be easy now for Richard to kill Somerset; to rid himself, and the realm, of this foxy traitor. But if he gave in to such temptation, how could he ever stand again as the champion of order and justice? Up to now, he had treated his enemies with scrupulous correctness. One murder would drag him down to the level of a mere brigand.

She prayed that Richard would restrain within himself the terrible temper of the Plantagenets and would act only on their honour.

As smoke billowed towards her, she had to fight waves of nausea. The child seemed to be heaving inside her. Not in the sturdy kicking movements of a healthy infant but with a convulsive jerking that brought pain worse than labour.

She felt the young squire frenziedly dragging her off her horse, then half-carrying her in his arms as he stumbled off towards the river... The last thing she remembered was feeling rather sorry for him: she was a big woman when she was so far advanced with child.

After a long while, she was aware of him shouting hoarsely for a boatman and of a voice answering from what seemed to be mid-river: 'All right, all right.' The voice, accompanied by much splashing, drew nearer. 'Such turmoil hereabout,' it grumbled. 'Earl o' Devon's barge near cut us in two a minute back. Racing for the Tower it was, carrying the Earl himself and the Duke o' York and –

would ye credit it? – *Somerset* cradled like a babe between them!'

'Oh, thank God,' she breathed as they set her gently down on rocking boards. But it was for Somerset's safety she was grateful. Her own pain doubled her up and she knew that she must lose this child.

Perhaps the tidings of its loss would gladden the barren Queen.

WITH SCANT CEREMONY Richard deposited Edmund Beaufort on the water-steps of the Tower, then leapt back into Devon's barge and ordered it to speed up-river again. He wanted to return at once to the scene of the disturbance; to make sure that Cecily was all right, and to take charge of the miscreants who'd fired Somerset's house – his men had already arrested the ringleaders before he'd left.

For all that his sympathies were with the ragged ex-soldiers from France, he knew that he dared show them no leniency: they had attacked the Constable of England with murderous intent. And he would give his own enemies no opportunity to say that York was following in Gloucester's footsteps by cultivating the mob. Still, just one hanging might be made to suffice...

In the sidestreet he searched hurriedly for Cecily and the squire but, not finding them nor their horses, he assumed they'd ridden on to Coldharbour House – the Neville residence in London where he and Cecily and the children were staying at that time. Delaying no further, he rejoined his escort who had rounded up about a score of rioters and bound them hand to hand.

'Who is your leader?' he asked.

'I am.' A villainous-looking fellow glowered at him.

There was only half an ear on one side of the fellow's head – the other half had been left nailed to a post long ago for some other crime.

'You know you must die for inciting men to violence against the Constable of England's person and property?'

'Constable – bah!' said the man, spitting. 'And that goes for the King too—'

'Enough,' Richard thundered. 'You have condemned yourself out of your own mouth. I sentence you to be hanged at once.'

The man shrugged. 'Hang me then, lord Duke. But one last request—'

'What is it?'

'That I be strung from the inn-sign of the Standard in Cheapside. Strongest ale in London at the Standard. And warmest landlord's wife abed!'

'Much good either will do you now, fool,' Richard said almost compassionately. 'But your request is granted if the sign be strong enough for your weight.'

'And if it break, lord Duke?' The fellow was laughing.

'You'll die today in any case, make no mistake of that.' Then Richard ordered his guards to take the condemned man to Cheapside and to hold the others bound while they witnessed the execution.

He himself departed without further delay for Coldharbour House.

THE INN-SIGN of the Standard bore its unaccustomed burden with indifference. A few apprentices had come out from nearby shops to watch the hanging but it was raining heavily so they didn't tarry long; as soon as the body had ceased to writhe, they went back to their benches.

The landlord of the inn requested that the corpse should not be cut down until next morning. It would be good for a wet night's trade, he said – something for his customers to gawp at and talk about since many of them had known the one-eared fellow who used to drink here... The landlord would also like his own good wife to hear the creaking of the rope after they went to bed together in the room above the sign. She'd always been at such pains to assure him how much she disliked this former regular patron of the inn that it must give her great pleasure to know he was hanging dead beneath her window.

But Mercer Wainstead came rushing over from his shop across the road, furiously demanding the instant removal of the felon's corpse. It was not right, he shouted at the captain of the Duke of York's guard, that a merchant who had supplied the late great Cardinal Beaufort with cloths and tapestries should have a sight like this hung up opposite his windows. Especially when his wife was yet weak from the birth of their infant daughter.

In the bedchamber opposite the inn-sign lay Mistress Wainstead; a grey-eyed little woman with hair like spun flax. She had once been exceedingly gay and pretty; but marriage to the short-tempered, money-grabbing Thomas Wainstead had wilted a spirit which had needed a sunnier soil. She knew now that she'd soon be as dead as the man on the end of that rope.

Weak tears filled her eyes and overflowed onto her pillow as she turned to look at the baby.

Such a pretty baby girl. Tiny and silvery-fair. With a moist mouth that seemed to smile always, even in sleep...

From across the road, Mistress Wainstead could hear the squeak of a knife cutting through the wet rope. Thomas was having his way again and was making the

Duke of York's men cut the body down, despite loud protests from the landlord of the inn.

Thomas would always impose his own will, whether for good or evil, with bluster and self-importance. He'd do it even to this child of his. Force her into marriage with some suitable, earnest, ungenerous man.

'Little Jane, I pray love and laughter for you,' her mother whispered.

THE SON BORN PREMATURELY to the Yorks at Coldharbour House was christened Thomas. He died before the baptismal waters were dry.

As soon as she could face the four-day journey, Cecily left London for the castle of Fotheringhay in Northamptonshire. There at least, in the broad placid countryside bordering the river Nene, the other children would be safe and healthy. London was overcrowded – full of disease and disorder.

The disorder had spread into Kent where the damped-down fires of Cade's rebellion were again flickering sullenly. There were no harvests to see to now, this bleak January of 1451, and men had time to remember the list of complaints which their dead leader had drawn up and which had been totally ignored, despite all promises. So there were stirrings – skirmishes – riots.

Richard of York rode down into Kent at the head of troops which Edmund Beaufort, as Constable, should have been leading; but Beaufort was too vulnerable by now to risk such an unpopular journey, which must end in trials and executions of rebels.

Twenty-nine Kentish men in all Richard had to condemn and see beheaded. Yet he contrived to lead many others into the King's path, when Henry himself rode into chastened Kent, knowing that Henry would pardon them if they threw themselves on his mercy. Henry wept, and pardoned without question.

The glowering populace cursed York. Many who had been his adherents in Cade's day now turned from him in hatred for what they bitterly called 'The Harvest of Heads'.

# 8

When Parliament was dissolved at the end of May, Richard joined his family in Northamptonshire but Cecily knew that he would not stay long. Nothing could hold him inactive now. And an even more furious energy possessed him when he heard that Somerset was to replace his brother-in-law of Buckingham as Captain of Calais.

'By the Mass—' a throbbing vein swelled in his neck '—the most prestigious post in France, commanding the strongest garrison, for the man who lost Normandy! And I was ordered to withdraw my few men from London's streets – *I wish now I'd let Somerset burn*!'

His rage frightened her but she could find nothing to say that might lessen it... He had not been thanked, last December, for saving Edmund Beaufort. Instead, three days afterwards, the King and his officers had ridden through the city in a massive show of strength and royal unity. Neither York nor any of his friends had been asked to take part in this procession which had been headed by Cardinal Kemp and smugly-smiling Somerset. The clear motif of the progress was: the King is strong enough to rule this realm with his chosen advisers and no outsiders are needed.

The snub to York was obvious to even the rawest apprentice, and many of his less-dedicated followers had left him soon after – excusing themselves for that 'he is doomed to fail when the Queen champions Somerset'.

But Cecily knew that her husband would never accept failure. He had pledged himself to reform the government; and he had tried, by the constitutional means of Parliament, so to do, only to be blocked at every turn by the clever Cardinal Kemp. Now there was but one course remaining open to him: the course of armed challenge. She'd realised he was committed to this when he told her he was leaving Fotheringhay and heading for Wales; and that he was taking his two eldest sons with him among his pages and body-squires.

She had no grounds for protest against the boys' going. They were nine and eight years old respectively and had been their father's pages since they were six. But her heart turned over at the thought of days without sight or sound of them when Richard too would be gone – days that would be filled with apprehension for their safety.

Richard stoutly upheld his decision. 'Time the lads learned something of their own country, Cis. They're virtually foreigners, the pair of them, what with being born in France and then living in Ireland. The heirs of York must be English to the backbone; and good soldiers – knowledgeable of the people – as well.'

Of course. That was as true of a royal Duke's sons as it was of a king's... She nodded, but she couldn't speak for the painful tightness in her throat.

Now it was the morning of departure. Fotheringhay's fetterlock-shaped courtyard rang with arms and horse-gear and men's voices – a peculiar medley of sound which she acknowledged as the background to her entire life. There was nothing quite like it, not even the same men and animals returning made a remotely similar noise to that of riding out.

Clutching the hands of her daughters Elisabeth and Margaret she watched the two young Earls, mounted, positioning themselves on either side of their father; Richard had allotted them the 'haunch-places' behind the leading squires so that they could proudly call themselves his 'hench-men' – he was always at pains not to favour one son even a fraction more than the other although his tenderness for little Edmund of Rutland betrayed him sometimes when he was brusque with the strapping Edward of March.

Looking at Edward's straight back now, Cecily had to blink away tears. Dickon didn't understand his son who was so unlike himself, so much a Neville. But his mother understood him: there was an extraordinary bond of affection and confidence between them... To Cecily alone, he'd uncovered his childish heartbreak at leaving Ireland during the last frenzied days of packing in Dublin Castle – '*I think I will die without Mary FitzGerald!*'

Ah, love, so soon... Recovering from her astonishment, she remembered how much time Edward had spent in the Dublin mansion of the Earl and Countess of Desmond. So he'd chosen one of their daughters for his first passion! A tiny splinter of pain lodged in her heart with the realisation that she must begin to share his affections with strangers; and that, for handsome outward-going Edward, there must be many loves in the future.

For the moment, however, her eldest son was entirely caught up in the excitement of this tour of estates with his father—

A tour of estates was what Dickon insisted he was

embarking upon. Yet Cecily well knew what he'd look for on his wide holdings: the number of tenants capable of bearing arms. These last few weeks here at Fotheringhay many men had visited him. There had been long private talks with some of them – particularly with Sir William Oldhall whom Dickon had recently created his Chamberlain. And secret documents had been drafted by the most trusted clerk.

Now the blue banners were being unfurled, the cavalcade was on the move. A lofty nod from the two boy Earls as they passed their mother and sisters. A blown kiss from the gauntlet of the Duke of York...

When the courtyard was quite empty, Cecily went to the castle chapel and remained on her knees a long while.

ALL THROUGH THAT summer and autumn of 1451, Cecily kept the younger children close about her at Fotheringhay and knew little of her husband's doings. He seldom wrote and then only briefly, as though there were matters afoot in which he did not wish to involve her. He'd left the boys at Ludlow in the care of Sir Richard Croft (who'd been on his staff in Normandy) when he himself had ridden to Devon in September.

The Devon business she knew about. People were still talking of it: how Richard had ended the nobles' war there which had terrorised the countryside for so long. By doing this he'd shown himself a public-spirited man with a far greater sense of urgency than the lethargic government. He'd made peace between enemies, dispersed private armies, restored order – all before the King had stirred out of Coventry. She was immensely proud of him. But she realised that, by acting without formal royal commission, he was now likely to be more unpopular at Court than ever. Especially since he'd chastened young James Butler, Ormonde's son, who was one of the Queen's favourites.

Thought of Ormonde saddened her with a sense of acute loss. The White Earl, whom Richard had left as his Deputy in Ireland, had died at the end of a long and vigorous campaign against rebellious chieftains. He'd worked himself to death in the service of the House of York. In a way, Cecily had loved Ormonde ever since the old days in Rouen; and the Dublin period had brought them closer than before, with its difficulties and its tensions. In the loneliness of Richard's absence, she'd often felt herself called towards the older man's side, but she'd deafened herself to the clamourings of that Neville blood which always took what it wanted. For Richard's sake, and for the children, and for her own friendship with the Countess of Ormonde, there must be no scandal involving her name again with that of James Butler, as had happened without cause in Rouen. So she'd held herself coolly apart from him at all times. But he'd known her thoughts – he'd understood the fullness of her nature.

Now he was dead. And his heir – the Queen's Earl of Wiltshire – had inherited the Deputyship of Ireland, as young Warwick had foreseen. It mean that Richard, who was still Lieutenant of Ireland, was virtually cut off from his interests and revenues there, unless he went back.

Cecily shivered despite the firelit warmth of the solar where she was helping her small daughters with their embroidery. Remembrance of Dublin Castle in the wintertime always made her shiver and she had no desire to return; but she'd go without complaint if Richard felt that he'd be more his own man there. He'd achieved nothing by leaving, and coming to the King. Somerset was advanced to greater and greater power while the country disintegrated into riot and ferment. There were rumours of unrest on the Welsh Marches and – uncomfortably nearer home – in Cambridgeshire, Rutland and Lincolnshire. The latest news from France had been responsible for the newest outbreaks of violence at home: Guienne had been attacked by the French and had appealed to England for aid, but of the army of 3,000 which had cost England dear, not a man was sent to Guienne. So the people there, seeing they were deserted and left to face a united France, proceeded to make the best terms they could for themselves. They agreed that, if no relief came by the 18$^{th}$ day of August, they would formally surrender and swear allegiance to the King of France... On the appointed day, the heralds had mounted to the walls of Bordeaux and blown a last summons to England. England had not answered. So the city opened her gates and again became part of France—

Elisabeth raised her head from her embroidery. 'There's someone at the postern, Mother.'

Margaret ran to the window and cried: 'It's Sir William Oldhall!'

Cecily put her needle and silks away quickly. Sir William might be bringing news from Richard. She sent the reluctant Elisabeth and Margaret to join their brother George in the nursery; then she called servants to light candles because the short November day would soon be drawing in.

But Oldhall brought no messages from Richard. He said he hadn't seen him lately although he was riding about on the Duke's business.

'Many men from His Grace's old Normandy staff are so travelling,' he told Cecily as he rubbed his hands before the fire. 'We've all worked hard on behalf of the House of

York, ma'am. And now, everything is prepared.' He seemed glowingly satisfied.

Without having the least idea what he was talking about, she nodded as she poured wine for him.

'Yes,' he went on, 'we have planned – recruited – stirred up risings. There will be demonstrations in the towns of Fotheringhay and Grantham tomorrow. In Stamford the day after that and—' He stood there, a sober respectable man who'd been Speaker in the last Parliament, calmly telling her that he was going about fostering rebellion! – a crime for which he could pay with his life.

'Sir William,' she asked softly, 'what is the purpose of all this?'

'Why, Madam, to create enough popular unrest to overawe the Court, of course. King Henry may yet be *frightened* into dismissing his corrupt ministers and equipping a new army for Guienne. But, if he proves obstinate or unheeding, the forces which His Grace of York is now collecting will surely alter the royal mind. Everything is arranged for early spring. Letters have been sent by the Duke to many towns, telling them of his aims and asking their support.'

'Will the King not be shown these letters?' she enquired – wondering wildly if Richard had actually signed them.

'Perhaps.' Sir William seemed undisturbed by the possibility. 'But the forewarning will do the Court no good. York is now prepared to meet the entire royal army; to arrest Somerset and all the other enemies of the realm and then to take upon himself, with every true lord, the direction of the King. So we will have proper governance at last *and* an army for the recovery of Bordeaux. The 3,000 men standing idle under Woodville's captaincy have cost us £13,000 already but will never be sent as long as Somerset has need of them. It's the Kyrielle and Suffolk story all over again.'

'Then my cousin Edmund Beaufort fears something?'

'Aye, ma'am: he fears your husband. And with good reason.' The knight finished his wine at a gulp; then drew on his thick riding gloves.

'You're not staying here tonight?' Cecily asked, surprised.

'No, Your Grace, I'm for Stamford. There's a Dominican friar there named John Deeping who's done our cause much good by preaching all around Lincolnshire, urging people to support the Duke of York. With him I'll lodge so we can spend the night planning further operations...' He kissed her hand, bowed, and left hurriedly. She heard him ride away into the thickening dusk – a man so dedicated to her husband's cause that food and sleep and safety seemed to interest him no longer. There might be dozens – hundreds – like him.

Overwhelmed by the magnitude and seriousness of this insurrection to which Richard was putting his name, she stared unseeingly into the fire. Sir William had outlined only the results of success: but what if failure were the outcome?

# 9

March winds reddened the noses of the crowd gathered around St Paul's. A man's high beaver hat blew off and went bowling into the path of the King's horse. Henry rode over it with eyes downcast but unseeing; it was soon trampled flat by the hundreds of slow-pounding hooves that followed him.

Edmund Beaufort, Captain of Calais, rode on the Queen's right side, old Chancellor Kemp on her left; all three faces registered pleasure and triumph. Behind them came the imposing figure of the new Constable, Henry, Viscount Beaufort, his escort surrounding the rebel Duke of York whom he'd lately brought prisoner to London.

People craned their necks for sight of York but all they could glimpse between the armed ranks was the billowing blue of his mantle. 'A shame——' some muttered '——so to humiliate him.' But others argued he was lucky not to have been tried for treason: 'He raised an army against the King, did he not?'

Now and then, Cecily could see the wind-blown plume in her husband's cap. She kept her eyes fixed on its whiteness and paid no attention to her brother-in-law of Buckingham who was riding alongside her, nor to Salisbury, Warwick and the Bourchiers just ahead: she'd quarrelled violently with all of them over Richard's betrayal, though they'd sworn to her that they'd acted in good faith – *'Would we have damned our own fame by carrying lies to him?'*

Her anger had cooled now and she could examine the whole wretched affair objectively, as much as she knew of it...

AFTER BEING REFUSED admission to London, Richard's forces had faced the royal army in Kent. The King had sent a delegation of lords and bishops to Richard, promising that his demands for Somerset's removal would be met, so he had dispersed his army at once and gone joyfully to the King's tent. Whereupon the Constable had arrested him, dragged him prisoner to London and shut him up in a lodging there eight days ago. Never had an honourable man been so shamefully tricked. He'd trusted the royal word, borne by his own kinsmen so that, alone and unarmed, he'd walked into the trap which Somerset and the Queen had laid for him.

Now, his army broken up and all his captains imprisoned, he was being taken to St Paul's to make a public statement as the price of his liberty. He was to beg the King's pardon for resorting to arms; he was to withdraw all charges against Somerset; and he was to swear to live quietly on his own estates henceforward – exiled from the King's presence and from all place in the country's government. It was tantamount to a renunciation of his heirship to the Crown. Truly his enemies' triumph was complete this 10th day of March, 1452.

Cecily looked up at the lightning-damaged steeple of St Paul's so as not to have to see the faces crowding around the West Door. *Aye, citizens of London*, she thought, *you shut your gates against my lord when he came to deliver you from bad government. You forced him into hostile Kent where the memory of the Harvest of Heads is still green. But yet he could have gained his objective had not treachery been put into the mouths of his kinsmen.*

One knew not whom to trust now, when even the pious King could lie.

As soon as the painful ceremony in St Paul's was over (during which even the Lieutenancy of Ireland was taken from Richard) he and Cecily set out for Fotheringhay. There, with the younger children – Edward and Edmund remaining at Ludlow with tutors – they faithfully lived the private life which Richard had sworn to follow.

Visitors were few. Many of their old friends were still in prison or lying low. No new friends sought them out. And those kinsmen who'd formed the royal delegation in Kent were too embarrassed to come – they'd suffered from the flail of Cecily's anger and the cool disillusionment of Richard's eye – so they stayed away, with their wives and families. The isolation was completed by the withdrawal of John Mowbray, Duke of Norfolk – that nephew of Cecily's who was always designated '*young* John' although his namesake father had been dead these twenty years. Cecily never really discovered why Norfolk had deserted Richard, whose ally he'd been. But she suspected that the death of his stepfather, Tom Strangeways, and the re-marriage of his mother had much to do with it... The irrepressible Katherine, finding herself a widow for the second time, had married the Viscount Beaumont – the man who, as

Constable of England, had arrested Richard and who was firmly of the Queen's party. So Cecily saw no more of Katherine now than she did of Ann of Buckingham – that sharp-tongued sister she'd avoided for years.

Still, she felt no great need to contact with the outside world. Fotheringhay enclosed all her interests and there were frequent letters from the boys at Ludlow – mostly complaining about their tutor, Sir Richard Croft, whose fearful disciplines irked them, or asking, with as much urgency as if they lived at Court, for new clothes to be sent to them.

Their father would smile patiently over these letters; and, in answer to Cecily's probing about whether Sir Richard might actually be too hard on them, would reply: 'All boys regard their tutors as tyrants, sweetheart. When they grow up they'll worship his memory. Croft is a good man.'

Satisfied for the time being then, she would put her sewing-women to work on caps and doublets, hose and mantles to be packed off by the next carrier to Ludlow... She'd had to engage many extra sewing-women from the town lately. There was a trousseau to be got ready for daughter Anne who was soon to wed Henry Holland, Earl of Exeter. And there was a layette to be prepared for the new baby expected in the autumn.

Cecily hoped this latest child of hers would be a girl. Too many of her boys had died and she wanted what might be a last healthy baby for her approaching middle-age; one to whom she could give all the attention for which public life had never allowed her time before. She was turned thirty-seven, and although her body was still slim and resilient, she doubted if she'd conceive again. She doubted it because her husband was no longer the vital man of last springtime when he'd been planning his great coup against Beaufort.

She'd been with him at Ludlow during the few brief tension-filled weeks while his army gathered. She'd seen him sign his famous letter to Shrewsbury town, '*Your good friend, Richard York*'. And she'd watched him ride away from her after a night of joyous loving: a taut, confident commander at the head of a loyal army.

Now she scarcely recognised him for what he'd been then… Wearily apathetic, he tried to fill his days with interests which did not engage his brooding mind. And at nights he lay passionlessly wakeful beside her, or tossed and muttered in nightmares.

Failure, frustration and disgrace had destroyed the husband she had known. She tried to accept the destruction but she could not. Deep in her soul there was a rage — a defiance of fate.

ON THE EVENING OF MONDAY, October 2$^{nd}$, Cecily gave birth to a tiny, dark-haired boy. He looked so delicate that the castle chaplain was called at once to baptise him in the Keep apartments instead of in the courtyard chapel or the splendid new collegiate church of Fotheringhay. Cecily felt that any journey through the damp autumn air would extinguish her son's feeble life.

'What name do you want for him, sweetheart?' Richard whispered. They had only discussed girls' names — she'd been so certain, or she'd hoped so hard, that this child would be a girl.

'I want him called for you, Dickon. Even though he's weak and little, he has a look of you. I suppose it's his hair...' The infant was the only one of their sons to be born dark.

'Very well—' he signed to the priest '—Richard it is.'

She could tell by his tone that he felt it didn't make much difference what name was given: it would only be a short time in use. She began to weep quietly, despairingly. This baby, conceived in hope of power but born to its loss, was now the final symbol of his father's youth. And it seemed impossible that he could survive the night.

Yet, a week later, the new infant was living still, and Cecily's spirits lifted although it wrenched her heart to watch what a struggle it was for him to breathe and feed.

Then— 'Our youngest lord is a fighter,' she overheard one of the nurses say to Mistress Fletcher. 'If he's reared, God willing, he'll make as good a soldier as his sire!'

*He* must *be reared*, she thought. *I cannot part with him now...* This sad, fragile, obstinate babe had crept into the warmest corner of her heart, and pleas for his survival dominated all her prayers – prayers which she sensibly backed up with arrangements for him to be kept in the same room where he'd been born. The nursery suite was still occupied by Margaret and George – rumbustious children both, who never shut doors behind them – so little Dickon would be better off, for the winter, remaining in his parents' apartment.

He was only once carried down to the Hall. That was when King Henry paid an unscheduled visit to Fotheringhay during his autumn progress through the south-eastern counties. Neither Somerset nor Margaret was with the royal retinue at the time (the Queen having pushed impatiently ahead to see her new College at Cambridge, and Somerset having stayed close to her as usual) so Henry had decided to take this rare opportunity of visiting his isolated kinsman without fear of being ordered otherwise.

Margaret would be cross afterwards, of course, when she heard. But then, Margaret was mostly cross these days. Unless the Earl of Wiltshire or young Henry Beaufort, Somerset's heir, were around.

Richard and Cecily received their King in the torch-lit courtyard and walked with him to the Hall where the oriel window still held the last glow of the autumn evening. Cecily's greeting to Henry had been stiff, formal – she could not forget his treatment of her husband – but when those pale wistful eyes rested upon her, uncomprehendingly, she failed to maintain hostility to them. Whatever Henry had done must have been in ignorance or blind obedience. And he looked so frail – so old almost – though he was yet two months off his thirtieth birthday.

In the Hall, she presented Elisabeth and Margaret to him. Elisabeth was so rigid with awe that she stared straight in front of her all the time; but Margaret's bold dark glance travelled mercilessly from the King's lank hair to his rounded shoulders, and down the travel-stained length of his gown to his strange old-fashioned shoes, then up again to the long pallid face.

'I have a new brother, Sir,' she said brightly.

The royal countenance registered nothing but gentle pleasure at this news. 'Right glad we are to hear that, little lady. May the Virgin Mother and all the Saints keep him.' Then, to Cecily with the first glimmer of animation, 'Madame, could he be brought? For it is good to look upon the composition of Heaven's Kingdom: a child newborn and baptised.'

'Of – of course, Sire.' Wishing that Margaret had kept her prattling tongue quiet, she despatched a page with orders for little Dickon's nurse to carry her charge down. While she waited, she quieted her own fears: Anne Fletcher would see that the girl wrapped him well, and the

Hall was warm in any case. Besides, it would hurt Henry less to be presented with this weakling babe than with apple-cheeked golden George who wasn't allowed to meals in Hall yet. Next to Edward, George was the most beautiful of all the York children – even though his sunny charm often clouded over unpredictably and he'd drag away, wary-eyed, from those he'd kissed a moment before! Cecily sometimes wondered if the changeable Irish weather hadn't somehow affected George from his birth in Dublin.

She saw Richard talking to the King, his expression warm, relaxed. Clearly, he bore Henry no malice – even though the King had humiliated him still further lately by allowing Somerset to preside over the trials of York tenants and retainers at Ludlow Castle, home of the spring rising. But, like herself, Richard could neither blame nor hate Henry for anything that was done against them.

The royal attendants were crowding noisily around the trestle tables now as the smell of the evening meal wafted in from the kitchens. The few nobles Margaret and Somerset had left with the King were mounting the dais.

'Ah, sweet brother,' Henry said anxiously to a young man passing by, 'are you feeling better than you did this morning at Holy Mass?'

Edmund Tudor, Earl of Richmond, replied, 'I thank you, my lord King. Yes – much better—' But even this short speech was broken by a jagged rasp of coughing.

Cecily continued to look at the young Earl of Richmond who'd gone over to lean against a window. He had sunken cheeks and pale eyes. There was an air of feverish exhaustion about him, and she could see that the thin hand which he put to his mouth was unsteady... Concerned, she went to him.

'My lord—' she noticed the film of sweat on his gaunt face '—would you like to retire to a private chamber?'

'No, Madame—' he choked. 'This will pass – in a moment.' With his sleeve he wiped a red fleck off his lips. He was trembling all over like a winded horse.

She signed a page to bring him wine. While he drank, she watched him unobtrusively; seeing, in his long mobile throat and Valois nose, the marked resemblance to the late Queen Catherine, his mother.

'Ah, that's better. I'm grateful, Madame.' He met her eye. 'Perhaps I can repay your kindness sometime at Baynard's Castle?'

'There's nothing to repay,' she smiled. 'But maybe I shall see you when next I visit London. You may even be wedded by then. If so, I wish you and the Countess Margaret much joy.' She felt it was a hollow wish, and she turned away to hide the pity she felt for this eldest half-brother of the King. *Though more like,* she reflected, *it's little Margaret Beaufort who deserves the pity.*

A young nurse had brought baby Dickon to the curtained doorway of the solar behind the High Table and was frenziedly trying to catch Cecily's eye to know what to do next. Cecily took the infant from her – even with his shawls and swaddlings, he seemed to weigh nothing – and carried him to the King.

Henry gazed benignly down at the wizened little face. Baby Dickon opened blue-grey eyes and seemed to focus them on the royal countenance. There was a moment of heavy silence while the frail King continued to regard the frail infant; then he made the Sign of the Cross over the child's forehead with his fingertips and said simply: 'May God bless him. And may he grow up to be as fine a youth as either of his brothers whom I saw at Ludlow.'

Cecily bowed her head – touched by the childless

King's ability to admire, without envy, another man's heirs. Then she sent the nurse back quickly to the Keep apartments with the baby.

During the meal which followed, she heard Henry telling Richard how the relief army had gone out at last to Guienne under the leadership of John Talbot, Earl of Shrewsbury. Richard appeared to be trying to share the King's sense of achievement for this belated act but Cecily could read his dismayed thoughts:

*Shrewsbury, the last of Henry the Fifth's great captains: he must be well over seventy years of age by now. What a pass has England come to when she summons to arms such old men from their hearths and their slippers, and leaves younger ones to rot at home under the Queen's spite.*

## 10

Richard followed reports of the Guienne campaign with morose concentration. By Christmas, the valiant Talbot had managed to relieve Bordeaux. But, come the spring, the French were advancing against him in three great armies, with King Charles commanding a reserve in the rear. These armies were said to have siege and field guns among their equipment.

'Has Talbot any guns, Dickon?' Cecily asked.

'No. And probably wouldn't use them if he had. He regards the longbow as sacred.'

'Must he fail then?'

'As sure as judgment day, poor old warrior. Weaned on tales of Crécy and Poitiers – taught his strategy by Henry the Fifth – and now sent out with an inadequate force and no artillery – how could he win, Cis? And I'll lie idle here while he's murdered; while my friends are persecuted; and while twenty thousand archers are kept at home to support a villainous government.'

Richard's gloom had deepened during this present

Parliament which had outlawed his Chamberlain, Sir William Oldhall. Oldhall's goods and properties had been distributed to members of the Queen's party. And whatever small hopes of reform had been gained in the previous Parliament had been dashed in this one. Unworthy officers were now packed tighter than ever about the King (Henry would be unable to visit Fotheringhay so casually ever again!) and it was for their protection that the huge force of fighting men was being kept: a force which should have gone out to Guienne long ago, with or without guns...

By July, the French army was entrenched at Castillon, only thirty miles from Bordeaux. A fortified camp on the east side of the town had been specially designed by Jean Bureau, master gunner, to give the French artillery a maximum of oblique and enfilade fire. Talbot attacked this camp frontally.

'It was sheer suicide, Your Graces,' a broken survivor of the battle of Castillon related afterwards at Fotheringhay. 'We were all on foot except great Talbot himself – he was so old and stiff that he remained mounted on a little white palfrey, though it made him a target for the French guns. The palfrey was killed under him by a cannonball. Afterwards, he fought on until his thigh was broken by another ball. Only then did he and his son begin to retreat towards a ford over the river. There they were both killed and the army broken up...'

Richard covered his eyes with his hand and remained silent a long time. Talbot had been his friend since the siege of Orléans, twenty-four years ago. Now, the prophecy which the Maid had spoken during that siege was truly come to pass: the English were driven out of every foot of France (except for Calais) and the dowry which Eleanor of

Aquitaine had brought to Henry Plantagenet three centuries before was lost, along with all the blood-soaked conquests of Edward the Third and Henry the Fifth.

Leaving her husband with the soldier from Castillon, Cecily went to her own solar. There she took out pen, ink and fine white paper: she wanted to write to John Talbot's widow Margaret, Countess of Shrewsbury, whom she'd known in Rouen – Margaret had been quite young then, being Talbot's second wife.

But what could one say, even to the closest friend, as consolation for losing a husband and a son? The unlucky Countess would not even have her eldest daughter's company now either, because young Eleanor Talbot had been wedded recently. She'd married Thomas Lord Butler, the Baron Sudely – a brother of that Lady Elisabeth Saye who'd stood godmother at the heir of York's christening in Rouen. The irrepressible Lady Elisabeth had come to Fotheringhay to tell Cecily all about the wedding; and had raved, in her usual extravagant manner, about the bride:

'She's entirely beautiful, I tell you! Tall and dark and of *immense* dignity for all she's only fifteen. Great strength of character too, I should say – but that's only to be expected, isn't it, with a sire like Earl John?'

Aye, John 'Good Dog' Talbot had been a man of iron principle. Even his enemies, the French, had called him *le roi* and not entirely for his obstinate pride – he had a kind of presence which had quelled even the Irish who hated him. It seemed that his daughter Eleanor had inherited this presence; and perhaps the obstinacy and pride also.

Sighing, Cecily began to write to the Countess Margaret, the young woman's mother, who was remote kin to the Nevilles.

It was given out officially that the news of Castillon had so greatly distressed the King that he had retired, with his consort, to the royal hunting lodge at Clarendon in remotest Wiltshire. Weeks went by without a report of either of them being seen.

'Henry must be very ill, Dickon,' Cecily remarked at last early in October, 'else Margaret wouldn't be away from the hub of affairs for so long. I haven't heard of the Queen making a journey or a public appearance since – oh, it must be July...' Which was odd for the energetic and gregarious Margaret of Anjou.

Richard merely grunted, as though the matter had no interest for him. Yet she knew he'd been having inquiries made. And he'd travelled to Westminster several times lately although he had no place on the royal Council. Something strange was afoot, she was sure of it... But Richard said nothing until he rode home to Fotheringhay from London late on the evening of October 14$^{th}$. Then he drew her at once into the solar with him and carefully shut the door.

'Cis,' he said abruptly, 'I have two things to tell you and you'll find both of them startling – maybe even distressing. I think you'd best sit down.'

She sat, gripping her girdle-Rosary and staring at her husband who paced before the fire.

'The first news,' he said grimly, 'is that the King has been out of his mind since about last August.'

Her hand, still holding the Rosary, jerked to her lips. 'You mean – like his French grandsire – *mad?*' How ironic that poor Queen Catherine's legitimacy should thus be proved—

'I don't know whether Henry's illness is the same as Charles' was or not; only that they've both been stricken at about the same age. But, from what I hear, Henry is neither violent nor raving as the late Valois was – just completely senseless and without ability to move.'

'Catalepsy,' she whispered – remembering a man's rigid body which she'd once helped Anne of Bedford to tend. Anne had told her that the man had suffered a great shock just before he'd fallen into this pitiable state. Then another, older, memory intruded: of a small boy in royal robes at a knighting ceremony. That day in Leicester cathedral, Henry's eyes had gone blank as if his spirit had taken flight. *And Queen Catherine had wept.*

'Whatever his condition is called,' Richard was saying harshly, 'no one has been able to communicate with him for almost three months. Yet the Council has gone on acting as though with the King's approval – backing Margaret's pretence that all was normal. God knows how long this charade would have been kept up had it not been for the second occurrence.' He went on pacing, his hands knotted behind his back.

'What is it, Dickon?' she prompted, a splinter of fear at her heart.

'This: I am no longer heir to the throne, even in theory.'

She sprang up. 'You mean Somerset's claim has been allowed?'

'No. Neither his nor mine now – the battle is over. Cis, yesterday Margaret gave birth to a son.'

It was fully a minute before she could grasp what he'd said to her. Margaret. Mother of a boy-child. After seven barren years. But she couldn't be. Henry was too feeble – too childish himself ever to have been fully a husband to her… Gropingly, she asked: '*Can* the infant be Henry's?' And answered her own question with an emphatic, 'No.'

'We must never say that.' Richard grasped her hands painfully. 'Slander must be no weapon of ours against the Queen. There is no proof of her son's bastardy. There never can be—'

'But *everyone* will say the child is not Henry's, Dickon! Are they not saying it already?'

'Yes. Yes.' He released her hands to run blunt fingers through his own greying hair. 'London is frenzied with all manner of tales. That the infant is of Somerset's begetting — or of his son's, young Henry Beaufort's. Wiltshire has also been named and heaven knows how many more — Margaret's noble blood hasn't saved her from a charge of whoring with half the Court! But I'll not lay tongue to these charges, Cis. I'll swear allegiance to the new Prince as soon as he's brought forth in public.'

She found herself marvelling at his patient loyalty while, at the same time, an obscure anger stirred in her. She hadn't realised until this moment how confident she'd been these past few years that either her husband or her eldest son would eventually succeed Henry. Now they were both put aside forever — by a child whom she had little doubt was a bastard... Margaret had either given in to the temptations of the flesh (as Queen Catherine had done before her, albeit in widowhood) or else she'd conceived cold-bloodedly after being convinced by her councillors that it was the only way to uphold Henry's tottering kingship and reverse her own unpopularity with the people.... Oh, the Queen's churchmen would be quick to absolve her from sin — Kemp and Booth both owed their positions to Margaret's patronage; they would argue that she had only ever done her duty to the impotent Henry. And her women friends (of whom Alice Chaucer and Jacquetta Woodville were the leaders) would convince her that she owed satisfaction to herself, as a passionate and beautiful Queen still only twenty-two years old—

But Somerset? Would *he* further a scheme by which his own claims would be destroyed at the same time as York's? Yes, Edmund Beaufort was spiteful enough. And the advantage would still be his, of retaining power until the Prince grew up, without the embarrassment of York's title always hanging over him.

'I think you should not be so quick,' she said tightly to Richard now, 'to accept this child who puts your own heir aside.'

The implied accusation of loving Edward, Earl of March, too little, stung him: it was a friction that had always lain between himself and Cecily, unspoken. Now he lashed out: 'Mayhap my heir's title is flawed too!'

She felt herself go white to the lips. 'Richard,' she said in a voice that was not her own, 'you must be under great strain to speak so to me.' And she swept away from him, her mind seething.

He came after her at once; spinning her around to face him; grasping her roughly by the shoulders so that her bodice dragged across her breasts.

'Hear me out. Flawed by rumour bred of your own recklessness, Cis! It's what people say, not what I believe. And you are strong enough to accept that they will always say it—'

'Yes. I know.' Suddenly the tension went out of her and she leaned against him. 'It will always be said that Edward of March is John Blaeburn's son…' Present pain reached forward to the future: one day, Edward would hear himself called 'the archer's son'. And he would come to her, bewildered and accusing… No matter what defence she put up, her authority over him would be undermined for all time.

And, worse, perhaps his own confidence in himself was shaken—

She straightened up, disentangled herself from Richard's grasp and pulled away from him, saying very calmly: 'Let us discuss this present business and nothing else. The King has been out of his mind for near three months and we were not told – not called to take your place at the head of affairs as his heir. Now there is a Prince. What will happen?'

'I don't know.' He walked away from her. 'There is no precedent. But I think the country must be ruled again as when Henry was an infant: that is, by a new Council chosen from among all the magnates of the realm and acting under a Protector. I expect a summons to attend this Council election in a day or two...'

It was ten days before the summons arrived. Somerset fought to exclude York altogether but the other magnates had refused to allow this.

Richard arrived at Westminster on October 23$^{rd}$. There, by a majority vote of his peers, he was appointed Protector and Chief Councillor of the Realm, with special responsibility for the country's defence.

Almost the first act of his Protectorate was to lock Somerset up in the Tower, on the treason charge he'd waited so long to bring against him.

'Removing the Duke of Somerset from office,' he explained, 'is the best means I know of defending England.' Beaufort would be brought to a fair trial in due course.

Meanwhile, Richard acted with moderation, humility and restraint so that many of the great magnates now adhered openly to him and opposed the furious Queen who was petitioning to be made Regent.

Some observers of the widening gulf between the two parties saw mystical banners of war unfurling. On the one side was the restrained White Rose of York maintaining its long-denied rights. On the other was the passionate crimson bloom which motherhood had brought to full flower in Margaret's heart.

## 11

For nearly fourteen months now, Richard had been Protector of the Realm, and the country was beginning to right itself under his steady hand. In Derbyshire, he had settled the dangerous conflict between the Blounts and the Longfords; up in the north, he had quelled the Percy-stirred risings; and over in the southwest, he had carried out the painful duty of imprisoning his own son-in-law, Henry Holland, Duke of Exeter.

That this duty had cost Richard dear in sleeplessness and worry, Cecily knew, for she travelled everywhere with him nowadays and shared his vigorous life. Yet he'd had no choice except to imprison their eldest daughter's husband who was getting up to all sorts of dangerous mischiefs – even to claiming the Duchy of Lancaster on the grounds that John of Gaunt had been his great-grandsire!

But the pain of the matter to herself had been of another kind, arising out of her daughter's heartless indifference to the young man's plight. Anne had made no plea to her father on the prisoner's behalf and still gave no sign of caring what happened to him although she'd borne his child last August. Cecily feared that this attitude boded ill for the resumption of the marriage when Exeter would be released at last. Still, one could only wait and see if time would plant some flower of affection in Anne's flinty heart: there had never been a Neville who could not love.

Meanwhile, Cecily prepared energetically for her second Christmas at Court as wife of the Protector. Among other things, she had to have many new gowns fitted for the constant public appearances demanded of her. She was an acknowledged leader of fashion; and, at thirty-eight, was one of the most beautiful women in England, regal and fair. She enjoyed the high social positions she now filled with such distinction – it was like a homecoming after years in that wilderness of obscurity which had irked her with a sense of waste. *This* was her life: at the top of the power pyramid with all her kinsmen holding important office around her. It was like being queen to Richard's king…

The real Queen was living in total retirement with her sick consort and her infant son. Margaret would see no one, nor allow anyone outside her own intimate household to visit either the King or the Prince.

The only shadow on the splendour of Cecily's life was a loneliness for her own children – the two oldest boys at Ludlow and the two younger ones, with Elisabeth and Margaret, at Fotheringhay. Sometimes she was smitten by guilt for the little time she'd spent with fragile Richard since his birth just over two years ago. But then she'd quiet her conscience by reminding it of flying visits; occasional overnight stays at Fotheringhay on the speedy way to somewhere else – someplace where the Protector's presence was urgently required for the good of the realm. Richard liked to have his wife with him at all times now: the stronger he himself became, the more it seemed he needed her. So they would sweep into the fetterlock-shaped courtyard of Fotheringhay – two vital, busy people surrounded by an army of magnates, administrators, clerks, guards, servants who swarmed over the castle, imposing their alien noises on its normal tranquillity – and the very haste of their arrival would foreshadow their equally hasty departure.

But Cecily always spent at least one hour alone with the children on these occasions. The irrepressible Margaret and George would hurl themselves upon her, aware of her finery but reckless of how it fared under their wild embraces, while Elisabeth would stand in the background, awaiting her turn. Elisabeth was a gentle child who demanded far less attention than the younger two, and who seemed increasingly awed by her mother's beauty and fame. It took a deal of persuasion to make her even talk, let alone accept the lavish gifts her mother brought her. And Cecily would sometimes think uneasily, as she watched her retire behind the affectionate onslaughts of George and Margaret: *This poor little mouse will always abdicate her own position to stronger claimants.* She wished she had more time to put some Neville spirit and confidence into the child. But there was never time these urgent days. Just a few minutes left to look in again on baby Richard.

He was an unnaturally quiet baby, small and delicate still. His nurses said he slept little though seldom cried. Certainly, whenever Cecily had seen him this past year, he'd been awake – alert to a point of awareness that was somehow unnerving in one so young – but she'd never heard him utter any sound louder than the singing of a little tune to himself. At her approach he'd become silent, and would lie tensely unmoving while she bent over him. Then the long grey eyes would accept her unfamiliar presence, though with a certain reserve, as though some instinct warned him how transient this would be: 'The strange, beautiful lady is your mother, Dickon, but she has only come to say goodbye to you—'

Dickon's eyes were the sharpest pricks to Cecily's maternal conscience. This youngest child of hers was so frail – so withdrawn and apart somehow, though in a quite different way from Elisabeth's self-effacement – that his condition tugged at her heartstrings and she had a constant fear that he would die young. She wanted to give him time, love, attention. She wanted to observe constantly the growth of an intelligence which, she felt, would far outstrip one day that of any of her other children if he were spared to grow up. But there was never time in this high summer of the power and importance of his sire.

'Goodbye, little Dickon.' No, she could never let any of her children intrude on the intense unit which she and Richard the Protector formed. She must always be free to meet her husband's demands, proudly and passionately.

On Christmas morning in the Palace of Westminster, good cheer was heartier than it had been for many years, and the dress of the courtiers and their ladies proclaimed new hope for the prosperity of the country. The ladies (no longer fearful of pious King Henry's censure) had lowered their necklines; and men of all ranks were going gay in slashed outer garments through which were drawn the vivid fabrics underneath. Many of the younger generation, both male and female, now wore hats or caps with little gold knobs on top while their elders affected odd cushion-shaped eastern headgear, latticed with cords or braids. And the sheen and glitter of spangles was everywhere; on ruched and pleated veils and mantles; around the cuffs of vast oversleeves; on cauls, on ear-muffs and on gorgets...

Against a background of crisp new-fallen snow, the jewel-and-precious-metal colours of the Court's costumes glowed with a painted richness. It was the first time in years that anyone had dared be outrageous in dress and all were now enjoying the experience – talking and laughing animatedly, even flirting a little, as they came out from hearing the Third Mass of Christmas together and tramped noisily towards the Hall for games and dancing and gift exchanging. No one noticed that the empty chairs there of the King and Queen had been hung with new tapestries.

Cecily and Richard came in to greet their friends. The more perceptive of those friends observed that Their graces of York were not quite themselves today: they seemed graver than was their wont, as though some uneasy news had reached them; and they were much inclined to go into huddled conference with their Neville and Bourchier kin of the royal Council.

Now almost the entire Council was gathered in a tight group near the dais, and those members who had their backs towards the door behind the royal chairs kept turning to glance over their shoulders. At last, the door opened—

A hush fell on the Hall. Queen Margaret was standing there, looking down on everyone with that arrogant, chin-lifted gesture of hers; her high breasts prominent in a magnificent cloth-of-gold gown; and her raised left hand, ablaze with the gold and ruby of her wedding ring, reaching back into the doorway to clasp the hand of another figure which hesitated in her shadow.

'My lords and ladies,' Margaret cried, 'the King!'

The entire company fell to its knees. Henry shuffled forward onto the dais and made a vague motion for them to rise. Staring at him, they did so.

He looked well enough – or at least as well as he had ever looked. The long pale face was no paler and no thinner than it had ever been, though there was an increased transparency about the complexion, and an odd hunted expression about the eyes. Someone had dressed and groomed the King with more than normal care today; arranging his thinning colourless hair in a neat roll below his jewelled cap and setting the great Lancastrian collar of golden 'S's straight for once upon his sloping shoulders and hollow chest. Yet there was a faint unsteadiness about him which spoilt the whole outward show of well-being: the head bobbed a little, the over-white hands fumbled and plucked—

'Are you well, Sire?' Richard advanced to ask.

Henry seemed to have difficulty in focusing upon the Protector's figure although it stood straight in front of him, below the shallow steps of the dais.

'Ah, forsooth cousin,' the King said then in a nervous rush, 'I am quite recovered. May God, and my beloved consort here who nursed me, be thanked.' He reached out a visibly trembling hand to the Queen.

Margaret came to stand very close beside him – an unshakable buttress to his weakness. On her face, as she stared down at York, was a look of exhausted triumph. Then the fever-bright eyes moved restlessly over the members of the royal Council until they fastened on Humphrey Stafford – the husband of Cecily's least-favourite sister, Ann of Buckingham.

'My lord Duke of Buckingham,' Margaret said, 'I pray you do now as I instructed you.'

'Aye, Madam.' Solid Stafford bowed low and then went out of the Hall – narrowly watched by his wife who had entered behind the Queen.

Cecily looked up at Ann Stafford, Duchess of Buckingham, whom she had never much liked; and whom she knew had disliked her since earliest childhood. Ann's close friendship with the Queen was founded, Cecily had no doubt, on their joint hostility to the House of York. The friendship had been cemented last year by Her Grace of Buckingham having been chosen as godmother to the infant Prince; after which ceremony she had gone into retirement with Margaret. How the pair of them must have looked forward to this day when the King would be well enough to return and break the Protector's power! – for Henry's reappearance could mean only that, an end to Richard's office: there could not be a functioning King and a Protector of England at the same time.

More of the Queen's friends were pressing in now upon the dais. There were so many of them that one hardly noticed the absence of Edmund Beaufort, Duke of Somerset, who was still in prison awaiting trial on the treason charge Richard brought against him. But Somerset's son, Henry Beaufort, was there, close to the Queen, who was smiling at him: a young man with reddish-sand-coloured hair like his father's and the thrusting nose of all the Beauforts. Involuntarily Cecily wondered if the infant Prince bore either of these characteristics; for the Beauforts, father and son, shared equally in the common speculation about the Prince's paternity.

Now here came another contender for the glory of that deed: the Earl of Wiltshire, great Ormonde's unworthy son. And here was Alice Chaucer, Dowager Duchess of Suffolk, with *her* son, the new Duke of Suffolk; a young man credited with having stepped into his murdered father's shoes in more respects than title.

Immediately behind the Suffolks came Jacquetta Woodville, Dowager Duchess of Bedford – looking more witchlike even than Cecily remembered her in Rouen! Jacquetta was attended by a young woman who, though quite beautiful, was clearly her daughter: the bone structure of both small, pointed faces was alike; and the younger woman's body was remarkably slight, just as Cecily recalled Jacquetta's having been before Sir Richard Woodville, her second husband, began to broaden it with a strapping child of his every year. Yes, that was certainly a Woodville daughter. Probably Elizabeth, the eldest, whom Cecily had seen in Rouen some years ago at an eccentric supper-party given by Jacquetta. Cecily had been struck, then, by the child's curious gilt-fair colouring and the light, cold eyes she'd inherited from her Woodville sire. Now it was the slim, sinuous body that held her attention; reminding her in some odd way of the Melusine legend so often recounted in France. Of a woman who turned into a serpent; a winged serpent that flew, slender as spun cloud, across a witching moon...

The young woman moved across to the Queen's side and stood there with easy familiarity. She must be one of Margaret's new ladies, chosen for the triumphant return to power. Margaret would hold in high esteem the noble French blood of St Pol which Jacquetta had transmitted to the Woodville brood—

Humphrey Stafford re-entered the Hall attended by many more knights and ladies of the Queen's party. In his arms he carried a sturdy, dark-haired child who sat upright against the knotted badge of Stafford on the Duke's shoulder.

'Edward, by the grace of God, Prince of Wales and Cornwall!'

Again the entire company knelt. But, this time, Henry did not bid them rise: he was watching Buckingham's approach with an apprehensive, sidelong glance and, simultaneously, trying to grasp something Margaret was whispering to him. Between the two he seemed bemused, anxious; and yet pathetically eager to comprehend and comply—

He sat down suddenly, as if his knees had buckled, on the tapestried chair behind him just as Buckingham began to ascend the dais. Margaret lowered herself to her knees at his slippered feet. 'My lord sovereign,' she said, 'His Grace of Buckingham presents to you our royal son, Prince Edward.'

'Our – our son?' The King's head was unsteady as he drew it back against the chair tapestry – his frightened eyes flitting over the child in Buckingham's arms and then coming to rest on the kneeling Queen. 'Our son, Margaret?'

'Yes, my lord King.' There was a slight edge to Margaret's voice. 'You have been shown him before now, many times.'

'I – I disremember. I have been ill for so long—'

'He was born during your illness.'

'Aye. A son. I heard it said through the darkness that surrounded me...' Henry's gaze slid away to some distant point between the Queen's head and the Prince's, and his lips closed with what appeared to be finality.

'My lord King—' the edge to Margaret's voice was sharper now, as though trying to penetrate the opacity of his consciousness '—this is the first time you have been well enough to recognise our son before the entire Court. I pray that you say something directly to him, as his royal sire.'

The kneeling, watching throng held its breath, waiting for the public recognition of her son which Margaret must have from the King if gossip were ever to be silenced. It was clear from Margaret's tone that she had tutored Henry in what he was to say. It was equally clear from Henry's clouded gaze and increasingly troubled mien that he could not remember.

Then, suddenly, the royal eyes cleared as if a light from heaven shone inside the brain. The bobbing head steadied;

the nervous hands ceased to pluck; and the frightened – almost tortured – expression vanished from the visage, leaving it radiant with innocence.

'This child,' said King Henry with utter certainty, 'is the work of the Holy Spirit.'

~

UNTIL LATE THAT CHRISTMAS NIGHT, there was still argument and conjecture in every room of the Palace.

'I maintain,' Cecily said fiercely, walking up and down before the bedchamber fire, 'that what Henry said was no acknowledgment. Even though he took the child in his arms afterwards and kissed and blessed him – why, that was little more than he did with our own Dickon at Fotheringhay! Listen Richard—' she interrupted her pacing to stand still before her husband who was sitting thoughtfully on the settle-bench '—Margaret was six months pregnant before Henry fell ill a year gone August. Granted that he's too ignorant of such matters to have noticed anything; but, by that time, *if the child were his*, she must have told him. And he would remember now. He would remember everything instead of looking so strangely on the Prince and saying such an odd thing.'

'*Not* such an odd thing, Cis. Not for Henry...' Richard was watching an apple-bough burn bluely on the hearth.

'You mean – his intense piety? Giving the Holy Spirit credit for something which he himself had done? Except that I can't believe he ever did it!'

'*He* doesn't want to believe it either.'

'What?'

Richard sighed for her apparent lack of perception. 'Cis, did you not mark how Henry's whole being altered when he came to that glorious conclusion about the Third Person of the Holy Trinity?'

'Yes, certainly, but—' She sat down beside him on the bench.

'Up until then, in the Hall,' Richard continued, 'the King had been sorely troubled. And for more than year prior to that, remember, he'd been insensible to every word and image presented to him and could not move a limb. Yet he recovered today, suddenly and totally, before our very eyes – although, even up to last evening, it was still doubtful if he'd be well enough to appear. *He recovered on the instant that he pushed responsibility for Margaret's child over onto the most unimpeachable agency!*'

Cecily stared at Richard as though he were raving.

'That would still apply,' she protested, 'if Henry knew deep in his heart that the child was *not* his. It would also account for his illness: at the precise time that Margaret's condition could no longer be kept secret, Henry fell ill from a great shock – as it was given out, the shock of our soldiers losing Guienne. But I think it was the shock of discovering that his consort had a lover.'

'No, Cis.' Richard shook his head. 'Henry's mind would never accept that, even if proof incontrovertible were put before it. He adores Margaret. She can do no wrong in his sight. But he is, himself, a man of most scrupulous conscious: a man, I would say, innocent of all sin.'

'And how could it be sin to father a child on his own wife?'

'How indeed? For the answer to that, we'd need the presence of Bishop Ayscough; but the good Bishop is dead – murdered by his people.'

'You mean – when Ayscough was Henry's confessor—?'

'Aye, I think the tale is true enough in essence: that he convinced Henry it were sin to have intercourse with Margaret... God alone knows why Ayscough did this – possibly he feared the Queen's influence over Henry would supersede his own if she had opportunity for love-whispering – but we do know that the Bishop's power over Henry in spiritual matters was total. Henry would have regarded as the Word of God any confessional advice of his.'

'So—' it was Cecily's turn now to stare unseeingly at the burning apple-bough '—after nearly ten years of sharing a marriage-bed with Margaret, you contend that Henry gave in to the temptations of the flesh – once – just before?'

'Knowing his nature, yes, I believe so. Then he struggled to forget the fall from Ayscough's peculiar grace, since he couldn't ask a dead man's absolution. Afterwards, he sought to regain his own innocence in the sight of God by denying, even to himself, that he had carnal knowledge of Margaret. But Margaret was growing heavy with his child. By her sixth month even Henry had to be aware of it. He retreated into paralysis – deafness – blindness – for nearly seventeen months. I believe he'd have stayed like that indefinitely if Margaret hadn't exerted her will to cure him... We must give the Queen her due, Cis: she's a strong woman for her consort and her son. And I will not credit that she is an unchaste wife to the King.'

Cecily knew it was no use arguing further with Richard. He had worked out a theory in which he believed absolutely. And he had knelt to the baby Prince this day and sworn his allegiance to him.

But in her own heart she would never accept that Margaret's infant had been fathered by Henry. And Margaret knew this: in the one piercingly intuitive look that had speared between her and Cecily today, the Queen had read Cecily's utter scepticism of her claims on her son's behalf – that son who favoured in appearance neither Beaufort nor Butler nor de la Pole but only the dark blood of the House of Anjou.

## 12

Behind the Neville castle of Middleham in North Yorkshire, the green park known as Sunskew rolled gently upward towards the crown of tree-shaded William's Hill. The trees formed a circle there, marking what had once been the Keep of an earlier castle; no trace of which now remained except this terraced ring of root-woven earth, criss-crossed by sheep paths – the hollow at its centre dense with briar and thorn bush and long grass.

Up here on summer days the ladies of the household gathered, to breathe the fresh air off Middleham Moor; or to watch the Monday market gathering in the town, or the constant activities on the jousting field that lay alongside the park, east of the moat, where all training and practice of arms was done; or just to enjoy the wonderful sweeping view of sky, castle, church, town, river – the River Cover that joined with the Yore to run through the rich lands of Wensleydale towards Jervaulx Abbey.

Cecily had a lifelong affection for this vantage point above her brother's castle. On childhood visits here with her family, she'd always led the race to William's Hill for a game of 'kings and queens' with her betrothed and the multitude of her brothers and sisters and cousins. Later on, dignity and heavier skirts had made her slow her pace a little; and, later still, she'd shortened her stride to accommodate a succession of stumbling, clinging children – her own, or those of her kinsfolk... Now, this Maytime of 1455, there was a Neville grandchild (Isabel, two-year-old daughter of the Warwicks) amid the scramble of youngsters all around her.

Laughing, she flung out her arms to the two littlest ones – Isabel, and her own son Richard who was nearly three – to help them up the last steep, hot incline; while Richard's governess, the young Lady Agnes Croft, walked alongside with Elisabeth and George – Margaret having just streaked ahead with the three youngest Neville girls.

'Your Grace ought to exert less effort in this heat,' Lady Croft said severely, relinquishing her grip on the two older children to take over firm charge of the toddlers. George went scrambling away at once over the brow of the hill, calling 'Margaret – Margaret – wait for me!' to his favourite sister; while Elisabeth wandered off by herself to pick flowers.

'Yes, I suppose I ought,' Cecily said a little breathlessly. Unencumbered by the toddlers, she'd quickly gained the highest point of the sheep path and was standing looking about her at the sunny countryside. 'After all,' she continued with a smile, 'I'm forty years old; seven months on in my twelfth pregnancy; and a grandmother this year past into the bargain!'

'*Your Grace, I didn't mean—*' Lady Agnes was but twenty herself and only a short time wedded to Sir Richard Croft, the young Earls' tutor at Ludlow.

'... That I'm too old for keeping pace uphill with youngsters? No, my dear, of course I know you didn't mean that!' The chuckle in Cecily's voice belied the assurance. 'But, nevertheless, I agree I should be more careful just now, with my next confinement but a few weeks off and all my kinsmen away.' York, Salisbury and Warwick had set out eight days previously – their combined escorts forming almost an army – to attend a meeting of the royal Council at Leicester. They were all three still members of this Council, though in the teeth of the Queen's bitterest opposition to their continuing attendance at its meetings. So they went now strong-armed, prepared for the attack which they realised must come one day—

God alone knew how matters would go henceforth. No Yorkist had held any official position in the realm since the King had formally dismissed Richard from the Protectorate last February...

Cecily tried not to recall that bitter day in London when her lord and his followers had been mercilessly stripped of all power. Seeing the hand of the triumphant Queen in everything that was done, they had not tarried to try conclusions with her (nor with Somerset, whom she'd brought from the Tower prison to be again First Minister of the realm) but had quickly gathered their households and headed north. All the way out of London, people had stood silent in the rain, watching the upholders of good government leave the capital: York, who had given them a period of firm justice; his sister's husband, the Viscount Bourchier, who had put the Treasury in order for the first time in years; and the respected Neville Earls of Salisbury and Warwick with their peace-keeping force of north-country men. In these responsible men's going, the citizens of London had obviously seen a return to the chaos and bankruptcy of Henry's nominal rule, because there had been hearty and widespread agreement with an old man who'd shouted:

'The King's cure was a disaster for this land! A fatal day that gave us back Henry of Lancaster and his Frenchwoman in place of Their Graces of York—'

The words had found a vehement echo in Cecily's mind at the time but she'd gradually silenced them within herself. First, in the tranquil atmosphere of Fotheringhay, where she'd been able to tell her delighted children that they were to travel north with their parents; then at Richard's castle of Sandal for a while; and, finally, in the tumult of York's city celebration of Corpus Christi, where she and Richard were given positions of highest honour in the Guild processions. The city of York had displayed the White Rose with more than normal enthusiasm this year and had entertained its namesake Duke and Duchess with most lavish hospitality. After which, it had been almost a relief to come here to Middleham, where there was little else to do when the menfolk were away except play with the children or gossip with the many noble ladies of the great household.

Idly, Cecily sat down on the sloping bank and watched her youngest son making meticulous arrangements of daisy heads on the sheep-cropped grass. As usual, Dickon was utterly absorbed; unaware of Lady Croft's voice prattling nonsense rhymes to his cousin Isabel; unaware of the shouts coming from the far side of the hill where the elder children played. Cecily had noticed that he never asked to go anywhere with Margaret and George: it was as though he'd learned that their friendship was a unit which excluded him – that he, Dickon, however coddled by adults for his delicacy, was alone in his childhood. He made no overtures to his fair cousin Isabel. He made few demands upon his governess except to ask her sometimes for a story – nearly always the same story, that of 'Tantony pig'; about the littlest pig of a litter who had to fight hard to grow up and become as strong as the others... Cecily had felt unaccountable tears prick her eyes the first time she'd heard Agnes Croft telling Dickon this north country tale; and, on impulse, she'd given Agnes a little white marble boar which had always graced her own apartments, so that the story might have more point in the telling. 'See, Dickon, how Tantony pig *did* grow up – into a strong great boar with tusks and bristles!' It had been worth parting with the ornament (legacy of the much-loved Duke of Bedford long ago in Rouen) to see Dickon's face light up with hope for his own future; and to hear his determined prayer afterwards to Saint Anthony, the patron of swineherds, for prowess in the forest hunt one day...

It seemed unlikely that his prayer would ever be answered, Cecily thought sadly. Compared with the rest of her sturdy brood, Dickon was still a weakling although he'd made some physical progress these past few months, and was learning to ride a very small, very quiet pony here in Middleham's jousting field. To his riding lessons he brought the same concentrated attention which he gave to everything else he was taught. No ordinary noises could penetrate his intense absorption. Yet he was always the first to notice unusual sounds, sometimes from a great distance—

Cecily saw him lift his head now from the flower pattern he'd been making. She saw him turn to look intently eastward, his eyes narrowing as they sought some distant focus.

'What is it, Dickon?' she asked, scrambling down the bank towards him. 'What do you hear?' She liked to ascribe his acute hearing to the Neville talent for music, fostered over many generations. It seemed it might be the only Neville characteristic he would ever have.

'A horse,' he said after due consideration; and pointed

to the road leading to the main gate in the castle's north face.

'I see no horse—' she scanned the road that swept up steeply towards the drawbridge over the moat '—Are you sure?'

He nodded, his gaze moving along with some object still invisible to her. Then, suddenly, the rider swung into view in a cloud of summer dust. Only a rider in a desperate hurry would drive his mount so—

She began to walk quickly down towards the castle. The smells from the brew-house and bake-house caught her throat, making her giddy with momentary nausea. She turned aside into the chapel and knelt awhile, head down, until the sickness passed. In the quiet, she heard the hollow beat of hooves crossing the wooden drawbridge, and then a voice urgently asking for Her Grace of York.

Gripping her girdle-Rosary, she left the chapel by the north door. There was a knot of people near the main gate opposite. A dishevelled figure broke away from them and came towards her. Through the dust caking his face, she recognised the puckered eye-scar of Robert de Vere; that loyal friend of her husband's whom she'd last seen in Dublin Castle. A sense of profound apprehension overwhelmed her. 'Robert – what is it?'

'There's been a skirmish, Madame, at St Albans.' He kept his voice low. 'All Your Grace's near kinsmen are safe. But the Duke of Somerset was slain and many others of the Queen's men.'

She held the Rosary in a fierce grip – dread flooding her soul that it was Richard who had killed Somerset. Robert de Vere rushed on unbidden:

'My lord Duke wished to parley with the King before the Council meeting at Leicester. He wished to give the lie to certain rumours concerning the young Prince's safety –

Somerset was putting it about that York planned the murder of the Prince... Anyhow, that's how we came to be so far south. Our combined escorts numbered about 3,000 men... We reached the fields north of St Albans late last Tuesday night. We encamped there until dawn – knowing the King had arrived in the town on his way to Leicester. At first light, my lords of York and Salisbury sent their heralds with letters to the royal lodging but, after three hours, the only reply was that the streets were barricaded against us. Then my lord of Warwick said: "No conclusion will be reached this way, Somerset is not allowing our letters through to the King. So let you, my father and my uncle, assault the barricades while I seek another passage into the town." With that, he rode off across some back gardens, accompanied by many of his own men, while we fell upon the obstructions across the streets... The next thing I saw was Warwick's company galloping through the town – their weapons bared, and royal troops fleeing before them into houses and alleyways. There was terrible din and confusion – men falling left and right before the red jacks with the Bear and Ragged Staff badge of Warwick on them... A few minutes later, we managed to break into the town near St Peter's where the King's banner was. The fighting was thick and fierce there. I saw Lord Clifford fall; and, immediately after, I witnessed the Earl of Northumberland pierced— Madame, I grieve to bring you this news: though he was a Queen's man, he was first Your Grace's brother-in-law.'

'Yes, yes...' Cecily crossed herself for her sister Eleanor's husband. A loud-mouthed, swaggering Percy he may have been, and certainly no friend of the Middleham Nevilles whom he'd raided and harried all his life; but great Harry Hotspur had been his sire. 'What other lords were killed?' she asked.

'None. Except – well, there was one sore wounded in the face. But he may recover.'

'Who?'

'Your Grace's nephew Humphrey; Buckingham's heir.'

Young Stafford... She closed her eyes on a vision of his father carrying the infant Prince into Westminster Hall – his mother standing on the dais behind the Queen. If the heir of Buckingham were to die, then indeed would her sharp-tongued sister Ann have cause to hate her and the whole party of York... 'Go on,' she said quietly to de Vere; and he continued.

'I saw the royal standard fall, revealing King Henry himself leaning against the wall of St Peter's. He was wearing no armour of any kind, and blood was spurting from his neck—'

*'The King? Wounded?'*

'It was only an arrow graze, Madame. But the Duke of York rushed to him at once and carried him into a cobbler's shop. Almost before the wound was dressed in there, the battle was over outside. Queen's lords began fleeing while the common soldiers of both sides gathered up their dead – about sixty men in all... Then my lord of Warwick came to St Peter's with the body of Edmund Beaufort lying across his saddle...'

So, she thought with guilty relief, it was my nephew of Warwick who killed Somerset. Yes, immediate despatch would be that peremptory young man's way with an enemy – not for him the patient process of law which York and Salisbury would surely have preferred.

'Where is my husband and my kinsmen now?' she asked de Vere. 'And were is King Henry?'

'They were all preparing to ride together to London, Your Grace, when I left St Alban's. The Queen too, I heard, was to go with them – though she was sore distressed by the Duke of Somerset's death.

'Yes. She would be.' Unlucky Margaret, violently bereft of yet another favourite! And she had not even the wily old Cardinal Kemp's support to fall back on now, for Kemp had died last year. How alone she must feel on her way to London with the men who had scattered her army – the men who would now control the King: York, Salisbury, Warwick. *And how she must hate them all.* Much more henceforward than ever in the past.

Cecily was well aware that the concentrated hatred of a woman like Margaret of Anjou would be both venomous and lifelong – especially if she were given the slightest grounds for believing Somerset's final lie: that York's aim was to harm somehow, the little Prince of Wales. Only God knew what the Queen would do if she felt her son threatened in any way; either in his health, which she guarded with an army of physicians; or in his importance which she'd begun to bolster lately with a household far more magnificent than her own or the King's.

Margaret would be ruthless as a tigress in her precious child's defence. She would be swift, cunning and merciless.

*'My lord, tread warily,'* Cecily wrote that night in a long letter to her husband, *'for the Queen knows nothing of that knightly honour on which you base your whole life's conduct.'*

Worried, she sealed the letter and called for William Botoner, her clerk, to arrange for its swift transport to London.

'Then see about our own removal back to Fotheringhay,' she ordered Botoner. 'I shall not go to London myself until after my confinement but I wish to be nearer my lord Duke at this time.' Middleham was suddenly too remote – too cut off from the south where Richard must now surely remain; especially if it were true that the King was sinking into yet another pit of oblivion.

She frowned, trying to recall de Vere's exact words when she'd questioned him a second time about the royal neck wound.

'... He seemed to be in a kind of trance, Your Grace. His eyes were glazed and unfocused and he gave no evidence of hearing anything that was said to him. He moved if guided; but otherwise sat still, like an effigy in wax...'

Yes, without doubt Henry was again slipping from a world that pained and shocked him by its violence. For how much longer could England pretend to be governed by such a King? – grandson of a usurper, he should have retired to a monk's cell long ago and allowed the real heir, Richard Plantagenet, to reign and govern.

Botoner cut in on her treasonous thoughts: 'When does Your Grace wish to set out for Fotheringhay?' His long face was creased with worry for her unborn child. Too often, his pen had recorded birth immediately followed by death in the records of the House of York.

'The morning after tomorrow,' she said decisively. 'That leaves ample time for packing and preparation. Were it not for the children I would leave sooner.'

Yet she was glad enough of the excuse to stay an extra day with her sister-in-law, Alice of Salisbury, and her nephew of Warwick's little Countess, Anne Beauchamp – Isabel's mother. Anne was expecting her second child very soon and there were great hopes for a boy: it was unthinkable that the virile Earl of Warwick should have no son! Cecily had hoped to be at Middleham for the birth but, now, it seemed unlikely that she would be.

Early next morning, however, the Countess of Warwick began her labour and, by mid-afternoon, had been delivered of another daughter; who was baptised at once because she looked so weak and frail. The name Anne was chosen for her, after her mother and her Beauchamp granddame.

Cecily held the tiny infant at the font in the private chapel, while all the other children crowded around for the hasty, informal ceremony at which they sang an anthem with the resident castle choir. Then each youngster was allowed just one look at the delicate baby before she was taken back upstairs.

Dickon's turn came last, after Isabel's. He stared solemnly at the new Anne Neville but made no comment.

## 13

Within a month of the battle of St Albans, King Henry had again collapsed totally so that Richard had to be called to the Protectorate for a second term.

This time, however, he had Queen Margaret to contend with at close quarters. With her own party members thick about her, the Queen stayed at Court, fixing on the Protector a lynx-like stare and countering his every move by some act of reckless hostility – such as seeking aid against him from England's most dedicated enemies, Scotland and France. King James gleefully attacked the northern marches while King Charles sent a marauding fleet along the south coast.

Richard's rage finally exploded against the Queen for these acts of gross disloyalty to her adopted country.

'Blood of God, Madame,' he roared, 'can you not see that if our government topples, James and Charles will divide England between them? What do you want for your royal son – *a vassal's crown?*'

'I want for him,' Margaret ground through her teeth, 'a land wherein there is no murdering party of York!' And her fingers clenched around a medallion which had been given to her by Edmund Beaufort just before his death at St Albans.

CECILY REMAINED at Fotheringhay until mid-autumn; by which time she had completed preparation for moving her household to London. There was an air of finality this time about the packing and the locking up: Richard had announced his intention of keeping a permanent home in London from henceforth, '... so that, no matter how my power may wax or wane, I shall be entrenched here to combat any further treacheries of the Queen.' He had looked at many properties within the capital's walls; and had finally settled on Baynard's Castle which the young Earl of Richmond wanted to sell – it being too near the river for the ailing Tudor lungs...

On the feast-morning of St Catherine, Cecily was ready to quit Fotheringhay with her children, her servants, and more baggage than she'd ever travelled with before: the old Northamptonshire home on the Nene had been stripped bare to furnish mighty Baynard's Castle on the Thames.

She looked back tearlessly once, across the water-meadows, at the familiar outlines of church and village and double-walled keep. Within the shelter of those stones stood a new tomb: that of her infant daughter, Ursula, born in July, dead by September... This twelfth child was the first girl she had lost. She'd hoped, right up to the end, that the mite would cling to life as miraculously as Dickon had done. But it was not to be so—

Resolutely she turned her face towards London and a new home.

BAYNARD'S CASTLE was a massive place. It even daunted Cecily a little at first. Hemmed in as it was by all the other buildings crowding between St Paul's and the Thames, it sought its space upwards – floor upon floor climbing about a dark central courtyard which had its own arched ways to the busy river... The top storeys were crowned with turrets that stared proprietorially all around the city: eastward, along the private landing-stages, wharves and docks to the Tower; northward to the bulk of St Paul's; and west, to where the Convent of the Black Friars stood in an angle of the city wall above where the River Fleet tumbled into the Thames.

Yet she had a feeling of coming home once she and Richard had taken up their residence in this royal mansion that had lately been Edmund Tudor's and, before that, Humphrey of Gloucester's. The delicate Tudor and his Beaufort child-wife had left no trace of themselves here, but Humphrey of Gloucester's presence was still strong: in the vast library; in the Hall that had seen both royal banquets and rowdy gatherings of the commons; and in the spacious tower which he'd given over to poor scribes and scholars.

Cecily accepted her dead kinsman's ebullient ghost as part of the heritage which she saw daily enveloping Richard more and more completely – people even referred to him nowadays by Gloucester's nickname of 'the Good Duke'. But she was careful not to make her own those apartments which had been private to the unlucky Duchess of Gloucester: for the brooding presence of the yet-imprisoned Eleanor Cobham might call up the uneasy spirits of those executed after her witchcraft trial... The atmosphere of the nurseries, in particular, disturbed Cecily. Eleanor

Cobham had lavished an obsessive care on this suite of apartments which she was never to need, and their pathetic detail was eloquent of a barren wife's anguish. It may even have been in here that the waxen image of a child was made—

Hastily, she shut the door on the nursery rooms. She'd decide later what use they were to be put to; since there was now no child of York young enough to need them for their original purpose – Dickon was turned three since October and seemed determined to be adult in all things.

Cecily went down to the Hall where servants were unpacking silver and rare glassware – the discarded lambswool wrappings of the latter looking like an early fall of snow for the approaching Christmas.

She heard riders enter the courtyard through the Thames Street gate which was near the Hall; a few seconds later, Richard's decisive step on the cobbles. He'd been at Westminster all morning.

She looked enquiringly at him as he approached her through the Hall. He seemed angry or at least disturbed in some way: the long moustaches which he'd allowed to grow these past few months were bristling at their tips. He swept her along with him towards the solar.

'Cis—' he kicked the door shut '—I've seen Henry today, by Margaret's order. There's a noticeable improvement in the King's condition.'

'Oh, my God!'

'You may well say that. Inside a month Henry will be back on the throne.'

'With Margaret in full charge again?'

'*No.*' Richard brought a fist down into the palm of a hand. 'This time I'll fight her. I intend to remain head of the Council after I cease to be Protector.'

'She'll thwart you at every turn.'

'I know that. Also, she'll block each move I make for the country's good, if she can. And no efforts will be spared to get rid of me: either to the far north to fight James, or – as was suggested this morning – back to Ireland.'

'*Ireland?*'

'Aye. But I'll not go into that exile again unless I'm desperate. No, here I'll stay, close to my poor bewildered King—'

'Margaret could poison Henry's mind against you.'

'She could. And probably will. But I'll continue to prove my loyalty both to the King and to the Prince.'

'Enemies may accuse you of some treachery.'

'They've been doing that since St Albans. And now I hear I'm supposed to be at the bottom of the Welsh unrest also! Ah, well, my back is broad—' His anger at the King's inconvenient and futile return to health was beginning to cool under the breath of his own normal philosophical patience. But Cecily was convinced that this time, when he ceased to be Protector, he would remain the true leader of the realm. For his life was at the full of its summer's fruiting and it must be used to the purpose of its early seed and long maturing. Even though the Queen's shadow lie dark across it.

Cecily picked a strand of lambswool off her sleeve. 'Yes, you must fight to remain where you are, Dickon,' she said with objective calm, 'even though Margaret will strive to have you removed because she sees you as a threat to her Prince's inheritance.'

'But, by all the Saints, I have no designs on Henry's throne nor on his heir's succession!'

'The Queen has always been convinced that you have – ever since Edmund Beaufort put the idea in her head. She knows your blood-right is stronger than Henry's. And that your popularity is great with the commons; who fear nothing, by the way, more than a minority.'

'There'll be no minority. Henry will live for years yet—'

'Will he, Richard? Well, maybe: like the creaking gate, he may outlast the building. But if he were to die before his son come of age, then you could certainly look forward to several years of power – a power you might not be willing to give up, at the end, to a usurper's great-grandson whose legitimacy will always be in doubt— Thus, I think, may Margaret be reasoning. And it is why she will always hate and fear you.'

'Nay, Cis,' his arm went around her, 'Margaret fears me for the strong upgrown sons you have given me. How would you like to visit them on the western marches in the spring, eh? I could do with seeing my Welsh estates then – satisfy myself that the recent troubles have caused no great damage.'

Her heart leapt at the prospect of a reunion with her boys – *boys*: why, they were men now, the Earls of March and Rutland!

MEN INDEED... Cecily decided this was true when, at last, she met her sons at Wigmore.

Though Edward would be only fourteen in April, he was so tall that he looked much older – a golden giant standing nearly six feet high, with broad shoulders and a slim waist. And Edmund, just a year younger, already had his father's solid authority of manner: plainspoken, quietly decisive. Indeed, he was so like Richard at the same age that his image caught Cecily's breath; the unruly brown hair falling to one side of the square forehead; the honest eyes – unnarrowed as yet against life's threats and treacheries. No wonder Richard loved this son who was so much a mirror of his own youth.

But Cecily's spirit reached out as it had always done to Edward of March; and Edward's response to her love was instant. Within minutes of meeting, they were laughing together – more like brother and sister than mother and son – and Edward was telling her all about his armed exploits around the castle of Ludlow, and about his passions for various maidens in the vicinity – there seemed to be a great concentration of these young ladies, all of them beautiful!

'Then you've forgotten little Mary of Desmond?' she teased.

'Long ago, Mother, I fear!' he laughed exactly as her father, Earl Ralph Neville, used to laugh – a hearty sound that warmed the rather dank apartments here at Wigmore in the heart of the woods. She was glad her maids had built the fire up and closed the shutters this March evening.

'And the queen in the Mortimer tapestry?' she asked, lifting mulled wine up from the hearth. All attendants had been sent away so that she might talk alone for a little while with her eldest son.

'What queen? What tapestry?' Edward seemed puzzled. Clearly he had no recollection of the matter.

'Oh, when you were still quite small – in Ireland I think it was – you told me you'd wed a fair lady like the one in an old piece of arras your uncle Mortimer left to your father.' Having poured wine for her son, Cecily set it down by his elbow; then smiling, she began brushing his sleeve velvet merely as an excuse to touch him. 'You remember the tapestry I mean? We hung it in the Hall of Dublin Castle where it dropped to pieces from the damp. Well, your much-admired lady was the central figure in it.'

She felt his muscles stiffen under the sleeve.

'I – I didn't know she was only a woven figure,' he said then. 'I believed I actually saw her once. In Rouen—'

'But you were less than four years old when we left Rouen!'

'Nevertheless, I remember...' He began to frown, '... I remember a table laid with white linen and silver, but the candles were of black wax. The room, too, was draped in black, decorated with silver stars and planets....'

Cecily felt her spine prickle. Edward was describing Jacquetta Woodville's upper room in Rouen as it had been that night of the strange party. *But he hadn't been born until seven months after that!*

Still, he could have heard her telling some of her friends about it. He'd always stayed close to her when he was little; and he'd been an alert child from the start, with almost a mental greed for colour and intricate detail.

Now he was going on, still frowning in intense concentration:

'... There was a girl sitting at the table. She had long straight gilt-fair hair – it gleamed like gold spun-silk in the candlelight with that dense darkness behind: I think it must have been black velvet on the walls – surely you recall such an unusual room, Mother? – and such a girl? I wish you would tell me where I saw her and who she was; for her memory has always haunted me.'

With enormous effort, Cecily smiled, although her face felt tight under the icy breath of superstitious fear. How could a child in the womb see through his mother's eyes? – unless the witch, Jacquetta, had cast a spell that night— Oh, God, protect Edward from sorcery! And tell me now what to say to him—

'It was the tapestry.' Cecily's voice was firm, confident, relaxed. 'You describe it precisely. But as that picture was woven for your Irish ancestress, Elisabeth de Burgho of

Ulster, more than a hundred years ago – ah well, I fear, Edward, that you will never find your gilt-fair lady!'

The implied lie came forcefully, to convince him. He must never know that it was the eldest daughter of Jacquetta Woodville, Dowager Duchess of Bedford, whose image had, somehow, lodged in his mind... This young woman would now be about twenty years of age; and Cecily remembered hearing of her marriage to John Grey, Lord Ferrers of Groby, quite a long time ago; a marriage arranged by the Queen when Elizabeth had been her lady-in-waiting... Cecily had no intention though of giving focus to her son's imaginings by admitting to any knowledge of Elizabeth Woodville.

Edward was smiling his lazy golden smile.

'You have released me from a dream, Mother. I thank you. Henceforward, I will only fall in love with *dark* ladies. Do you suppose that Alençon's daughter is dark?'

The French Duke of Alençon, one of the nobles opposed to Charles the Seventh, was seeking to have his heiress betrothed to the Earl of March. It was a purely political move which Cecily was doing her utmost to thwart. She knew that Alençon would expect a reopening of the French war, to his own advantage, if the House of York came to supreme power in England; and Cecily had no wish to see this dangerous temptation dangled before either her husband or her eldest son – energetic soldiers *both*, by all accounts, if Edward's saga of defending Ludlow could be entirely believed.

'I think,' she said hurriedly, 'we can leave the question of your marriage undecided for a while longer yet, Edward. It's too important a thing to rush into without much and long thought.'

'If I were in love—' Edward stretched himself like a lion '—I'd leap without any thought at all.'

'Then you'd deserve to fall over a precipice,' she said sharply, 'like the Fool in the Tarot cards—' There it was again, the link with Jacquetta; Jacquetta had read the Tarot cards that night after supper, and had accurately foretold the fall of the Duchess of Gloucester, whose house the Yorks now owned.

'What are Tarot cards?' Edward was swirling his wine thoughtfully.

Cecily groped for a definition of the ancient, evil pictures.

'In a witch's hands,' she said then, 'they're tools of the devil. Have nothing to do with such things, my son; nor with people who dabble in strange practices. You promise me this?' she concluded quickly, catching the light of intense interest in his eye which was fixed on her, sidelong, over the rim of his wine cup.

'I promise, Mother.' He laughed. But the warmth had gone out of the sound, and out of the room.

She shivered. Wigmore Castle was a place she had never liked. All those trees, growing right up to the walls in parts; darkening the rooms within as though for secrets and questionable deeds. And the chapel windows were so overgown with ivy and hornbeam that they scarcely allowed a chink of light through…

She'd be glad to move on towards Ludlow tomorrow. Ludlow was an open, healthy castle with its village spread out around its feet where it could be seen – not skulking in a wood three miles away, as here at Wigmore!

## 14

At last, Cecily's solar in the South Tower of Baynard's Castle was entirely to her liking. For two years she'd been having improvements made to it – a carved fireplace that connected with the massive flues from kitchens and Hall; oak-panelled walls; felt-lined shutters for the oriel window that had needed expensive new clear-glass panes – but now everything was finished, from fresh gilt paint on the beams down to polished new floor-planks. Flemish velvet cushions, corded and tasselled, glowed from window-seats and bench tops. Strange Irish embroideries on linen and silk decorated walls and chests. And creamy lambskins from the flocks of Jervaulx looking like patches of foam on the water-smooth floor.

It was a beautiful room and Cecily was well pleased with it. In its ordered tranquillity she'd decided to spend henceforth her leisure hours; sufficient unto herself for entertainment (she had her books, her needlework and a variety of musical instruments) but accessible to her husband and family if they needed her.

Richard was now the country's leading statesman and

had almost no private life. Cecily was with him a great deal in public but his growing children saw little of him. The deprivation seemed not to worry the older three, Elisabeth and Margaret and George; but Cecily had noticed how Dickon watched his busy father, wistfully, from a distance.

Poor Dickon, he was such an odd, quiet child that one never knew what was going on in his head. He was making brilliant progress in the schoolroom and the chapel choir; he was even pleasing the sergeant who taught him riding and archery and tilting, and the steward who took care of his Hall training. But Cecily still worried about this youngest son of hers – that he would overstrain his small body at sport, in his efforts to outdo stronger companions; or, simply, that he would fail to be happy. For, though he often smiled, she had never heard him laugh aloud in all the five-and-a-half years of his life.

Still, though yet thin and undersized, he was growing heather-root strong through determined physical effort, and she knew she ought to be grateful for this miracle. But his face continued to disturb her: it remained the face of a delicate, inactive child, more accustomed to observing than to participating. The long grey eyes were the eyes of a thinker. And the mouth was tense from silent grappling with problems and tasks for which George would have instantly demanded help. In this quality of earnestness, Dickon was even more like his father than Edmund of Rutland was. What he lacked was the outwardgoingness of both sire and older brother – the need to communicate and be popular with people at large. Dickon had a few special friends for whom he would do anything; but even their approbation seemed unnecessary to him, for he neither explained nor excused himself to them as he went his own inscrutable way.

'We have a proper north-country man here,' Cecily's

brother Robert, Bishop of Durham, had remarked with a wink after meeting his youngest nephew for the first – and, as it turned out, the last time. Bishop Robert had died recently, leaving vacant the great See which he'd had to obtain dispensation to fill, many years ago, at the age of only twenty-four... Cecily remembered him much younger than that. At Raby. A boy like all the rest except that being very clever and destined for the Church had set him a little apart until he'd left home altogether. Now he was dead: the first adult member to die of the large family which Joan Beaufort had borne to Ralph Neville, Earl of Westmorland... The Bishop's funeral had brought the remaining brothers and sisters together for a short time. From all parts of the country they'd converged on the high rock of Durham – wealthy, successful, powerful Nevilles all; proud of their rootstock but not too tolerant of one another. Once the Prince-Bishop was interred, they'd gone their separate ways again, unchanged except for a heightened consciousness of death: Ann of Buckingham to Penshurst; widowed Eleanor of Northumberland to her Bishop-son's palace at Carlisle; thrice-wed Katherine of Norfolk to her new husband's apartments in the Prince of Wales' household; Jane the nun back to her convent; Richard of Salisbury to impregnable Middleham Castle; William, Lord Fauconberg, to his mad wife at Skelton; Edward, Lord Abergavenny, to Wales; Thomas, to the rich widow, Lady Willoughby, whom he'd wed three years ago, thus ending his joint bachelor life with his brother John at Sheriff Hutton; George, Lord Latimer, to God alone knew where, for George was growing very strange and absent-minded lately; and Cecily – the youngest member of the entire family – to royal Baynard's Castle. It was here that Cecily had heard the news a few weeks later of the appointment of Bishop Robert's successor: Queen Margaret had moved her own candidate, Lawrence Booth, into the See of Durham. This was an even greater blow to Neville interests in the north than Robert's death had been; for Lawrence Booth would almost certainly use the episcopal lands and their arms-bearing tenants for positive support of the Queen, who was now busily gathering an army.

All this spring, Margaret had behaved like a madwoman. In appalling weather, she'd travelled openly on horseback about the country, enlisting fighting men to her son's bodyguard – as though the four-year-old Prince were in some mortal danger! Many a discontented veteran of the French wars was now wearing the White Swan that was the Prince of Wales' cognizance, after swearing to protect the royal child '…against those evil men who would do him hurt and steal his birthright.' Even the dullest soldier knew that the 'evil men' of the oath referred to the Yorkists, about whom Margaret was becoming increasingly hysterical as the King grew weaker: Henry was now reputed to 'sleep overmuch' – not the sign of a healthy mind or body. He could collapse again at any time; and people were saying openly that, if the Protectorate fell again to Richard of York, it must be made permanent until the Prince came of age. The inference was that Henry should renounce the throne; and it was this hint of her consort's abdication that was driving Margaret to frenzy after two quiescent years…

Cecily was well aware that any passion of the Queen's was dangerous. She was also aware of a growing number of White Swan badges in the streets of London; of a tension that had not been there a few months ago; and of clashes becoming more frequent between the followers of York and of the Queen.

But she would not allow her mind to dwell on those matters, for very fear of courting a fear which would destroy her inner serenity. The children needed her to be calm. She was the centre of their world and they all came to her with their troubles... Fourteen-year-old Elisabeth was in a constant state of anxiety about whom she would be made to marry – her reluctance in this direction had caused her parents to postpone any betrothal arrangements for her for the time being. Margaret, at not quite twelve, was more advanced than her sister, both physically and emotionally. Indeed, looking at this dark-eyed, red-lipped daughter of hers, Cecily was always struck by the likeness to her own sister Katherine; and – Katherine having demonstrated her need of men – Cecily worried about Margaret's marriage. The girl for whom the Queen had stood godmother in friendlier days was headstrong, passionate, and beginning to be a beauty; early wedlock was an imperative in her case. But it would be a severe blow to Elisabeth's confidence if her younger sister became a matron before she did; so one must wait for Elisabeth to develop. Rush a girl like that to a marriage-bed and she might lose her reason, Cecily thought. On the other hand, keep one like Margaret out of it for too long and she would certainly lose her virginity elsewhere! It was an exercise which occupied much of their mother's time, preparing one of them to accept adult life and restraining the other. Sometimes – very privily – Cecily felt herself punished in her girl-children. This feeling was most strong after a visit from the eldest, Anne, Duchess of Exeter.

The discontented Anne would come to Baynard's Castle, bringing her own small daughter with her. Cecily doted on this sole grandchild and loved to play with and talk to her. But Anne would never allow them peace together. She would interrupt any game, any story, by an intrusion of herself, demanding attention for her unhappy state. Then she would rant about her husband, Henry

Holland – calling him a coward, a criminal, a traitor to York interests; although he was now out of prison and fully reconciled with Richard, who had engineered his recent appointment as Admiral of the Royal Fleet. Cecily usually had to be sharp with Anne in the end. The result of which would be that Her Grace of Exeter would storm off in a rage; sending no message for weeks to her worrying mother who seldom knew where she was to be found... Emphatically not in Henry Holland's company. Though, it seemed, more and more with a certain Sir Thomas St Leger—

Cecily grieved much over her twenty-year-old daughter who was recklessly throwing away marriage, reputation and a child's life. But she felt helpless to do anything except pray for the ungovernable young woman, and knew, in that very helplessness, the greatest torment of parenthood...

Shaking her head now over the whole wretched business, she began absent-mindedly to rearrange one of the ornaments in her new solar. This was the little white marble boar which Agnes Croft had insisted on returning before she'd left to join her husband at Ludlow.

'Dickon would miss it if I took it away with me,' Agnes had said. And indeed Dickon was much devoted to 'Tantony pig' whose story he still loved to hear.

So Cecily had resumed ownership of the ornament. She now placed it on the writing-desk which stood in the window embrasure, between her silver inkwell and her box of quills.

'There's a splendid view for you, Tantony,' she remarked aloud. And then thought: *Heaven, I'm growing old – talking to myself.*

Almost forty-three... Compulsively, she studied her face in a wall-mirror. Her skin was still firm and clear, with only a few lines imprinted with grief and worry; and the lightness of the new butterfly headdress, which was all the fashion just now, was kind to her neck and jawline. But the little tendrils of curl that escaped the gauze band were no longer in bleached contrast to the rest of her hair when her serving-women brushed it out at nights: it had all gone from gold to silver-fair... Still, it was a gentle change which deepened the blue of her eyes.

Objectively, she acknowledged that she was still beautiful; and glad to be so for Richard's sake. An end to childbearing too, had fined down her figure – had restored her to an almost girlish slimness.

But she'd lost the ability of youth to remain absorbed in its own image. Increasingly, as the children grew, her interests had moved outward with them – away from herself, into the wide world which they would inhabit. She'd even chosen this room in the South Tower for her own use because, from it, she could see so much of that world: her brother of Salisbury's town house by Puddle Dock (where all the city's horses came to drink, 'puddling' the water with their hooves) and her nephew of Warwick's lodging, Barclay's Inn, in Adle Street. Then there was the great river where bright-awninged barges bustled up and down, their brass fittings gleaming; or wine ships with scarlet sails made for Paul's Wharf. If she leaned against the window, she could see further downstream to London Bridge where all the shops were brightly new – they'd had to be rebuilt after Jack Cade's burning of the Bridge – so that, from here, they looked like polished gems strung between sky and water on a chain of sun-gilt arches. The air was so clear this twenty-fourth day of March that she could almost make out the royal arms above the premises of the Court merchants.

*Oh, I love London,* she thought. *Life is here.*

Life with a constant threat of death though. For, since January, it had needed Mayor Boleyn's 4,000 men to patrol the streets in an effort to keep peace between those magnates who'd crowded in for the latest Council meeting.

Tension came, now, not only from the Queen's hatred of Richard but from the many blood-feuds begun at St Albans. Kin of the slain lords were thirsting for vengeance; Somerset's heir, Henry Beaufort, the third Duke, had made two attempts already to murder Warwick; the Percys were out in force to avenge their father, Northumberland; young Clifford was nursing a vow to let both York and Neville blood flow for his dead sire; and Humphrey Stafford, whose oldest boy had died recently from the face wound received at St Albans, was turning a grim countenance on York.

Cecily heard her husband's step on the stair. She hurried to open the door for him and was glad to see that he was alone.

'Is the Council ended?' she asked.

'Aye – God be thanked—'

His breathing was still laboured from the steep ascent as he flung himself on a cushioned bench and drew her down beside him. This shortness of breath in Richard worried her sometimes until she reminded herself that it was normal enough in a heavily-built man nearing fifty.

Casually, she gave him time to recover by drawing off his gauntlets for him and unfastening the fur collar of his pellard.

'Now tell me,' she asked, 'what terms are agreed?'

'Terms that may, or may not, satisfy dead men's kin! Salisbury, Warwick and myself are to establish a chantry at St Albans; masses to be said there in perpetuity for the souls of the slain. And we're to pay compensation to heirs and widows…' He went on to give her details of those payments.

'I see,' she said when he'd finished. 'Is that all?'

'No, not quite. Henry, bless his simple soul, has arranged a little pageant for tomorrow, the Feast of the Annunciation.'

'A pageant? In the season of Lent?'

'Aye, the city criers are going about already proclaiming it. There is to be a "Love Day" procession to St Paul's. We're all to walk hand in hand with former enemies, and promise eternal friendship from henceforth.' He leaned his iron-grey head back against the wall and surveyed the ceiling. 'Warwick is to walk with young Somerset,' he said grimly. 'Salisbury with Northumberland. And – I with the Queen.'

If it had not been for his sober tone, she'd have thought he was joking. Then he went on, a sharpness of cynicism edging his voice: 'Maybe our daughter Anne ought to join young Exeter in his progress: it is, after all, a forced coupling of adversaries!'

She flinched at the reminder; then asked, 'Is that how you see the whole thing, Dickon?'

'I fear so, sweetheart. This "Love Day" of Henry's will be but a public statement of enmities for the next battle; and people will remember whose hands were joined after all the vows of friendship are forgotten.'

'Yet the vows may *not* be forgotten, surely? They may bring real peace. After all, Henry is a saint and perhaps he has been inspired—'

'No, my love. Henry is but a weak and childish man who will collapse again and again under the pressure of his great office. But Margaret is determined now that I shall not be Protector a third time, to hold the reality of power while her son is still a minor. So she must destroy me. And soon.'

This fatalism, which was so unlike Richard, struck dread to Cecily's soul. She knew that he'd been weary for a long time of the seesaw of power and the constant intriguing of the Queen. But he'd never talked like this before... He needed a rest, she decided desperately.

'Let us go to Ludlow,' she suggested as calmly as she could. 'Let us leave London for a while as soon as tomorrow's business is over.' She put her arms about his neck; felt the roughness of his long moustaches and the wind-whipped cold of his face against her cheek. He was infinitely dear to her, dearer than any ambition for the boy-Earl, Edward, who would succeed him. And yet, she wanted him to recover his will to fight on, for that was the essence of his being – of his whole life's obstinate struggle: to fight for good government in England.

Not at the price of deposing Henry though: Richard would never consider that. Last year, when James of Scotland had made overtures to him – promising him help in a bid for the Crown to which James said he believed York had a better right than Lancaster – Richard had written James a stiff refusal; and had then marched north to wage war on the border-raiding Scots.

But Margaret, hearing of the affair, had become more alarmed than ever; and had told Henry that York was collecting an army out of Neville lands to force his abdication.

'Aye, we'll go westward again soon, love,' Richard promised. 'I have a mind, in any case, to talk to our lads.' He put an arm about her shoulder and they sat on, in companionable silence, watching the view through the oriel window. But Cecily's mind was already far off, hungry for sight and sound of her boys. She'd had much news of them from her brother, Lord Abergavenny, at Bishop Robert's funeral; though Abergavenny had been more anxious to discuss the Tudors at the time, it being only a few months since Edward Tudor, Earl of Richmond, had died.

'Did you know that his widow is living in Wales, Cis? Under the protection of her brother-in-law, Jasper, at Pembroke Castle?'

Yes, Cecily had heard that Margaret, Countess of Richmond, intended to live permanently in Wales, now that her lord was dead. 'But isn't it rather odd,' she'd asked her brother, 'for so young a widow – she can't be more than sixteen – not to want to have a place in London any more? Of course I hear she's very studious. Though not given to melancholy, I trust, like her unfortunate father, God rest him.' The rumour had never died that John Beaufort had taken his own life when royal favour waned.

Abergavenny's loud laugh rang out. 'She didn't seem melancholy to me,' he said, 'at her young lord's funeral, which I attended at the Grey Friars in Carmarthen last November. Her infant son would be only a few months old then but there was nothing helpless about the Countess Margaret. No; for all she's no bigger than a wren, she was as firmly in control of everything and everyone as only a Beaufort *could* be at such a time. And Jasper Tudor – the lord of Pembroke and half-brother of the King! – was running around asking her advice as if she were a middle-aged matron with experience of fifty funerals. Oh, her son will go far with a mother like that at his back; you mark my words, Cis!'

'What has she called the boy?'

'Blessed if I know – oh yes, Henry. A good Lancastrian name.'

Henry Tudor, Cecily had thought absently. Great-grandson of the eldest bastard of John of Gaunt and Katherine Swynford. If the infant hadn't inherited his father's lung disease, he might live to be invested with the

Earldom of Richmond one day... But that was all she ever expected to hear of the Beaufort widow's son.

～

THE MORNING of the Annunciation Feast was chilly but bright. Vast crowds had been gathering since dawn along the processional route from Westminster to St Paul's. A mood of intense optimism prevailed: spring was in full flower today and the threat of civil war removed.

Here were the King's bishops and household officers now, clattering along Fleet Street and through Ludgate. Outside the Bishop of London's palace the Earls of Salisbury and of Warwick were waiting, with unarmed retinues, alongside the Percys from Northumberland House – a sight wonderful to behold, Neville and Percy in one place without a gleam of steel between them! And now the Duke and Duchess of York were riding up past the Great Wardrobe from Baynard's Castle.

Leaving Richard to await the Queen's arrival, Cecily handed her horse to an esquire and went to stand among the throng of ladies by the West Door of St Paul's. The only space she could see was near a trio for whom she had no great love: her sister Ann, Duchess of Buckingham; Alice Chaucer, Dowager-Duchess of Suffolk; and Jacquetta Woodville. But, in the spirit of the 'Love Day', she took her place near them and murmured a pleasant 'Good morning' as she passed – though she couldn't help thinking, *Lord, how old-looking they've all become; Jacquetta is as wrinkled as a raisin; and Alice and Ann do their faces no good by scowling at me like that.* Then her sister-in-law, Alice of Salisbury, touched her arm and she moved over gratefully into the friendly circle of the Middleham Nevilles – Warwick's delicate little wife, Anne Beauchamp, was there; and his sister Katherine who'd recently wedded Lord Bonville – thus breaking the heart of an obscure young man named William Hastings.

But there was no time for gossip. The King, surrounded by his officers, was already dismounting; walking now towards the West Door and leaning on the arm of Humphrey of Buckingham.

Henry, Cecily thought, looked transparently pale this morning although he was smiling and obviously much pleased by the occasion; but happiness didn't straighten the stoop of his shoulders nor give any lift to the dragging step under the long ceremonial robes. Thirty-six years old, he seemed like a man of seventy; his sparse hair, almost totally grey, wisping about the small crown which he wore to give full dignity to this event.

Her brother-in-law of Buckingham, holding the royal arm, was clearly solicitous of Henry. But Buckingham himself had now grown old and slow: the death of his heir, after a long paralysis, had had a terrible effect upon him. Looking at Humphrey, Cecily wished to God that the ill-judged battle of St Albans had never taken place.

Now came Richard of Salisbury. Always an imposing figure, he appeared magnificent today in the saltire-decorated Neville colours of scarlet and silver. His thick mane of grey hair gleamed like polished steel about a face that grew more like his father's with age; he was almost sixty; but his blue eyes retained the typical marchman's alert clarity and long-sightedness. He looked around serenely for the new Earl of Northumberland who was glowering at him from the Percy ranks; grabbed this troublesome nephew of his by the hand and hauled him unceremoniously into St Paul's – the gesture saying clearer than words: 'Now look, lad, your father was killed in a fair fight so quit grouching like a damned foreigner. Englishmen don't support blood-feuds: that's a notion the Queen has put into all your heads for her own ends.'

After blunt Salisbury came his eldest son, Warwick, now Captain of Calais. Tall, blade-thin and more dangerous looking than ever from the sea-fighting that was lately his chief occupation, Warwick strode beside Henry Beaufort, third Duke of Somerset, whose father he had slain. But the Neville didn't look at the Beaufort. Even when their hands clamped together at the cathedral entrance, Warwick stared straight ahead, his wind-chiselled profile sharp in nose and brow and chin. And Beaufort, though regarding him sidelong with intense animosity, seemed ineffectual as a rabbit beside a golden eagle.

Cecily watched the bared heads of these cousins (one foxy fair, the other copper dark) disappear into the gloom of St Paul's. She knew she wouldn't give much for Somerset's chances in any straight encounter with the ferocious Warwick. But the weakly-handsome young Henry Beaufort had the full support of the Queen, whose lover he was reputed to be, so that his potential strength needed to be calculated on that. Which left Warwick, with only the Calais garrison, matched against the entire royal army! Any other Captain would have handled the Queen's favourite more warily, but the never-defeated Warwick was as arrogant and as headstrong, alas, as he was brilliant: an ally who might well make further trouble for York.

Several other hand-fasted pairs went by. Cecily glimpsed the ravaged face of her son-in-law, Exeter, and felt the familiar guilt she'd taken upon herself for her daughter's heartlessness and disloyalty in his regard. Then the murderous eye of the young Lord Clifford raked the Neville ranks where she stood, and she turned her head aside from the almost physical impact of its blood-lust.

Clifford would either avenge his slain father or go out of his mind...

The growing tension all around now proclaimed the approach of the Queen.

Margaret stalked rather than walked, majestic in a crimson robe, her blue-black hair gold crowned... As she drew nearer, the cold harsh sunlight showed Cecily the changes that time and torment had wrought in the lovely royal countenance: still strikingly beautiful, it had a ruthless strength now. As if all the old diverse passions had been channelled into one course: a relentless torrent of hate that glinted behind the green eyes fixed on Richard, Duke of York.

## 15

Queen Margaret made full use of the passions stirred by the 'Love Day' to arouse all the enemies of York.

After further attacks upon his followers in the capital, Richard quietly withdrew and journeyed towards Wales with Cecily and the children. He was sick to the heart of the futile struggle against the Queen who was now intriguing again with France, so that the south coast of England was in constant danger from a French fleet under Pierre de Brezé. Only Warwick's patrol of the Channel with ships from Calais had kept the enemy at bay for a while; but then Margaret had broken Warwick's Captaincy of Calais.

With his mighty father, Salisbury, she employed other methods: ravage by Scots: harassment by Percy's and Bishop's men of Durham. After more than a year of desperate defence, Salisbury set out to confer with his brother-in-law of York in Wales but, on the march, he was set upon by the Queen's Cheshire levies at Blore Heath and suffered heavy losses – including the arrest of two sons and of faithful ally Sir Thomas Parr of Kendal. The depleted north-country force struggled on to Ludlow where the Yorks had been living quietly for the past eighteen months, and Warwick had just arrived.

The presence of the three main Yorkist leaders under one roof made Ludlow Castle the focus of the Queen's implacable hostility. She had determined long ago upon their destruction, even if it meant plunging the country into civil war; now she moved against them with her main force.

This autumn of 1459, the sky rained blood over a little town in Bedfordshire after the royal army had passed through. News of the omen was spreading rapidly over the entire country so that people were waiting, everywhere, for some disaster.

The October midnight was black around Ludlow Castle but lights burned behind the shutters in the Great Hall where a tense conference was in progress.

Richard stood near Cecily, who was seated at the bare High Table. Salisbury and Warwick paced about on the dais, talking loudly. The young Earls of March and Rutland, surrounded by captains and household officers, listened from the body of the Hall into which hundreds of north-country soldiers were packed; many of these soldiers had been wounded at Blore Heath on September 23rd.

Salisbury was growling: 'I did everything I could to avoid clashing with the Queen's levies. But now two of my sons are prisoners and near a thousand men lost or incapacitated. So I say we cannot take on another fight, alone, against the odds out there.' He swung a fist in the direction of the River Teme beyond which a royal army, 10,000 strong, was encamped.

'I suppose you're blaming me, sire,' his heir fumed, 'that those scoundrels I brought from Calais have deserted?' Warwick was still white with rage and shock at the discovery that the troops he'd led from France, through a cheering London, had suddenly slipped away from him in Shropshire. He'd been dumbfounded at sight of their empty quarters; then humiliated; then blindly furious—

'Nay, lad,' his father said soothingly, 'one could expect no other from the men who lost Normandy under Edmund of Somerset.'

'But these were *my* men. I retrained them myself when I took over the Captaincy of Calais.'

'Mayhap, nephew,' Cecily said sharply, 'you only taught them how to pirate ships, and to laugh at royal messengers who came to take your Captaincy from you.' She was impatient of all the arguments. Time was running out for what she knew must be done in the end. But Warwick remained obsessed about the reasons for his troops' desertion which had cut his pride to the quick.

'That's it,' he shouted, brightening, 'that's it! The King appointed young Somerset in my place, only I wouldn't give it up. So now they've gone over to *him* – they think he's the legal Captain of Calais. But, by God, I'll hang every mother's son who has exchanged the Ragged Staff this night for the Beaufort Portcullis. I'll—'

Richard brought his fist down on the table. 'Let it be, Warwick,' he said. 'Your men have gone. So has Sir Andrew Trollope and my Welsh levies. God knows why but there it is: maybe they looked across the river and came to an intelligent decision! But the fact remains, now, that we have no one left here except the personal retinues of myself and my sons, and your father's loyal marchmen – Herbert's reinforcements not having turned up. So we have to decide, quickly, what to do before the King's offer of pardon expires.'

'Pardon!' Warwick exploded. 'If the ambush at Blore Heath is any example, we'll all be executed anyhow. I'm for holding out here.'

'This castle is not prepared for a siege,' Richard said quietly.

'Why not, Uncle? You had eighteen months to prepare it!'

'I was being careful not to provoke Queen Margaret whose spies followed me like gnats from London—'

Eighteen months, Cecily thought, as her menfolk went on arguing... That short space of time had seen a great lessening of Yorkist influence on the Council as Margaret filled each arising vacancy with her own candidate. Even people who had no great love for the Queen had begun to side with her since the hand-clasping outside St Paul's because it had been so obvious from that day that she had decided on the extinction of York.

Warwick's exploits in the Channel had set her to arms. He'd sent captured French vessels up the Thames, to the huge delight of Londoners; and he'd made overtures of friendship to Burgundy, that enemy of all Angevin kin. So when he'd come home to attend last autumn's Parliament at Westminster, Margaret had tried to have him murdered; and, failing that, had ordered him to give up Calais to young Henry of Somerset – an order which he flatly refused to obey even when Somerset went out with troops to besiege him and his uncle, William Fauconberg.

By the summer, Margaret had her own vast army in the midlands with – incredibly – the King at its head: she'd convinced Henry at last that York and Salisbury were behind Warwick's defiance, and that they had to be crushed.

So there was Henry – wearing armour and living in a tent – with his 10,000 armed men drawn up just south of the River Teme. This morning, they'd tried to storm across Ludford Bridge, but the Yorkists had turned their artillery on them.

'They're firing on the King!' had been the cry. 'Treason – *treason!*'

It was from that moment, Cecily judged, that pardons became out of the question. Despairingly, she'd watched all day from the top of the Keep as her kinsmen's forces held the town and the riverbank. But the desertion, tonight, of the Calais men and the Welsh levies, meant that even the holding operation could not continue. There were only two alternatives. One was to barricade the castle for a siege. The other – which every commander was loathe to suggest – was to evacuate it and flee.

Decisively, she stood up.

'Let there be an end to this profitless talk,' she said. 'There are yet enough hours left until daylight for you all to get away. Richard—' she swung around on her husband '—let neither me nor the children put your innocent head on a block. Leave us. We shall be safe. No one would dare molest us. Now go – *go* while still you may. Take Edmund with you and sail for Ireland where you are loved… And you, my brother and my nephew, convey Edward of March to Calais. That way will the heirs of York have hope of survival until a better fighting day dawns.'

Her urgent common-sense impelled everyone, except Richard, to final agreement. He agonised over the decision of leaving her and the children defenceless.

'For God's sake,' she shouted at him, her nerve cracking, 'of what use to me or my little ones is a dead lord? And what becomes of the York inheritance for March and Rutland if you do not save yourself to fight again? Oh, take horse, I beseech you, for the coast; then ship to Ireland.'

'She's right, Uncle,' Warwick muttered. 'Your death is certain here. But Ireland will receive you and Edmund gladly. And we'll guard Edward at Calais which William Fauconberg keeps for us. So may God speed us all.'

For a moment longer, Richard hesitated – looking from the main body of the room which was fast emptying as Salisbury sent his marchmen out, to the still figure of his wife by the High Table. Then he crossed swiftly to her, took her in his arms and kissed her.

Unmoving, she watched him and young Edmund hurry away together with Sir David Hall and Sir Richard Croft; while Salisbury and Warwick bustled Edward of March before them so that there was only time for a look between mother and son.

After they had all gone, the Hall was ghostly quiet – a quietness intensified by the sound of hoofbeats from the mountain road, filtering up through the blank shutters.

Unsteadily, she made her way to the chapel and prayed for the safe passage of those whom she loved. Then she gathered all the household servants and told them to be ready to evacuate the castle at first light, because it would almost certainly be sacked by the royal army.

'Agnes—' she turned to Lady Croft '—you will ride north with the ladies Elisabeth and Margaret until you reach some religious house which will give you all sanctuary.' The girls were both old enough to excite soldiers' lusts: at whatever cost, she had to get them out of Ludlow.

'And – and the lords George and Richard?' Agnes Croft asked.

'The boys and I will go into the town here. We will wait at the market cross to submit York property to the King. The royal army will see at once that we are undefended: that should prevent looting or – or other outrage to the inhabitants.'

*Though maybe not to me*, she thought, suddenly sick with apprehension.

She kissed her daughters, gave all the money she had left over from servants' wages to Agnes Croft, and then, without a backward glance, went on directing the disbandment of the household – leaving George and Dickon to sleep for as long as possible.

Those small boys, aged ten and seven, were all that remained now of the House of York. She didn't know if she'd ever see their father or their elder brothers again. She didn't know what treatment to expect for herself in Ludlow town.

Cold with fear, she changed her clothing to a dark green riding gown and mantle; then she went in to rouse the children.

George was sleeping heavily – his corn-gold hair tossed about his flushed face and his mouth slightly open. But Dickon's quiet grey eyes reflected the taper glow at once: Dickon always slept light as a cat. She wondered how much he'd heard from Hall and courtyard.

It was chilly in the hour before dawn. Grasping the children's hands under the folds of her riding mantle, Cecily began the steep descent from the castle. She'd ordered the main gate to be left open behind her. And she took away no possessions except the clothing and jewellery she and the boys wore. Choice of what to save became absurd in the end, she'd found.

The path from the castle to Ludlow town had seen many a game among the York children; but it was still too greyish this morning for even George's fantastic imagination to devise much entertainment from it, so he chattered as he walked along – seeming quite unaware of abnormality in the situation. But Dickon was silent, tense. *He knows*, Cecily thought in helpless sympathy with his fear that echoed her own. Yet he walked without faltering, keeping just one step ahead of her; while George, growing even more erratic than usual, either dragged behind or leaned over to touch the ghostly hedgerows and grasses.

The houses of Ludlow were crowding closer now. People, warned by messengers from the castle, huddled behind windows or doorways, waiting for the submission of their town to be made to the royal army. Silently they watched the Duchess and her sons go by in the grey light. Many blessed, and some cursed the House of York; but no one remained unmoved.

JUBILANT TROOPS CAME SWEEPING across the Teme bridge. They were howling like a horde of barbarians and totally outstripping their officers.

Wildly, Cecily looked for some responsible man to accept the town's submission from her and to control the troops, but all she saw, as she stepped forward into their path, was a confusion of badges and drawn weapons.

Pressing her sons close against her, she held her ground, even when it seemed that to be trampled was inevitable, but the charge divided at the last moment, surrounding her instead – a jostling, terrifying mob without leader or discipline or decency. She could feel its heat, smell its sweat.

Her only defence was to summon every shred of dignity and pride she possessed. She drew herself up to her considerable height and ordered:

'Stand back. Make way for your commanders to come to me.'

For an instant, she thought she had won. The men paused; shuffled like a herd of bullocks bewildered by some invisible force. She held them with her eyes, willing them to back away— But then, a Calais deserter bawled:

'Ha, look at proud Cis – still giving the orders like a true Neville! But where's Salisbury and Warwick? Where's great York, come to that? – for we've heard they've all flown.' Then the rest began to laugh and to crowd in upon her again.

Someone else shouted: 'The Rose of Raby – ripe for the picking!' and a huge fellow loomed over her, demanding, 'Do you still keep your taste for tall archers, lady?'

She'd managed to back against the steps of the market cross. Gripping Dickon with one hand and her skirts with the other, she mounted the steps until her spine was pressed against the cross. But the men had surged upwards with her and now the big fellow was leading a chant of:

'Where's the archer's son? Blaeburn's boy, the Earl of March. Blaeburn's boy—'

She had a nightmare sensation of having been brought here for execution. *This is how Jeanne d'Arc felt in Rouen*, she thought.

Now a soldier was wrenching the White Rose ring off her finger, and another was trying to undo her jewelled cincture without breaking its clasp. She felt Dickon kicking out like a wild horse – there was no sign of George – but still the men swarmed; jeering; shouting; touching her – one kissing her neck and trying to reach her mouth.

Suddenly the man slumped forward, his embrace loosening. The weight of his body fell on her feet. Dickon was sidestepping the spurting blood.

She looked up to see Humphrey of Buckingham wiping his sword. He must have charged his mount right through the crowd... Now he was swinging her up onto the saddle before him while he bellowed orders to the troops to disperse.

'Mother of God – Cis, are you all right?' was all he managed to pant as he wheeled about, shielding the boys.

The mob took to its heels through the town and up towards the castle. More and more armed men were swarming over the bridge – no one seemed able to stop or control them. Helplessly, Cecily and her brother-in-law watched as the looting and pillaging began, as women were dragged out of their homes, and as hearth-fires were scattered up onto the roof thatches.

Somehow, Buckingham got her and the boys to the safety of the King's tent.

Henry was kneeling in prayer, oblivious of the carnage across the river. The Duke said to him: 'Sire, I pray your protection for the Duchess of York and her young sons, my nephews. They are innocent of their menfolk's treachery.'

'It was – *no treachery*—' Cecily gasped in protest; but her brother-in-law silenced her with a look until the King crossed himself and murmured:

'Of course the Duchess Cecily is innocent. Come and talk to us, dear cousin.'

'Oh, my lord King—' she flung herself to her knees before Henry '—the town of Ludlow is burning: *the people are being massacred*—'

A spasm of pain twitched Henry's face.

'Try to stop it, my lord,' he said weakly to Buckingham. 'And then send Her Grace here, with her sons, into the care of your own good Duchess.'

Cecily stared aghast at the King. *To be put in Ann of Buckingham's charge—* Sweet God, though kindly meant, it was worse than any sentence of imprisonment!

## 16

The castle of Penshurst in Kent had been given to Humphrey Stafford from the estate of the late Duke of Gloucester. Thither, Cecily and her sons were brought from Ludlow through a sad, autumnal countryside.

Their reception by Ann of Buckingham, in the timber-roofed Great Hall, was brief and bitter – Ann was still garbed in heaviest mourning for the death of her eldest son.

'So,' she said tightly, 'you are paying the price of your lord's ambition at last, are you, my sister? It is a judgment from God which I shall make no effort to soften in your regard, be sure of that.'

'I never expected that you would, Ann,' Cecily replied. 'But at least you can be kind to my small boys.' She put her palms behind the shoulder blades of each and pushed them into a reluctant approach to their hard-faced aunt.

'Why should I?' Ann snapped. 'Their father caused the death of my eldest son as surely as if he had stabbed him. For thirty months after the battle of St Albans, I nursed his paralysed body. And now he's dead – dead—' Her eyes and nose reddened in her thin white face but she choked back the pressing tears to add: 'His widow and his heir are living here with me. Let you all look upon their grief, and upon mine: then you will not seek favours from any of us.'

Cecily expected none; not from Ann, who was the Queen's friend; nor from the young widow who was Edmund of Somerset's daughter. She hoped for only two things during this bleak winter's imprisonment which she faced without even a change of clothing: news of Richard and the other exiles: and some gentleness towards the bewildered small boys on whom Ann had not even bestowed a glance.

These hopes almost died in the bleak, north-facing tower where, it seemed, they were all to be confined. They would be allowed out, they were told, only for prayers, meals and one hour's archery or riding each morning in the park.

'We must escape from here,' Cecily said quietly to Dickon when he came to stand beside her at the window that looked towards distant London. She wouldn't have said that to George: George was a chatterbox, recklessly indiscreet. But she'd never known Dickon to breathe a word of any confidence reposed in him.

After that, matters didn't seem so bad: she had something for which to plan and keep alert. But if only she could hear some tidings of Richard, Edmund and Edward.

News came, unexpectedly, from Ann one morning in late November when she visited the north tower. She carried an open letter in her hand and she appeared to be in high good humour.

'I have a report here, Cecily,' she began without preamble, 'of the Coventry Parliament now in session. Your husband and all your kin have been attainted. Their property is forfeit, their titles extinguished. So I must see to it from henceforth that my household no longer refers to you as the Duchess of York.'

Cecily felt neither shock nor surprise at the sentences, which would have been dictated by the Queen. But, in her sister Ann's elated mood, she sensed a lack of caution today. Ann might be trapped into telling her something.

'Attainted – in exile?' she asked, pretending faintness.

'How else?' Ann's eyes narrowed as they rested upon her. 'York and Rutland in Dublin. Salisbury, Warwick and March in Calais.' She seemed to have forgotten the fact that none of these titles was now legal.

*So they'd all safely reached their chosen ports.* It was as much as Cecily could do not to hug her sister for these tidings. Instead, she put her head down and sighed deeply. 'Have attempts been made to arrest them?' she asked.

'Of course. They've been condemned to death, I trust you understand. But Calais is yet blockaded by Warwick's pirate ships: no one can get in until the royal fleet attacks and disperses the pirates. Still, that won't be long: Sir Richard Woodville is gathering vessels at Dover... As for the King's envoy, Sir William Overy, who went across to Dublin – well, he simply hasn't returned yet. There's some wild talk of the Irish having *executed* him but one can't believe that—'

*Can't one?* Cecily's heart exulted. *The Irish love Richard enough to flout any laws for his safety; and more than ever now should they strive to protect him after years of Wiltshire's bad government in the King's name.* Richard could have the entire country at his back: earls, chieftains, officials, from among whom he could gather an army. *He could return home in force.*

Her mind tried to anticipate what her husband would require to be done, here, by way of preparation. His friends in London would need a central meeting place where they could co-ordinate all plans – receive and send out messages to keep Dublin and Calais in touch for a combined invasion. And the opening of the city's gates must be certain when Richard reached them.

Somehow she had to get to London to form the nucleus of all this work. An escape plan, long brooded upon, began to chip its way to the hatching.

'...Oh, one good thing,' Ann was saying, 'if you're not too dismayed to take it in after the loss of all property and titles.' Ann seemed to enjoy repeating this. 'It is that the King has allowed you a grant of one thousand marks yearly, for your relief and that of your children, even though you're a condemned traitor's wife and deserve nothing! But I suppose it was done to unburden me of your keep.'

*A burden,* Cecily thought, *of which I will relieve you as soon as possible, my sister...* She was familiar with the countryside around here from having stayed with the Mowbrays at nearby Tonbridge Castle several times in the old days. Yet she realised that escape from Penshurst would be rendered daily more difficult as the winter deepened. The castle gates were locked between five in the evening and seven the next morning. Leafless trees in the park offered no blind from pursuers. And, soon, there'd be even harsher weather than now.

Turning to Ann, she said thoughtfully: 'From the King's gracious moneys, I shall require winter clothing for the children and myself. But, in accordance with our new position, I shall have the outer garments made of plain rough stuff: burel or fryse will do us very well, I think.'

Astonishment made Ann laugh sharply. 'Faith, 'twill make a great change for you, who've always been so fond of fashion! But then you're growing old, Cecily, are you not? – forty-four last Maytime if I calculate correctly; there can't be many years left of the famous beauty you have abused that all your children are suspect of being bastards!' Jealousy twisted Ann's narrow face. She turned abruptly towards the door. 'I'll see that the work of attiring you for a humble future is put in hand at once.' As if she couldn't wait to behold her sister's reduced condition, she hurried off.

Cecily glanced at Dickon and George, who were sitting in a dim corner of the tower room, to assess how much they had understood. George was sunk in the listless apathy that had quieted him almost to unconsciousness of late. Dickon was absorbed in carving a candle-end with a piece of sharp stick. Both of them disliked their aunt of Buckingham and kept themselves as far from her presence as possible, even though she had relented towards them soon after their arrival and sometimes had them brought down to the Hall.

Cecily wanted to discuss her escape plan with someone, to fix it in her own mind and have it checked for faults. And she would need Dickon's co-operation with it in due course because success would depend on his horsemanship. But she decided it was too soon yet to place such a burden of secrecy on so small a boy. He'd struck up an admiring friendship these past weeks with little Harry Stafford, the orphaned heir to the Dukedom of Buckingham. This cousin was almost his own age; and Harry was a child of easy charm who might be told the secret as some kind of compensation for Dickon's bleaker nature. Cecily knew that her youngest son was becoming aware of his own indrawn character. Only last night – after the supper which they'd all been allowed to eat in the Hall because there were no visitors – she'd watched him force himself to enter a clowning game with the uninhibited Harry; and then retire, smiling with relief, when it became apparent that Harry needed no partner for his dazzling antics. No, for once Dickon couldn't be trusted: he was under the spell of his handsome cousin. So she'd have to put off telling him what to do until the actual morning when she was ready for escape from Penshurst. Meanwhile though, she could pass on to him her own knowledge of the country lying to the northward.

Gently taking the pointed stick from him, she began to mark paths and landmarks in the dust of the floor with it. Dickon watched intently, his eyes narrowed and his lips compressed into a straight, colourless line – signs of his deepest concentration; while George continued to loll against the wall, his bored mind unstimulated by such dull games as trying to redraw the chart after it was rubbed out time after time. The only question George asked was: 'What does the candle signify?'

'*London*,' Cecily and Dickon replied in unison.

OPPORTUNITY CAME IN EARLY JANUARY, when the Duchess of Buckingham was occupied with the marriage preparations of her second son, Henry, to the young Beaufort widow of Edmund Tudor, who was still living in Pembroke with her brother-in-law and her child, but would leave shortly for Penshurst. There was a flurry of preparation for her coming so that less attention than usual was paid to the York family.

Dressed in their drab clothing, Cecily and her sons set out for their morning ride through the wintry park. Two armed men were in attendance as always – the Stafford Knot badges on their leather jacks covered up this cold morning by frieze cloaks. But they were less alert now than they'd been even a month ago: the lady Cecily never gave them any trouble and they were beginning to relax with her. She was always gracious, correct and undemanding in privilege.

"'Tis hard,' one of the men sighed to his comrade today, 'to think of a great noblewoman like that losing her title.'

'Harder still,' replied the other, 'to imagine what her lord has lost *besides* his title: lands, castles and all the wealth of a royal Dukedom! People are saying it isn't right, though, the way York property is given away to the Queen's friends. There's uneasiness among her enemies, I tell you, lest that kind of generosity should spread.'

'Aye, dangerous to be rich nowadays if the Frenchwoman loves you not, eh? I hear she's sending a mighty fleet against Calais to kill York's son, and to finish off "Warwick the Corsair" and his father and his uncle Fauconberg. A clean sweep of Neville that would be, with two more of Salisbury's' sons yet in prison and like to lose their heads.'

'I hear further that the Queen is keeping her own army intact for fear of invasion from Ireland. They say the rebel Yorks – I mean of course Plantagenets – have a mighty following there…'

Deep in conversation, the guards rode on by the familiar northward track. Cecily always chose to lead her sons north, towards the Downs. But she'd turn as soon as she reached the Sevenoaks road – they knew she would – and then she'd come back by the circular route under Crockham Hill to Leigh: she did this every time, without variation.

They could see the youngest boy turning now – breaking into a canter along the ridge – galloping westward.

'He's a brave sight on a horse, that little 'un. Look how

he goes, hell for leather! Fairly lying on the creature's neck he is…'

Expecting to see Cecily and George following close, the guards reined their own mounts to watch Dickon swerve towards them, along the usual track. But the headlong rider did not swerve. And they thought they heard a cry for help.

Panic-stricken, they both shouted at once: 'The lad's mount has bolted—' Then, at breakneck speed, they made for Crockham Hill.

They searched as far as Godstone, and up to Westerham, but found no sign of Dickon. So they went back along the track to Leigh – not relishing the prospect of telling his mother that her son must have been thrown, and that a search party would have to go out onto the Downs to recover his body.

But the lady Cecily wasn't at Leigh. Neither was she at Penshurst.

OUTSIDE THE DOWNS village of Warlingham, Cecily looked back anxiously. Not daring to halt, she still prayed that Dickon could catch up with her and George, although he'd seemed quite resigned to being captured by the guards once he'd given his mother and brother a good start towards London.

'You ride on north,' he'd said, nodding sagely when she'd outlined the plan to him. 'I'll decoy the men westward as far as I can. Then I'll either join you or – or I'll go back to Penshurst.' His understanding of every point had been clear and instant, and he'd carried out her directions precisely – indeed, his mime of being helpless on a runaway horse had been almost too good at one stage and his mother had almost set off in pursuit! Now she knew that some day, having learned so well how to obey, Dickon would make as good a leader as his father, God willing – unless Ann of Buckingham beat him to death for this morning's doings. Because he would not lie to minimize his guilt: he had a curiously undefensive honesty.

Desperately, she looked back again. A small mounted figure was coming into view, riding hard...

WITH BOTH HER sons safe beside her, she pressed on for London. There, she'd sell her jewelled belt to buy food and lodging. She'd sell it to John Shore in Lombard Street, with whom she'd often dealt in the past. Shore, though Court jeweller, was a shrewd old merchant whose only political thoughts concerned trade – which the Queen's 'war' had not helped of late years: therefore Shore was a Yorkist by conviction.

So Cecily reasoned in any case. And prayed she was right.

# 17

Leaving the boys at the Spurre Inn, Cecily made her way on foot through the crowded alleys of Southwark that led to London Bridge. Nobody paid any attention to her in her rough hooded mantle.

All the way from the leper-house known as the Loke in Kent Street to St Thomas' hospital in Thieves Lane, a concentrated human din arose from prisons and bordellos, tenements and market-stalls. Above that, sounding the baying of mastiffs and the roaring of bulls from the bear gardens, as well as chanting and bell-ringing from the many churches. Now the ubiquitous smell of cooking food was mingling with the low-tide stench of the river.

Cecily crossed the thronged bridge where the crowding shops on each side were doing brisk business – and where bodiless heads dripped fresh blood onto the spikes by the North Tower end. Sight of these heads brought home to her with shock the panic measures which the government was now adopting against all who aided exiled rebels. Invasion was expected, either from Ireland or from France, and Queen Margaret had thrown the country into a state of almost hysterical preparedness. Taxation – conscription – confiscation of shipping – forced loans – it seemed that the government no longer cared how much offence it gave, at home or abroad.

Descending at the north side of the bridge, she was careful not to glance to her left, up-river, in case she'd glimpse the turrets of Baynard's Castle rearing above the skyline of Blackfriars. It felt like a thousand years since she and Richard had lived there; and she wondered who occupied the mansion now; and whether anything had been spared of York possessions when royal troops had ransacked the place after the November Parliament – or 'the Parliament of Devils' as she'd heard it referred to at the Inn...

No, nothing would have been left she decided as she hurried across Thames Street. All Richard's properties in England and in Wales had been seized by the Crown before being bestowed on other lords. Nothing remained now of the mighty York estate. Even its retainers had been driven out; maltreated – murdered—

Anger, long-smouldering, blazed in her as she came into Lombard Street. That she, a Neville, wife of great Richard of York, should be penniless and homeless; her royal-blooded lord attainted; her children without inheritance... But she must fight for that lord and those children. *Fight.*

For a moment she forgot to walk humbly, hooded head bowed. Instead, her chin lifted; her body drew itself up; she began to move faster as people instinctively stepped aside to let her pass. In regal isolation she swept into the jeweller's shop beneath the royal arms and the gilt-lettering sign that said: 'Shore and Son, Court Jewellers.' She'd obtain enough money here to help her make a start – any kind of start – on a campaign to bring the Yorkists back to their rightful power near King Henry's throne. Henry *needed* York.

The fat old jeweller was rearranging his glittering wares on velvet-covered shelves which half hid the busy workshop behind him and the cramped office where a younger man pored over ledgers... With a leap of the heart, Cecily recognised on the shelves a medallion belonging to her son, Edward; and a mantle-brooch she'd seen her brother of Salisbury wear that last night at Ludlow.

Old Shore's eyes were as quick as her own.

'Your Grace,' he whispered after the swiftest glance at her, 'come inside I beg of you lest you be seen.' Ushering her through a curtained doorway, he called over his shoulder to the man in the office: 'William, my son, leave the ledgers awhile, will you, and attend to the new stock I was putting up?' Then he followed her into a dark passage that led to a wainscoted room... In the firelight she noticed that he was sweating although it was a cold January day. 'Your Grace—' he began agitatedly.

'That is not my title now, Master Shore,' she reminded him. 'It has gone, along with all my other possessions. Except for this gemmed girdle you once made for me and which I wish to sell.' She unclasped it from under her surcoat and handed it to him – the fire drawing shafts of light from the polished stones.

His chins and his paunch wobbled in dismay. 'Alas, Madame, I can offer but half its value. I am overdrawn and over-stocked—'

'Over-stocked? From Calais?'

'*No!* We-e-ell, yes, yes…'

'You've been there yourself lately?' She gripped his plump wrist.

'Most unwillingly I have,' he cried with much feeling;

and then poured out a story which, he swore, would soon be entertaining every rebel in the land...

The royal fleet, it appeared, had been gathered in Sandwich harbour on the night of January 19th. Its commander, Sir Richard Woodville, was in the town at the time, saying farewell to his wife Jacquetta and some of their many children. With them were several merchants – including Shore – doing some last-minute business before the fleet sailed to help young Somerset wrest Calais from Warwick and the other rebels. The Woodville lodging was guarded by those former members of the Calais garrison who'd deserted Warwick at Ludlow in October...

Under cover of darkness, two small ships stole into the harbour. They came in answer to a secret message from the townspeople who had hated Queen Margaret ever since her French champion, de Brezé, had sacked their port. The ships were commanded by two of Warwick's best men.

With the aid of the people of Sandwich the entire royal fleet was captured; then everyone in the Woodville house was made prisoner and carried off across the Channel.

When they arrived in Calais, the Earl of Warwick was waiting grimly on the quayside. He picked out every soldier who'd deserted him at Ludlow and bade them all stand before him.

'You swore to follow me and to fight for the just cause of York,' he said through clenched teeth. 'You volunteered. I did not press you. Then you betrayed me; held me up to ridicule before all my kin to whom I had boasted of your fidelity and your valour— Ah, false knaves, the world will be well rid of your like!' Then he ordered the execution of 120 men...

While their corpses lay bleeding on Calais quay, the Woodvilles – father, eldest son and their close attendants – were paraded past the bonfires that had been lit in the streets to celebrate the capture of the royal ships. At last they reached the square where the young Earl of March was standing between his uncles of Salisbury and of Fauconberg.

Jeweller Shore tremulously recalled the scene which followed:

'I thought my lord Edward of March was going to strike all our heads off with his own sword! I was there with the Woodvilles, you see – having run from the slaughter on the quayside – and I prayed so hard that I barely know what happened for a while. But I saw the Earl of Warwick striding up and down, conferring with his kinsmen... Then they all took it in turns to berate the Woodvilles for serving Queen Margaret. And my lord of Salisbury said with great scorn: "How dare you lackeys collect a fleet to sail against us! We have more loyalty to our King than ever you and the Frenchwoman can muster." After that, Lord Fauconberg called them "common rascals, unfit for any punishment except a whipping" – and he reminded the elder Woodville how he'd climbed from being a mere henchman by taking advantage of his late master's widow. Whereupon, the lady in question began to scream curses into the fire.'

Old Shore's chins wobbled increasingly. 'Oh, the Dowager-Duchess of Bedford uttered some fearful curses, Your Grace. Against both your noble brothers and your nephew of Warwick. Then against the young Earl of March.'

A stab of maternal fear transfixed Cecily. 'Wh-what did she say to my eldest son?'

'She said – well, some nonsense about the blood of Beaufort: that its passion would ruin his body and the heirs of it... Then she went on to predict that he'd spend the rest of his life making amends to the name of Woodville for the insults he'd heaped on it that night. Out of her mind she looked – liked a dancing witch: it shivered my spine to listen to her. But her husband and her son said nothing. And Your Grace's kinsmen only laughed and walked away...'

Cecily stared into the jeweller's little backroom fire. Part of it was black where the coals had failed to light. She visualised there Jacquetta's dark supper-room in Rouen long ago, and the gilt-haired girl whose memory haunted Edward... Had Edward known that old Woodville was sire to his dream-maiden, would he have joined so heartily in insulting his blood? She believed not...

'These doings—' old Shore interrupted her thoughts '—have greatly incensed the Queen. She's stepped up her persecution of all Yorkist supporters: Your Grace may have seen a few fresh heads on London Bridge today. One of them belongs to a north-country lawyer named Roger Neville who tried to organise supplies of bowstrings for Calais.'

Cecily replied soberly: 'I see that I'm going to have trouble in finding friends... but a small house to rent for myself and my sons cannot be difficult to procure, Master Shore? Do you know of one – preferably south of the river?'

'Umm, now, there's a place used to belong to Sir John Fastolf, God rest him: he left some property to the Paston family of Norfolk when he died last year... I could send a message to Sir John Paston in the Temple, inquiring if this house be his and if it be for rent. Yes, yes, I'll send a boy. Meanwhile, Your Grace must eat and drink; you look famished.' He went to an inner door and called: 'Jane – Jane, bring wine and wafers. On the *best* tray.' Then he explained, beaming, to Cecily: 'Jane is my son William's wife. They were wedded but a sennight ago. She's only daughter to Mercer Wainstead of Cheap – a pretty child, as you'll see.'

Jane Shore was both pretty and very young: no more than twelve or thirteen years, Cecily judged, as the girl served her… Small of build, she still had a childish softness which made her matronly garb look absurd; and her linen cap failed altogether to confine her yellow, curling hair.

'I hope your marriage will be happy, Mistress Shore,' Cecily smiled at her – remembering her own daughters whose whereabouts she didn't even know.

A pair of round blue eyes looked up with gratitude and admiration – eyes that had an irrepressible merriment in their depths although they were bruised all about just now from outraged weeping.

'Oh, it *will be* a happy marriage,' her father-in-law cut in. 'She'll settle down with my William. She'll be content here yet…' His protest was forceful to the point of anxiety. Clearly, little Jane's lack of contentment worried him, for he floundered about awhile and then went rushing back along the passage to the shop, shouting for one of the boys to take a message to the Temple…

To Cecily's sympathetic scrutiny, Jane didn't look as if she'd ever belong to this dark house in Lombard Street, nor to the earnest young man out there whom she'd glimpsed toiling over his father's dusty ledgers. For, despite her tear-stains and bruises, the child-wife had a joyous presence. And a little dimple in her cheek refused to be ironed out by marital care.

~

As soon as it became known that Cecily was living in Southwark, some of her old retainers crept back to serve her. Many Yorkist supporters also rallied around her, so that the Fastolf house became a place of secret meetings and smuggled messages. There, for the first time in months, she heard detailed news of her husband.

Richard had been joyfully received in Dublin. Hailed as 'Richard Plantagenet, Earl of Ulster', the extinguishing of his York title made no difference to Irish acceptance of him. He was protected by the Dublin Parliament from all royal attempts to arrest him; and a new coin was struck in his honour. Now all classes were rallying in arms to him and to his son.

BY THE MONTH OF MARCH, Warwick had sailed openly from Calais to confer with his uncle in Dublin. Hearing of this, Queen Margaret ordered young Somerset to redouble his efforts to win back the stronghold; but Somerset had no more success than previously against the remaining captains there, Richard of Salisbury, 'Little William' Fauconberg and Edward of March... Margaret also ordered the Duke of Exeter to take the remnants of the royal fleet to sea for the interception of Warwick on his return voyage. But, early in June, Warwick sailed contemptuously past young Exeter without even troubling to put about for a fight. 'Because—' as he explained later in Calais '—I did not wish to see damaged those vessels which I myself shall soon command.'

The Irish conference of the rebel leaders raised the Queen's apprehension to fever-heat. In Henry's name she issued orders for the guarding of the coasts from North Wales to Kent because she had no idea where the invasion would begin... Nor had anyone else in England – not even Cecily. All that was certain was that it would happen, overwhelmingly and soon. And that thousands of people would welcome invaders who brought Richard of York back to power. For the land was distracted and trade ruined by the reckless Queen who continued to court foreign aid – especially from England's most deadly enemies, Scotland and France. This was the sin for which she could not expect to be forgiven except that she committed it for the sake of her seven-year-old son...

On June 21st, warships from Calais tore a first gash in the south coast defences. Little William Fauconberg came ashore and was met by his kinsmen Archbishop Bourchier and Bishop Neville. Behind these prelates, the men of Kent began to rally...

Cecily was to remember that fourth week in June as a time of breathless waiting; the streets around her house shrill with rumour and alarm but the house itself quiet – tense until the midnight when its windows were shaken by the passing of royal messengers galloping through Southwark, to warn the King who was at Coventry: *the rebel Earls have landed – Salisbury, Warwick and March are coming up through Kent with a force of 2,000 men.*

The invasion had begun; and the Yorkists maintained a swift northwest march, pausing only at Canterbury to pay homage to Saint Thomas Becket.

On the morning of July 2nd, Cecily stood with her excited boys to watch the army – now more than doubled in size – go by towards London Bridge.

'There's my uncle of Salisbury!' George shouted, waving at the majestically ageing Earl who led his cavalry under a banner of Neville Saltires. The grey head turned. A gauntlet was raised in salute to Cecily.

'There's our cousin of Warwick,' Dickon breathed, his eyes fixed with awe on the tall thin man who'd become a legend of ferocity on land and sea... Warwick had a mighty following of foot-soldiers; the regulars displaying his cognisance of the Bear and Ragged Staff, white on scarlet, but the casual recruits who'd only joined him in Kent wearing roughly-made White Roses.

Following the Kentishmen were the Bishops Bourchier and Neville with the Papal Legate, Francesco Coppini, riding between them... Coppini had been sent to England by the Pope the previous year, to try to make peace between Lancaster and York; but, for some reason, Henry had refused to recognise him; whereupon he'd gone to Calais and joined the Yorkists – his presence among them doing much to bolster their position.

'Here comes our uncle of Fauconberg!' George was shrilling now; and Cecily watched her diminutive brother go past with his bastard son, Thomas, by his side. Together with the villainous-looking band of men following them, she knew they'd formed a pirate crew for the capture of many a ship... William had plunged into this dangerous career when the French wars had finally ended rather than return to his mad wife, Joan, in Skelton Castle again; he hadn't seen her since the day after Bishop Robert's funeral when he'd found her madder than ever...

Cecily strained to see beyond the corsairs towards the van of the army. There – surely that was a golden-haired rider taller than the rest? – he'd just taken his helm off and was waving it at the cheering crowds. She gripped Dickon's arm.

'Look, your brother Edward comes!'

Her throat grew tight with emotion as the young Earl of March drew nearer. He rode like a king – joyful in the bright nimbus of his youth and physical splendour. The crowd was cheering itself hoarse for very sight of him.

It was the happiest experience of Cecily's life when her son sprang from his saddle and came to embrace her for one brief, wonderful moment of reunion. Then he tousled the hair of George and Dickon before remounting and spurring towards the bridge.

Salisbury and Warwick were already there, demanding admission to the city… London had slammed her gates at the first news of the invasion but now it seemed that she was ready to receive the rebel Earls: the South Tower of the bridge was being unlocked – they were riding across the river, leading their men – the capital was theirs once they'd dislodged the Tower garrison!

When Cecily looked down again at Dickon, she saw that his thin cheeks were wet with tears from an emotion as intense as her own.

LEAVING Salisbury to besiege the Tower, the other leaders set off with the main force next morning to find the King.

On July 9th, they reached Northampton, where Henry was encamped in a loop of the River Nene between the de la Pré Abbey and the town. He had a force of only about 1,000 men (for the Queen had not yet joined him with her own army) but a formidable range of artillery pieces was visible through the spiked palisades of the camp…

In torrential rain, the Bishops went to the King with messages from the Earls. The Earls, they told him, were willing to make peace if the government of the country were given permanently into their hands, and if their attainders were reversed and their properties restored.

The Duke of Buckingham answered for Henry:

'You come not as Bishops for to treat for peace but as men of arms. I say the Earl of Warwick shall not enter the King's presence; and if he come, he shall die.'

…But it was Humphrey Stafford, Duke of Buckingham, who died in the next day's battle, when floods put the royal guns out of action. Victorious Yorkists found his body lying in the mud outside the tent where Henry knelt in prayer... With it were the bodies of John Talbot, mighty Shrewsbury's heir; of Lord Egremont, second son of Eleanor Percy; and of the Viscount Beaumont, Katherine Neville's third husband... Three hundred other Lancastrian lords, knights and esquires had also fallen – Warwick having ordered only the common soldiers to be spared.

The rain-swollen waters of the River Nene ran scarlet through Northampton town; and, scarlet still, they drove the mill-wheel of the Abbey.

CECILY SAW King Henry brought back to London – Warwick carrying the naked, pointless Sword of State before him... Henry's opaque eyes were focussed inward, unseeing of the honours which her kinsmen were careful to show him although he was virtually their prisoner – a docile, apathetic captive, still dazed with shock from the violent deaths he'd witnessed at Northampton.

Behind him on a draped cart followed the bodies of the four nobles who'd fallen while defending the royal tent... Cecily wept for Humphrey Stafford who'd saved her life at Ludlow. The Dukedom of Buckingham would now pass to his grandson – that brilliant child, Harry, who'd so fascinated Dickon at Penshurst...

The King was taken to the Bishop of London's house while the siege of the Tower continued. At last, the Tower was surrendered and its commander, Lord Scales, was allowed to go free. But he was murdered that night by bargemen on the river – his corpse cast up on the Southwark bank next morning... Cecily had the body taken to her house, to be decently prepared for burial. Looking down at it there, she remembered how this great lord had stood godfather for her firstborn son in Rouen eighteen years before. Now – thinking also of dead Buckingham and Beaumont, her brothers-in-law; of Egremont, her Percy nephew; and of noble young Talbot – she wondered how high the final toll of Yorkist victory must be. For the Queen had not been captured after the battle of Northampton; and, so long as she remained at large with her son, there could be no peace, no safety for the new order... Everything had happened so quickly that it wasn't even certain when news had reached Dublin. And no one was foolish enough to imagine that Margaret would remain idle while Richard of York marched back to power.

'She'll raise a bigger army,' Cecily said worriedly to Edward on one of his daily visits to her and the boys. 'You know what a talent she has for gathering men. Then she'll waylay your father when he lands in Wales – oh, when do you think he *will* land, Edward?'

'In his own good season, Mother,' Edward smiled. 'He's not as headstrong as Warwick, you know – Warwick had us all in Kent three months ahead of time! September was the planned invasion months, not June. But things happened to precipitate events. So we invaded without waiting for my sire.' Edward was gay and casual. And too much under Warwick's spell of easy success she was beginning to think. She wished Richard would return.

Everyone was prophesying now that York would be made Protector for life, or at least until the child-Prince reached maturity. Because Henry was only a cipher even if he did not collapse again. England needed a mature man by her King's side; a man experienced in foreign affairs – as Salisbury was not; and a soldier less reckless than Warwick... If only Edward of March were older! His mother regretted now the eight childless years of her marriage.

Yet she couldn't pretend that she wasn't enjoying this golden month of August which brought a visit every day from her favourite son, no matter how occupied he was. Edward had now taken over Baynard's Castle and filled it with his own soldiers. He'd wanted her to move back there; but she'd said she preferred to remain in Southwark until his father came. That was now the point of time on which all her plans were focused: *when Richard came home.*

The family would be complete again then. Edmund of Rutland would be by his father's side, as always. And Lady Agnes Croft had brought Elisabeth and Margaret safely to London a week ago, after ten months' wandering in the north with them... The only one missing would be Anne of Exeter. Anne had been in the Tower with Sir Thomas St Leger while her uncle of Salisbury was besieging it. Now no one knew where she and her lover had gone. The only certainty was that they would not have joined the Queen because Anne's husband was in Margaret's retinue – poor Henry Holland, Duke of Exeter; unsuccessful husband, rebel and admiral; now the dedicated champion of the fugitive Queen. He had been attainted after the battle of Northampton; and it was now rumoured that Anne was seeking to divorce him on the grounds that he was a traitor.

Cecily's worried thoughts on this subject were broken into by the sound of Edward's great laugh as he came up the stairs three at a time – trailed, as ever, by his adoring sisters and brothers... Everybody loved big, generous, handsome Edward. And – Cecily suspected – Edward was already an experienced lover of women... Arrangements would have to be made for a suitable marriage for him when Richard came home.

The golden giant strode into the room. She went

quickly to him and kissed him, then asked eagerly: 'What news from the council chamber today, my son?' Edward always brought news.

'Only that the King of Scots is dead,' he replied lightly. 'Queen Margaret's great champion has blown himself up with one of his own siege-guns at Roxborough! Serves him right for assaulting our northern marches.' Edward flung himself down on a bench and dangled his booted legs over the end. He still wore the functional clothes of a soldier and looked carelessly splendid in them. Old military garb had suddenly become fashionable in the city as a result.

But, for once, Cecily looked cold-eyed at her adored son. His youthful callousness had jarred upon her... She turned away to her prie-dieu to pray for the soul's repose of the Scottish monarch whose mother had been a Beaufort.

*The blood is thinning*, she thought as she prayed. How long to the final generation which mad Marion Watherwicke had cursed, that snowy day at Staindrop so long ago? The madwoman's words would always remain clear in Cecily's mind: 'Whore's blood of the bastard Beauforts! May their parents' passion be accursed in them! Even unto the final generation.'

Yet Cecily could smile at curses while her children were gathered about her. It was only in the lonely nights, waiting for Richard, that she became afraid of the Beaufort inheritance which she'd handed on to them.

This virile young man, Edward of March, sprawled at ease among her cushions – he had as much of Beaufort blood in him as he had of Plantagenet and Mortimer and Neville. And, all at once, she was cold with fear for him.

## 18

Autumn sunshine gilded crisp drifts of leaves as Cecily's chariot passed through Temple bar. She had left the children with Sir John Paston in his Temple lodgings where Edward would continue to visit them every day as he had done at Southwark.

The chariot, draped in blue velvet, was drawn by eight white horses – York colours that were repeated in the liveries of the escort. Cecily herself wore a cloth-of-silver gown under a dark blue broadcloth mantle lined with marten furs, and a magnificent jewelled headdress crowned her hair. But beneath the regal, straight-backed dignity which she maintained, she was hiding a pounding excitement: for she was going to meet Richard, who was nearing London at last after his long journey home from exile…

The cheering seemed louder in each successive town through which she passed. Slough and Maidenhead and Henley on the first day's travel. Then Nettlebed and Wallingford and Dorchester, all echoing to cries of 'York – York!' And at Abingdon the tumult was deafening because scouts had just galloped in to report that Duke Richard's banners were in sight along the Fyfield road.

Cecily retired alone to the hall of the market-house. From the height of this pillar-supported building she'd be able to watch the approach of her husband and son... As she hurried towards the west window of the hall, she could hear trumpets sounding in the distance. She gripped the sill and leaned out. The great banner of Richard's Earldom of Ulster was the first to come into view, its dragon ablaze against the evening sky. Then reared the Lion of March, and the Blue Boar which signified direct descent from King Edward the Third... A mighty force of men, wearing the York Fetterlock and White Rose, marched beneath these billowing emblems while their mounted officers clattered forward onto the cobbles of the market square. Among those officers, Cecily recognised many faces: from France – from Ireland – from Wales. Men who'd been in hiding, or in exile, for years. Men, like Sir William Oldhall, who'd been imprisoned and lost everything. They all looked grimly resolute now.

The horses were crowding one another on the cobbles – backing against the jostling townspeople and the pillars of the market house. Their riders were clearing a passage for the advance of a last huge banner.

Cecily saw the golden lions and lilies of the royal arms of England. She looked for the sign of difference upon them which a Duke must show when he rides apart from his sovereign. But these royal arms were being displayed without difference – *as for a king*—

The Irish Earl of Desmond was riding just forward of the two knightly supporters. Desmond was bearing a naked, unpointed sword upright. It was the Irish State Sword, which might be so borne in England only before the rightful sovereign.

Behind it rode Richard, Duke of York...

He raised his head as he drew near, and looked up at the west window of the market-house. A tight smile stretched his lips; but his eyes remained sombre under brows whose tense contraction altered his entire face.

He took off his helm and threw it to his squire. His hair was broadly streaked with white; and his moustaches, released from the chin-piece guards, showed totally white. He had aged by twenty years.

Dazedly, Cecily stepped back into the room away from the window. That man down there, claiming royal honours, seemed like a complete stranger to her: loyal Richard of York would never attempt the usurpation of his King's rights.

Now there were heavy footsteps on the stair; the scrape of a scabbard against stone; then Richard's voice saying to his attendants: 'Keep back awhile. I would speak in private with my lady.' And even his voice was changed: it rasped where once there had been a quiet sweetness.

She stood in the centre of the room and let him come to her. His hands closed hard about her shoulders. His mouth found hers in a long hungry kiss...

It was only in the kiss that she could recognise him then. But later – through the night while she lay beside him, listening to his desperate resolves – she found again the simplicity and the directness which had always been in him. And she knew that he was now a man caught up by fate. A man dominated by the very forces which he controlled.

He said quietly out of the dark: 'It was my officers who came to me at Hereford with the royal arms. After a while I gave up arguing. I agreed to ride to Westminster beneath the Lion and Lily banner – to claim the royal power for myself... It was what I had decided to do in any case, long since. The manner of it makes no odds.'

She said nothing. And, after a moment, he went on: 'In Christchurch of Dublin I begged God for guidance. And He put a memory into my mind... I recalled hearing, when first I went to Ireland eleven years ago, how the remote native tribes get their chieftains. A strong leader is not followed into power by his son if that son be a weakling, or stupid, or deformed. No: such a one is put aside and another kinsman made chieftain in his stead – *because it is not merely the blood, but the welfare of the tribe, that is accounted.*'

Richard had raised himself on one elbow. Cecily could feel him leaning earnestly towards her – his heartbeat strong and quick against her bare shoulder.

'Cis – can't you see – had we all not loved King Henry so much, we'd have deposed him long ago? He has never governed this realm. He never *will* govern it. And a Protectorate that can be terminated at his or Margaret's whim, is worse than useless: I am too wary to accept such precarious office again. So it must be the royal power for me. I shall demand it by right of service and of blood; but only for England's sake... Now tell me that I am right, Cis. Tell me that here is no selfish treason against the Lord Anointed.'

'I cannot tell you that, Richard,' she whispered. 'Only the lawyer-priests can say. And only your own peers can accept, or reject you.'

He fell silent and lay back, away from her. And she knew him wakeful until first cockcrow, when a restless sleep overcame him and she heard him mutter; 'In the act of usurpation is the murder of the King implicit?' She knew that her own father had spoken these words to him years ago at Raby; and that they had formed the background of nightmare for him ever since although he had shut them out of his waking mind.

By her husband's side, Cecily rode to Westminster on October 10th. Parliament was in session, the lords assembled; and it had been proclaimed that the attainders against all rebels were now reversed: she and Richard were once more Duke and Duchess of York. But would this Duke and Duchess yet be King and Queen of England, she wondered, as she watched the royal banner curl above them and the State Sword carried upright before?

Later, she was to hear many versions of what happened after Richard left her at Westminster Hall. But never from Richard himself. He never spoke of it after…

With his closest attendants he passed through the Hall and came into the House of Lords. All eyes turned towards him – there had been detailed news of his coming, and of the banner and the sword – but he looked at no one as he strode forward past his own accustomed place – straight to the dais where stood the empty throne.

He mounted the steps of the dais. Then, turning around to face the assembly, he put his hand upon the arm of the King's chair.

There was a terrible silence in the body of the House. Neither protest nor acclamation broke that silence around the isolated figure by the throne… Angry and defiant, York stared at his peers, willing them to accept the reality of what must be done. They stared back at him; startled; incredulous; and embarrassed by the choice which had been thrust too abruptly upon them.

The Archbishop of Canterbury walked to the dais and asked York if he wished to see the King. York considered this Bourchier brother-in-law of his for a long moment before replying:

'I know of no one in this realm who should not more

fitly come to me than I to him.' With that, he strode out, leaving the magnates to ponder his strange actions and stranger words...

It had been badly done: Richard was no diplomat. And both Salisbury and Warwick were angry with him for making his precipitate claim without prior consultation with themselves.

'Had we agreed to it at all,' Warwick said furiously, 'we would have handled it properly, through the lawyers. But now my uncle has outraged all the lords of the realm so I wash my hands of the whole affair.'

But Salisbury had regained his own composure. He waited for his heir to calm down and then said quietly:

'No, my son, you will never wash away your involvement with the royal claim of York. This past year, it has become your life's passion to further the interests of your cousin, Edward of March — is that not so? For you love him as the boy whom you yourself have failed to sire. And you have hopes of ruling him because he is easy-going, pleasure-loving: so you will continue to back the man whose heir March is... But as for myself — well, I have been a friend to York since he was brought, a little orphan boy, to Raby Castle in the year of Agincourt. By now I can allow him some blunders...'

THROUGH THE CONFUSED days which followed, Cecily lived at Baynard's Castle... At least Richard was calm now, and conferring with his lawyers; but she would never forget his explosion of violence after his rejection by the lords. He'd led his men to the Palace of Westminster and made them force an entry into the royal apartments there. Fortunately, the King had not been in residence and Richard had left after walking swiftly through the rooms. But the whole strained episode had been a sign that Richard's lifelong defences against the destructive and reckless rages of the Plantagenets were beginning to crack.

Legally, matters were going around in circles. An irrefutable York claim to the throne had been drawn up, based on double descent from King Edward the Third. This, Richard had presented to the House of Lords, and the lords had consulted Henry about it. Predictably, Henry had refused to hold any opinion: he'd dropped the problem back in his barons' laps, and the barons had called in the justices, the royal sergeants-at-law and the attorneys. These in their turn had stated the matter to be beyond their competence: the lords must decide what to do... Their eventual decision was to ask Henry to abdicate. They expected him to raise no difficulties...

As he replied to the delegation's request, Henry looked sadly at the Archbishop of Canterbury. 'I was born a King,' he said. 'I do not wish or enjoy Kingship. But what God imposes upon man, that he may not put away from him.'

From this stand Henry refused to move. But Richard was determined now to press the matter to a conclusion. He went again before the House which had so lately rejected him – and which, he knew, would reject him again and again because of one thing which he had overlooked the first time: almost every member of that House had renewed his Oath of Fealty to King Henry the previous November, after the 'Parliament of Devils'. No one would dare break this solemn oath although all now admitted York's claim to be sounder than Lancaster's.

'You swore to King Henry the Sixth,' Richard thundered from the dais, 'just as you swore to the Fifth and the Fourth Henrys. But was the Fourth not a usurper? Bolingbroke took by arms the throne to which my uncle Mortimer was heir. And then he based his legal claim on a proven lie—'

Lucidly, Richard went into the question of Harry Bolingbroke's lineage and exposed the fatal flaw which the House of Lancaster had always been at pains to hide: that Edmund Crouchback, its ancestor, had been only the second son of royal father and not his heir.

'The Fourth Henry,' Richard continued, 'was an unlawful ruler, *and he knew it*. Likewise his mighty son who fought as a lion in France – *he also knew the falseness of his position at home*. It was only the infant, coming to the royal dignity as King Henry the Sixth, who was innocent of this knowledge. But now the truth has been demonstrated, so that Henry of Lancaster and every man here must face one fact at least: that no lawful Parliament has been held in this realm for three-score years. Therefore, whatever was done at Coventry last November need bind no man's conscience. Nor need Henry of Lancaster feel himself called upon any longer to bear the royal burden for which he knows himself unfitted.'

Most of the lords were convinced by these arguments and they went again to Henry, begging him to retire quietly. But, when he still refused, York ordered that the King should not be harassed further.

'Let us find a new agreement,' Richard said wearily, 'before all our lives run out.'

THE AGREEMENT finally drawn up was that Henry should keep the Crown for life, with York as permanent Protector and undisputed heir to that crown: his eldest son, Edward of March, to succeed him.

The document was brought to Henry for signature. Unmoving, he looked at it a long while, then raised his mild gaze to the press of lords surrounding him... None of them – not even York – hated him: of that he was certain. Indeed, they were offering to let him live and die in a kingship which they acknowledged to be unlawful; and Henry was grateful for the offer because he did not know how to live as a common man and the idea of change terrified him. But what of his son – Margaret's son? A fugitive in the north with his mother, it was said. And, once this document was signed, a dispossessed outcast also. The Prince of Wales would never know what it was to be a king.

Henry's eyes filled with tears. He gazed pleadingly at the lords. But the lords hardened themselves against the love and the pity they all felt for him.

'Sire – your signature,' Norfolk prompted. And, obediently, Henry picked a quill out of the inkstand...

As it scratched over the parchment, he remembered how his royal grandsire of France had signed away his own Dauphin's birthright; and what years of blood and fire and murder had resulted from that one weak deed.

Sobbing aloud, he completed his signature.

## 19

Richard rode back to Baynard's Castle to tell Cecily what had been agreed with the King. A peaceful exhaustion weighted him down. He felt that everything was settled for the best – that he'd been too old anyhow for crowning and anointing. But Edward his heir would have these mystical honours one day, and without the spectre of a living Henry peering over his shoulder: Richard knew now that he himself could never have borne that. And he had no delusions about outliving Henry who was ten years his junior...

Still, a Protectorate assured for life meant that long-term plans could now be made. For a start, Edward must be rigorously trained for kingship.

'... So I have decided to send him at once to the Welsh marches,' Richard told Cecily. 'He can make Wigmore Castle his headquarters while he gathers troops to assist me in the north.'

*Wigmore*, Cecily thought uneasily, *that dark and secret place which I have always so disliked.* She recalled how the chapel windows were overgrown with ivy and hornbeam, making even the celebration of the Mass there a sinister act— But she must put such fancies out of her mind.

'When will you set out for the north, Richard?' she asked, picking up a ciborium cover she was gold-embroidering.

'As soon as possible, my love. Margaret and her ruffians have caused plenty of trouble there already, it seems – raiding our own estates and Salisbury's among other acts of violence. And God knows what she'll do when she hears that her son has lost the succession!'

Cecily kept her eyes on her needlework. 'It's what she always feared from you, Richard. So approach her warily now. She has many allies and you can't estimate the strength of her forces.' She visualised the Queen's army prowling the high wintry wastelands of the north. How many men might she have, under her commanders Northumberland, Exeter, Clifford, Westmorland-Neville? No one could even guess. And Richard was being so *casual* about marching to her defeat.

Putting the embroidery down, Cecily gripped her husband's arm and said with intense earnestness: 'I beg of you to wait for the troops which Edward will collect.' Thought of Margaret had long made her apprehensive. Now, a Margaret vicious with maternal outrage suddenly appeared as an inhuman creature – crouched and menacing.

~

Two days later – All Hallows' Eve – Edward was ready to set off for the Welsh marches. He was to repossess all Mortimer holdings there; raise an army from them; and try to stop Sir Jasper Tudor, Earl of Pembroke, and his old father, Sir Owain Tudor, from joining Queen Margaret, as it was rumoured they had a mind to do.

It was a large enough programme, Cecily realised, for a young man not yet nineteen years of age. Yet, as she fussed unashamedly over his departure, she couldn't help slipping in irrelevant maternal injunctions like 'Be careful not to catch cold!' which sent him into roars of laughter.

'Oh, Edward, be serious.' She tugged the saddle-cloth straight beneath his stirrup where the spur had rucked it. 'You've never been alone on campaign before and—'

'*Alone*, Mother?' He made a sweeping gesture with his arms around the courtyard of Baynard's Castle which was crammed with mounted members of his escort; and close to his own mount's haunches on each side was his troop-chaplain, Dr John Stillington, and his henchman, Sir William Hastings; the latter young man having been released by Salisbury from his Middleham household in order that Edward might have a companion near his own age and temperament to serve him. Hastings was gay and handsome…

'Alone *in command*,' Cecily corrected severely. 'For the first time in your life, Edward, you have neither tutors nor senior officers to tell you what to do. So I shall tell you one thing at least: keep clear of the Talbots of Shrewsbury… For all that Lady Talbot was once my good friend, she's not likely to forget that her son died at Yorkist hands last summer, at Northampton, nor that her daughter was widowed in the same battle.'

'Her daughter?' An attentive stillness came over Edward in the saddle. 'You mean the formidable Lady Eleanor Butler?'

'I had not heard that she was formidable; merely learned and beautiful and virtuous – she has done much for Corpus Christi College. Still, with the blood of old John

Talbot in her veins, she's likely to be a fighter rather than a forgiver of enemies. Remember that all Yorkists will be the enemies of her widowhood, my son... Go now, and God ride with you.'

But Edward, who had been so anxious to get away a moment before, now reined his mount in tight.

'Mother, where does the Lady Eleanor live,' he asked, laughing, 'that I may avoid the place like the plague?'

'At Haughmond Abbey,' Cecily replied unwillingly. She would have evaded the question if she could. For Haughmond Abbey was only two miles through the woods from Wigmore's gates. And she had observed her son closely enough these past few months to realise that he had a reckless passion for women; preferably married women, or widows...

She watched him ride out into Thames Street and was comforted only by the fact that Dr Stillington was with him, as chaplain and confessor. That wild young man, Hastings, would be no curb at all. But John Stillington was a discreet and sober cleric who would take care of Edward's soul.

George and Dickon came racing back from waving their farewells at the gate. She grasped their hands tightly. Soon, they'd be the only close male kin she had left in London; for Richard and Edmund were to set out shortly for the north, and were to be joined on the march by Salisbury from nearby Coldharbour House.

The sudden bleakness of spirit that assailed her at this prospect seemed to come on an icy wind from the river. The golden months of this year were over. Winter was almost here.

∽

A BLINDING sleet-storm rasped across the Thames and rattled the windows of Baynard's Castle. But, within, Christmas cheer still lingered among the berried evergreens that would remain on the walls until tomorrow, Twelfth Night, when their dryness would make a crackling fire as background to the last games and feastings.

Cecily's heart had not been in the Christmas celebrations this year although she'd done her best for the children... Her remaining menfolk had ridden off early in December, leaving Warwick to guard London. Since when, little had been heard of them except that they'd been attacked by the Queen's forces at Worksop on the 21$^{st}$ and had made a successful dash for Richard's castle of Sandal near Wakefield.

It was a strong castle, Cecily had been telling herself ever since. It should be able to withstand even a siege until Edward came up from Wigmore with reinforcements... Yet the Queen's attack had been a shock, for there'd been no warning that she'd left her northern lair – Margaret must have moved with the speed and stealth of a hunting tigress...

The Hall of Baynard's Castle was beginning to fill up for the evening meal at five. It was dark already as members of the household tramped in, bringing hailstones on their hoods, slush on their feet. They stood awkwardly about, whispering and muttering. There'd been rumour on the bone-chilling air all day, Cecily reflected uneasily. But no certainty. Only fear.

That fear clutched now at her own throat as she saw the bedraggled figure being helped in from the courtyard. It took her fully a minute to recognise it as that of Father Aspall – a chaplain who'd ridden with Richard's men.

At first the priest could not speak, he was near paralysed from the saturated cold of his garments. Cecily knew that no churchman rode in such desperate case without compelling reason, so she had him carried to the solar behind the dais where she ordered blankets and mulled wine to be brought. While she waited she rubbed his hands and face with towels, and so far loosened his numbed jaw that he was able to mutter something. She leaned closer, holding her breath...

Father Aspall said: 'Duke – Richard – is slain.'

She had no idea how long the blackness that engulfed her lasted. But when it cleared a little, and she could see the priest's eyes as pinpoints of light, she repeated blankly:

'Duke Richard is slain,' and saw the eyes blink away tears which she herself could not summon... After a long while she asked remotely, 'And his son, Edmund of Rutland?'

Father Aspall looked away; the movement a half-shake of the head on which sleet was thawing, sending rivulets of water down the gaunt cheeks.

'Slain too – the young Earl of Rutland.'

She wanted no details. She could take nothing in except that Edmund and his father were both dead. Though even this information remained apart from her conscious mind – she felt nothing. She even disbelieved the reality of the conversation until the priest fumbled from his habit folds the golden pyx which Richard had always worn about his neck – a wedding-day gift from herself, tooled with the Falcon, the Fetterlock and the Rose.

'When?' she asked, gripping the pyx.

The priest had begun to shake from head to foot. 'Th- the l-l-last d-day of the y-y-year—'

A week ago... For a whole week, her husband and her second son had been dead. And she had gone on living. Doing normal things as she was doing now – holding a mazer of wine against the chattering teeth of the priest until he had drunk deep...

She left Father Aspall with the page who'd brought the wine and wandered back into the Hall, groping her way like a blind woman.

The Hall was in a state of uproar. Strange, dripping figures stumbling in. Being helped towards the fire. Being plied with questions—

'What happened? *What happened?*' she heard one of her own servants bawling as he shook an exhausted man by the shoulders.

'... We were in the Castle of Sandal,' the man said dazedly. 'There was snow all about. More falling. Nine days we waited. Food getting short. So some of us went out to hunt. There was a Christmas truce, you see...'

'Where was the Queen's army?'

'Eh? Oh, it must have been all about us... Yes—' the man was less numbed now and able to speak more clearly, 'but when we saw a movement of men from the west, we thought it was Edward of March coming at least with reinforcements. It wasn't of course. He didn't come—'

'But the hunters were attacked, despite the truce?'

'Aye. All killed – except me. I got back and warned the Duke.'

'What did His Grace of York, God rest him, do?'

'He went up onto the ramparts. Scanned the countryside. But all he saw where the Queen's heralds approaching.'

'They brought offers of terms?'

'No. Only taunts. And their voices carried clear as their trumpets. We all heard them shouting, among other shameful things: *York, York, do you fear a woman still, even as you feared the Maid at Orléans?* At that, the Duke rushed back down into the courtyard – his face like none of us ever saw it before. He ordered every man to arms. The Earl of Salisbury tried to stop him – told him we were outnumbered and ought to wait for Edward of March. But the Duke was beside himself with rage. He swore he'd ride out, alone if necessary, to refute the Queen Margaret's charge of cowardice. So when it was clear that he meant to go, we all ranged ourselves around him... His son, Rutland, took up position on his left side and old Sir David Hall on his right – although Sir David had backed Salisbury's opinion that we should not attack. But the Duke had only cried to him: "Ah, Davy, Davy, have you loved me so long and would see me now dishonoured?" Before God, these were the last words any of us heard from great Richard of York—'

Cecily leaned against the dais curtain. She saw the narrator cover his face with his hands as he burst into tears. But still she could not weep, even with Richard's last words echoing through the tense stillness that had fallen on the Hall... *'Ah, Davy, Davy*—' Then he'd gone out to be butchered in the snow. And his eldest son had not come from Wigmore to save him...

She heard another man take up the tale:

'We charged down the slope from the gate. Before we even reached level ground we were set upon from all sides and our retreat cut off. Trees seemed to come alive: the Queen's treacherous men had been lying in wait... I saw Duke Richard fall; and, for a while after, Sir David standing astride his body; then Sir David went down... The Earls of Salisbury and Rutland fought on till there were scarce twenty of us to rally around them. At that, Salisbury ordered us all to flee however we might... I was with the young Earl of Rutland when his horse dropped under him. I turned – saw the boy on his knees in the snow. There was a knight leaning over him with couched lance. The knight was Lord Clifford. Rutland raised his hands: he had no weapon: he was pleading for mercy. But the knight drove the lance into his chest and shouted, "Thy Father slew mine and so do I slay thee." '

CECILY FELT the dry sobs tearing her body. She gripped the curtain so fiercely that it ripped from its hooks – the embroidered falcons and fetterlocks, within their garlands of white roses, crumpling at her feet. Everyone looked around, suddenly aware of her presence.

'My brother of Salisbury,' she choked, 'what of him? Tell me. For I must know all now.'

A soldier sank to his knees before her. 'Your Grace, the Earl was taken prisoner. He'll be safe for ransom—' But no sooner had this one glimmer of hope penetrated her despair than there was a further commotion at the end of the Hall and she saw her nephew of Warwick striding towards her, his face whitely set.

'Madame, I see you have heard the dread news,' he said tonelessly.

'Of my husband and my son, God help me, I have,' she replied. 'But there is hope for your father—?'

'No. He has been beheaded.'

This third catastrophe utterly crushed her. Sinking down at the table, she put her head on her arms while Warwick continued harshly:

'The Queen took his ransom money, and then had him

executed at Pontefract. On spikes above Micklegate Bar in York are heads hacked from three bodies: my father's, my uncle Richard's and my cousin Edmund's. On my uncle's brow is set a paper crown, mocking his claim to the royal dignity.'

Warwick walked up and down, his scabbard clattering against the table as he turned.

'Two other spikes of Micklegate remain untenanted as yet,' he went on grimly. 'By the Queen's order, they are to be kept for my own head and for that of Edward of March – who is now Duke of York and heir to the throne.'

## 20

Cecily had little time to mourn her dead. Margaret's great army was reported to be sweeping down from the north – tearing up whole villages in its path – killing – ravaging – burning.

A terrified London was preparing to resist entry by this murderous horde of which its commanders had lost control. And there was no sympathy anywhere in the south now for a Queen who'd given Berwick away to the Scots and who'd asked for guns to be mounted on French ships to sail against England.

But Cecily's sole concern was for the two sons of York still in her care – she had no knowledge of Edward's whereabouts – because she realised that they'd be in mortal danger if the Queen took London...

Through the frenzied city, she sent her stewards to the deep-water docks looking for a ship bound for the Low Countries. There would be few sailing in this weather, the very worst of the winter, but Warwick had allowed that his name be used to persuade some captain... It was a measure of Warwick's own fear of the Queen that he was permitting the boys to be sent out on such a perilous voyage: he knew as well as Cecily did that the whole cause of York was marked for destruction. Queen Margaret would show no mercy. And she was strong now, her victory at Sandal having brought her decisive help from Scotland and from France...

While she waited for the stewards' return, Cecily busied herself supervising the packing of warm clothing for the boys, and the sewing of money inside doublets and fur linings. There was no telling how long their resources would need to last – if indeed, they survived the voyage which she'd chosen for them in preference to Margaret's England.

There! – the last gold coin was slipped under a lambswool border and tacked all around. The coin was an angel; the only new one, apart from the half-angel, that had been struck during the present King's reign. Maybe the figure of St Michael on its face, and the cross-shaped mast of the ship on its reverse, would guard her precious sons.

She called them to her and sat with her arms about them; talking confidently to them; telling them how to behave in a foreign land... Both were still subdued from the shock of their bereavements. George had reacted hysterically and wept himself into an emotional emptiness, but Dickon had shown an extraordinary restraint in public – only his silence, and his indrawn brows and lips had revealed his intense grief. Though he must have wept in some hidden corner, for his eyelids were dark and swollen.

Cecily was careful not to let her voice falter; nor to admit that anything more than a boyish adventure was involved. But, while she talked, she was storing away every second of this last hour with her sons: remembering the feel of their childish bodies within her embrace – the indefinable scents of their hair and skin and clothing. She could not rid her mind of the idea that they were the 'final generation' of mad Marion's curse...

One of the stewards returned to say that all was arranged for a voyage to Bruges.

SHE WENT DOWN-RIVER with her sons in the castle barge. Her control of herself almost broke when the mid-channel water grew rougher. What would it be like in the open sea? Every wave seemed a threat to the boys. And there was a screaming wind around the northeast bend of the river beyond the Tower— She longed to turn and dash for home with them. But now her steward was pointing out a ship across the Narrows at Rotherhithe, and the barge master was steering for it while the oarsmen pulled...

An hour later, she was alone; the last farewell waved; the last glimpse of sail cut off by the loop of Millwall.

Chilled and empty, she went back to Baynard's Castle. Had her daughters Elisabeth and Margaret not been there, she'd have dropped the mask of faith and calmness then. But, at seventeen and fifteen years of age, the girls were pathetically dependent upon her in their bewildered grief. She could not fail them...

Elisabeth, always quiet, seemed to have been stricken dumb by the death of the brother who'd been nearest to her: some occupation must be found to take her out of herself. And the flashing vitality would have to be restored to Margaret's dark eyes – even though she'd been using it, of late, to flirt embarrassingly with every male in sight! Truly, a closer watch would need to be kept on Margaret's virtue—

Cecily submerged her own heartbreak in maternal and

domestic duties. With a great show of energy, she marshalled her daughters' aid for the feeding of the poor of Baynard's Castle Ward as food prices rocketed within the threatened city. The aged and infirm she brought to stay in the Castle, which was now double guarded at all points like every other foot of wall in London.

And, thus, everyone waited for the next news. The Queen's army had massacred an opposing force at Dunstable, and was now making for St Albans.

∽

WITH EVERY AVAILABLE man under arms, and the dazed King by his side, Warwick marched out through Aldersgate on the morning of February 15th.

The crowds who cheered him were buoyed up by hope at sight of the impressive artillery-pieces on the gun carriages, and the bright costumes of the Burgundian mercenaries who'd handle these complicated weapons. But Cecily, standing with the city dignitaries, wished that her nephew put less faith in such cumbersome defences: Richard used to say that guns slowed an army's progress, and were as like to kill their firers as their enemies…

She could think of Richard now with less acute pain. Under her mourning garments, she could even fondle without tears the golden pyx which was all she had of his from his last days of life – a tiny substitute for the unrecovered, headless corpse… But her son Edmund's death was still a throbbing wound: in him, she had lost not only a son, but the youthful image of his father. She mourned them both in him.

Yet she could thank God for other mercies. George and Dickon were now reliably reported safe in the city of Utrecht. And Edward had won a great battle near

Wigmore on the day after Candlemas – news of this had only reached London last night and she was still going over its details in her mind...

The Queen's Earls of Pembroke and Wiltshire had landed French troops in Wales. Edward – his Welsh army at last assembled – had thundered out from Wigmore Castle and made for Mortimer's Cross where the Lancastrians were reported to be. It was a morning of freezing fog; and, as he called his men about him for prayer before this first real battle of his life, he pointed at the sky where the sun was just beginning to show through the fog... By some strange alchemy of light on dazzling mist, three suns appeared – each so perfect a disc that reflection might not be told from reality.

'Be of good comfort, and dread not,' Edward had cried to his men, 'for this is the Sign of the Blessed Trinity. Therefore let us have a strong heart, and go forward with God against our enemies.'

And so they had done: killing 3000 Lancastrians at Mortimer's Cross and chasing as far as Hereford those who ran away.

The Earls of Pembroke and Wiltshire escaped. But Pembroke's father, old Sir Owain Tudor, was taken with seven other leaders to Hereford's marketplace for execution.

Cecily wished that Edward might have spared the old man who, in his handsome youth, had wooed the widow of King Henry the Fifth – there was little enough of such audacious romance left! But the Tudor had always been a troublemaker; so she supposed that Edward would have been foolish to give him freedom again for more intrigues with his son, Jasper of Pembroke, who was guardian-uncle to Margaret Beaufort's boy, Henry Tudor. Anyhow, the old man had gone to the block; but had kept one wily eye open for a pardon right up to the moment when the executioner had ripped the collar off his scarlet doublet. Only then had Sir Owain knelt down, saying philosophically:

'The head shall lie on the stock that was wont to lie in Queen Catherine's lap!' – and so took his death without further ado.

Now Edward was marching across from Hereford to join his forces with Warwick's against the Queen's.

TWO DAYS WENT TENSELY by without report... Cecily had formed a council of women for the care of London's poor in the event of siege, and this work had brought her once again into the company of her sisters Ann and Katherine. All three of them had now been widowed by the wars.

Ann was less flinty than Cecily had expected to find her; and Katherine even less altered than she'd dared hope; at well past sixty years of age, Katherine was still vital, striking-looking and interested in everyone's love affairs.

'Why, haven't you heard, Cis?' she gossiped now as they waited for other members of the council to arrive at the Hall of Baynard's Castle. 'As soon as Ann's year of mourning for Humphrey is over, she's to wed Lord Mountjoy! The handsome Walter began a discreet courtship of her – or of the Stafford fortune, I'm not sure which – last Martinmas. Since when, our Ann had blossomed like a flower in the sun. Ah, what a heartening thing it is to plan a new marriage!'

Cecily busied herself with some clothes-hampers which servants had brought into the Hall. She didn't know what to make of the odd look on Katherine's face. Surely this ageless sister of hers couldn't, herself, be planning to take another husband? Her fourth he would be! Yet anything was possible with Katherine.

'I hope Ann will be happy,' Cecily said dutifully. But Katherine snorted with derision: 'Ann is incapable of real happiness. It's *you* I was thinking of, Cis. You're the youngest of us all. And you've kept your looks. And you'll be enormously wealthy once the York estate is settled. You must have taken time to glance around by now——?'

Time, Cecily thought: six weeks – after thirty years of marriage! Even in six *years*, she doubted if she'd be 'glancing around'. But no use trying to explain to Katherine. She began sorting the children's outgrown clothing from the hampers for distribution to the poor.

Here was an under-tunic of Margaret's. It was pulled at the sleeve seams in front – lately, Margaret had been thrusting her young breasts out as noticeably as possible. And here were some leather-soled hose that must have belonged to George: they were too large in the feet, too broad in the legs, for Dickon to have worn.

'Isn't there *anyone* you'd like to wed?' Katherine pursued remorselessly. 'I mean, after a decent interval. When your life with Richard has become remote. As it will, I promise you.'

Cecily examined the yoke-piece of one of Dickon's shirts. It was splitting across the centre back. Dickon always used his arm and shoulder muscles far too vigorously in his tiltyard exercises…

'Kath,' she smiled, 'my life with Richard will become remote for me only when his children cease to need me. I left their bearing fairly late in life, so I'll be an old woman by then. Anyway, there's no man I could love now with my whole soul: that takes too long – too much of knowing. And I could not bed with one otherwise…' She knew that would not still be true had John Blaeburn lived; their souls had understood one another. But perhaps the years that had submerged her in childbearing and her husband's struggle for power would have killed, in any case, the feverish friendship with the tall archer.

There was a commotion in the street outside. A man shouted:

'Let me through. I must report to the Mayor.' But other voices were suddenly questioning; demanding to have full information first— *'Because our shops and houses will be in danger.'*

'Then board them up,' bellowed the first voice. 'Only let me pass, for the love of Christ, or the Queen will be on all our heels!'

Like wind-driven fire the news spread: Margaret had routed Warwick at St Albans and had regained possession of the King's person. Henry was reported to have laughed and sung to himself throughout the battle. It seemed that his mind might have collapsed again, so Margaret would now be supreme when she entered London with her rioting hordes.

'... We dare not refuse her admission,' the city fathers anguished. 'We have few fighting-men: she has many, and also the King's authority. Oh, she'll be at our gates as soon as she's finished looting St Albans and executing her prisoners!'

Details of these executions horrifically showed Margaret's training of her eight-year-old son; for she was reported to have asked him: 'What manner of death shall these knights, whom you see here, suffer?' And he to have promptly answered: 'Let them have their heads taken off.' Whereupon one of the condemned had cried out:

'May God destroy those who taught a little child this manner of speech.'

It was in terror of such ruthlessness that the

Common Council decided to surrender London. A deputation, headed by Ann, Dowager-Duchess of Buckingham, was sent to the Queen, offering her a peaceful entry if she would guarantee the good behaviour of her soldiers.

Ann of Buckingham took Jacquetta Woodville to St Albans with her. Jacquetta wished to recover the body of her son-in-law, John Grey, Lord Ferrers of Groby, one of the few Queen's men to have been slain. Lord Ferrers left Jacquetta's daughter, the gilt-haired Elizabeth Woodville, a widow with two small sons...

After some delay, Queen Margaret's reply to the Common Council was brought back, as from herself and the King:

'We have no mind to pillage the chief city and chamber of our realm.'

But could she control her men, Londoners wondered? Even some of her own captains seemed dubious about leading them into the capital. And the King was reported to be pleading with her to wait – *wait*. Meanwhile, fearful looting continued for leagues around the royal camp and details of atrocities flooded London. Every house and shop was now boarded up.

Still, the Mayor ordered the opening of the gates: 'We cannot refuse admission to our sovereigns.'

But the people refused. They would await deliverance, they plainly stated, by the Earl of Warwick and the new Duke of York, who must have joined forces by this time. The gates remained shut. Food trains being sent out to the royal army were attacked.

On February 27th, Warwick and York were within sight of London from the westward. They expected battle from Margaret's forces lying to the north. But no battle was possible because the royal army was now totally out of control – dispersed far and wide in its hunt for food, women and things to burn.

London threw open her gates to the Yorkists.

THAT NIGHT, in Baynard's Castle, there was urgent conference around Cecily's High Table.

'We can no longer pretend loyalty to Henry,' Warwick said. 'If we submit, Margaret will have us all executed. And if we do *not* submit, we have no choice except to proclaim our own new King at once.'

Cecily looked at the towering figure of her son, Edward. It was only six months since the crown had been flatly denied to his father by the lords.

'How can this be done?' she asked Warwick.

'By acclamation of the army and the London citizens,' her nephew replied. 'How say you, Edward?'

The younger man turned to his mother. He was very solemn for once; and, on his face, she read the question which she'd always known he must ask one day: 'Am I true heir of York and Plantagenet and Mortimer? Dare I be anointed with the sacred oil of kings?'

She thanked God that she'd kept faith with Richard long ago, in Rouen, when her whole nature had strained towards another man. For she could not have put a bastard on her country's throne. She thanked God also that her son, who was so careless and casual in many ways, should have enough respect for the royal dignity to worry lest a nameless archer's son take it upon himself.

As she nodded her head decisively, and smiled at Edward the confidence he needed for this irrevocable act, something in Warwick's gaze drew hers... Warwick's eyes were hard and bright and cruelly amused. In their sharp focus she read a memory, totally recalled from nineteen years previously... An autumn morning in Rouen. She and her nephew – then only a boy – riding towards the deserted house called Chantereine. The boy impatiently asking if he might ride on towards the city walls instead of going into the house with her. And her reply: 'Certainly you may go on the walls, nephew... But ask, if you please, a Captain Blaeburn to come to me here.' He must have so asked the captain of archers because Blaeburn had ridden at once to the deserted house where Cecily awaited him.

Now Warwick remembered – if indeed he had ever forgotten the incident or failed to associate it with subsequent scandal. But he was amused rather than perturbed at the doubt about the young Duke of York's legitimacy.

With shock, Cecily realised that Warwick simply did not care whether Edward were bastard or not. He would make him King because it suited his own policy; and because Edward was undoubtedly a Neville.

No other considerations weighed with Richard Neville, Earl of Warwick. He had no awed reverence of England's crown.

On Sunday morning, the first of March, in the wide fields outside Clerkenwell, citizens and soldiery were assembled. The Lord Chancellor – Warwick's brother, Bishop George Neville – demanded of them, 'Will you have Henry of Lancaster remain King over you?' 'Nay, nay,' they answered. 'Will you then have Edward, Duke of York?' And the roar of 'Yea!' carried into the city, with a thunder of hand-clapping and a beating of armour.

Three days later, in the Great Hall of William Rufus at Westminster, Cecily saw her eldest son seated upon the throne. He was dressed in royal robes. He held the sceptre. And he wore a cap of estate on his Neville-fair hair. All the lords present proclaimed him King of England...

But there could be no Coronation, everyone knew, until Edward had vanquished his enemies. Margaret, Henry and the Prince of Wales were known to be in the city of York, with bands of their reformed army patrolling as far south as Pontefract.

## 21

By dawn on Palm Sunday, March 29th, Edward and Warwick were positioning their 15,000 men in battle order near the Yorkshire village of Towton, where the Lancastrians were massed in a strength of 20,000. Among the Yorkists captains were Cecily's brothers William, Lord Fauconberg; George, Lord Latimer; and Thomas, Lord Willoughby. They had lately been joined by her nephews the Duke of Norfolk – Katherine's son – Thomas Neville of Middleham, and the Bastard of Salisbury; this latter a tall, shy man who had been fathered by the late Richard Neville in his bachelor days.

It was a deathly cold morning; an eye-watering wind rattling the banners, freezing men inside their armour. Now it was whistling snow from the north; lashing back the Yorkists at every step they tried to advance; blinding them… Hands grasping weapons were paralysed in an agony of cold. And the driving snow found chinks in armour where it lodged and froze.

Keeping Edward's tall figure in sight, on its great charger with the Arms of England saddle-cloth, billmen and archers stumbled into their places; mounted officers sat with tokens of white silk pinned to their shoulders for easy recognition by their own men in battle. All now respected Edward as a general as well as an uncrowned king, for he had saved the entire army at Ferrybridge when Clifford had attacked them there yesterday as they'd crossed the swollen river. 'Black Clifford', the slayer of young Rutland at Wakefield, would never draw sword again: he'd had his throat pierced by an arrow between helm and gorget. Looking down on his corpse, Edward had told his own followers that there was to be no quarter given in any future engagement with the enemy forces: leaders and common soldiers alike were to be killed. It was war to the death between Lancaster and York.

Snow was still falling heavily but it no longer blew in their faces.

'Wind's changed,' a north-country archer panted.

'Aye—' gasped his companion '—Lancastrians'll be getting it now. But whist! Here comes King Edward!'

He rode along the battle lines so that all might see, and know, their leader. As he rode, he exhorted his troops, declaring that any man afraid to fight could leave the field before the battle began; but, once it was joined, whoever turned his back on the cause of York would be killed and his slayer rewarded.

There was no movement in the ranks.

For a moment longer, Edward remained mounted, a giant figure in the swirling snow with his mantle billowing around him. Then, leaping suddenly to the ground and drawing his sword, he plunged the weapon into the horse's heart, killing the animal instantly.

'Mark you by this deed,' he shouted, 'that I will not forsake you in battle. I will be with you through victory – or death.' Then, on foot, he prepared to lead the first charge...

His decisive generalship was in marked contrast to that of King Henry, encamped upon the opposite ridge across the dale of Dinting. Henry had known, since yesterday, that Edward was bringing his force-marched troops across the river at Ferrybridge; but he'd refused to permit an attack upon the Yorkists who were at their most vulnerable just then. To the pious Henry, the Vigil of Palm Sunday was a great solemnity which should, he said, be spent in prayer rather than in bloody combat: the Lord would be more likely to grant victory to Lancaster on a secular day. So he stayed in his tent, telling his beads, while his army fretted in idleness, seeing its opportunity go by... But at last, this Palm Sunday morning, neither Margaret nor her captains would wait any longer. They were ready for battle: their centre, on the ridge, was under the commander-in-chief, Northumberland; their right wing, near the swollen Cock Beck, was under young Somerset and Exeter; and their left wing was strung out over the flat fields between the villages of Saxton and Towton and was commanded by the Earl of Devon and Lord Dacre. Northumberland was in a particularly strong position; for, to reach him, attackers would need to descend into the dale of Dinting and then climb again under a hail of arrows from above. But Edward and his kinsmen had already decided upon a plan, offered to them by the change in the snow-wind's direction.

They ordered their archers to fire one arrow apiece only and then drop quickly back out of range, so that the enemy should believe they were nearer than they actually were.

The plan worked. Peering blindly through the whirling curtain of snow, the Lancastrians fired volley after volley which fell short. When their fire ceased, the Yorkists gathered up the fallen shafts and returned them with deadly consequences for the Queen's forces.

But the Yorkists were still outnumbered and their position weak. A massive frontal assault on the Lancastrian centre failed. Northumberland's men came down upon them like an avalanche.

Now it was hand to hand fighting – men tearing at one another, hacking and slicing. Locked together, the armies struggled up and down the hill – the rattle of steel sharp above the shouting, and the soughing of the snow-heavy wind.

Twice, it seemed that the Yorkists were finished. But Edward and Warwick rallied their forces and led them back for another assault over the scarlet-splashed whiteness.

Norfolk had been holding their reserved troops. Now he brought them up and cut off the Queen's captain, young Somerset... Somerset retreated towards the flooded Cock Beck, his men dropping all along before Norfolk's onslaught. But still the main battle continued on the plateau – a muffled, heaving conflict of snow-caked figures, intent on each other's deaths.

The outcome was for many hours in doubt but the execution done by Edward's archers had given him an early advantage. This had greatly heightened the confidence of his entire army, which was already stimulated and encouraged by the sight of their young leader in the forefront of the fight.

King Henry was badgered into coming out of his tent at last to urge his own men to greater efforts, but after a few feeble admonitions he retired from the field altogether, accompanied by a few horsemen, and stood at a point from which he could watch the conflict in safety. This retirement, contrasting with the ferocious valour of Edward, took the heart out of the Lancastrians, who slowly gave way.

Yorkist victory became certain as twilight gathered, after the fighting had lasted ten hours. For miles around the battlefield, the snow was crimsoned, and the River Aire ran bright red.

In the swollen Cock Beck lay the bodies of Lancastrians drowned while fleeing: that of the Earl of Northumberland and the lords de Mauley, Wells, Dacre and hundreds more, including Sir Henry Stafford, another son of the unfortunate Buckinghams... On the battlefield itself were heaped 30,000 corpses, both Lancastrian and Yorkist. Among them lay Cecily's brother Thomas Lord Willoughby and her nephews Thomas Neville of Middleham and the Bastard of Salisbury – their death-stiffened limbs being patiently rubbed by her other brother, George Lord Latimer, now gone suddenly mad after years of mild oddity.

~

THROUGH THE GATHERING GLOOM, Edward and his remaining captains set their faces towards York. They hoped to capture the royal family there; put Margaret and her son into safe confinement and commit Henry to some monastery's care. But the three had fled northward, with Somerset and Exeter who had also escaped from the battlefield.

Parties of Yorkist horsemen were despatched at once to seek the fugitives. Messengers coming back reported that the hunt had almost closed in at Newcastle-upon-Tyne but had lost its quarry to Berwick. There, the royal family was awaiting safe conduct into Scotland.

Meanwhile, Edward entered the city of York with full

royal dignity on the morning after the battle of Towton. With his men – some riding, some marching – he passed in procession through the gates and along the narrow, snow-slushed streets, while priests and aldermen came out to greet him.

He looked up above the black arch of Micklegate to the ancient coping where night-torches still flare. In the raw light he saw the faces of his uncle, his brother, his father; their flesh perfectly preserved by the unbroken cold of this springtime of 1461; and the paper crown still in its mocking place on Richard Plantagenet's head.

'Take them down,' he ordered – his expression more murderous than it had been in the thick of battle. 'Place them in jewelled caskets and give them temporary burial with their bodies at Pontefract: they shall be brought home to a great tomb when I am crowned King. Meanwhile, the spikes are needed for other heads.' Then he ordered the executions of 42 Lancastrians brought prisoner from Towton.

WHEN NEWS of the Yorkist victory reached London, the city went wild with joy. On Easter Eve, a *Te Deum* was sung in Saint Paul's and in every parish church. Then preparations were put in hand for Edward's return to his capital for his Coronation.

With intense interest, Cecily followed reports of her son's progress. He'd left York city on April 16th and journeyed north and westward to receive tributes and oaths of allegiance from all classes of his subjects. Towns opened their gates to him and showered him with gifts. Magnates and clergy alike paid him homage. By the time he reached the midlands, on his way to London, he was the most universally popular king England had ever known.

On June 14th he rode through Cheapside to Saint Paul's amid fanfares of trumpets and the acclamation of thousands of people. Below the water-steps of Baynard's Castle, the gaily-decked royal barge waited to take him to Westminster Palace. It was clustered about on the sparkling river by hundreds of other barges belonging to knights and barons, churchmen and merchants. No name but Edward's was on anyone's lips. No eye looked elsewhere than at the new King – just twenty years of age, six feet three inches tall, and so fair and handsome and radiant that he seemed to have been cast in gold.

Cecily – who was to be known henceforward as Her Highness, the Princess of York – shared in her son's triumphal progress through the city. Her cup of happiness spilled over at every new token of affection for him by the people. And when she looked at him who was every inch a king, her happiness was fired by a passion of maternal pride which was obvious to everyone who saw her... 'Proud Cis' she was fondly dubbed by the crowds lining the streets and riverbanks.

She heard the nickname being tossed good-humouredly about. But she cared nothing for what the people called her, so long as they called Edward their King. Her pride, her happiness, was for him alone this unclouded June day. There had never been a more wonderful day in her entire life—

A breath of apprehension blew cool in her mind as the Palace of Westminster came into view beside the shimmering river. Everything was too wonderful: it could not last. Somewhere, the shadow that had dogged her entire life was lurking. *Somewhere close at hand.*

Tense with watchfulness she sat through the ceremonies

and the banquet at the Palace, where Edward was installed in the royal apartment as prelude to his Coronation at the end of the month.

Yet nothing untoward occurred; no rent appeared in the golden fabric of the day. And, by nightfall, she could smile at her fears as she stepped into her barge for return to Baynard's Castle. Tomorrow, and every day from now on, she would see Edward. He loved and honoured her, and had made her promise to be always his counsellor. The first thing she would counsel would be an early marriage for the bachelor King. Some wealthy and beautiful foreign princess perhaps, or a great English lady. In any case, a Queen-consort to match his own passion and give him lusty sons…

On arrival at Baynard's Castle, she felt suddenly very tired; so she bypassed the crowded Hall and, dismissing her attendants, went up alone to her solar in the South Tower. The candles were lit in the sconces there, illuminating all her treasures, and the shutters and casements of the oriel window were open, letting in the soft June night air. When she looked out, upriver, she could see that there was still a faint sunset glow behind brilliantly-lit Westminster Palace where Edward and his friends would be enjoying themselves until the early hours with the tireless vitality of youth. She smiled, thinking of him whose summer was beginning in such splendour; a summer which would never be ringed about with shadow as hers and Richard's had been.

Without warning, the apprehension of earlier in the day stirred again below the surface of her mind. How long could this present perfect state of affairs last? How long before restless Margaret of Anjou began to make trouble again, in Scotland or in France? Or before arrogant Warwick tried to tighten the screw of his control over

Edward? – Warwick, whom people were now calling 'the Kingmaker'...

Shivering, she leaned out to close the casement; and, in so doing, heard the sounds of a barge being moored below the castle. Presently, the guards at the water-gate were shouting their challenge to someone approaching up the river path; and a woman's voice carried clearly in reply on the still air:

'Margaret, Lady Talbot, Dowager-Countess of Shrewsbury, come to beg audience of Her Highness, the Princess Cecily of York.'

THE TWO WOMEN faced one another across the solar. It was twenty years since they had last met, in Rouen; and nearly ten years since Cecily had written her letter of condolence to the newly-widowed Countess, on the fall of great John Talbot at Castillon. Time, and the recent deaths of her son and son-in-law, had dealt hard with Margaret Talbot. She had become an old woman – wearied now to grey exhaustion by the latest demand upon her strength: a journey in haste from Shrewsbury to London...

'Madame—' Cecily could still not believe what the Dowager-Countess had just told her '—do you say that – the King – actually *wedded* your daughter – at Wigmore Castle last Christmas?'

'I do, Your Highness.'

'The Lady Eleanor Butler herself has told you this?'

'She has. No one else knows except the priest who performed the ceremony – Dr John Stillington, who rode to Wigmore with the Earl of March, as the King then was.'

*As the King then was*: an Earl who might likely take to

wife a childless young widow. But the Lord's Anointed was expected to wed a virgin consort.

Cecily held herself very still. 'There must have been witnesses to the ceremony,' she said. 'Else it would have been unlawful.' A guilty hope stirred in her that this had been merely seduction blessed by an irresponsible priest committed only to his lord's pleasure.

Margaret Talbot replied with sudden harshness: 'There were no witnesses by the bridegroom's order. And if the ceremony were unlawful, and the marriage be thereby invalid, then the child in my daughter's womb is a bastard.'

A child. Edward's child. Perhaps a son with great Talbot's qualities in him, waiting to be born to the splendid Neville King who must father a whole new royal line... One did not play with legal niceties in such case.

'How – how long until the lady's confinement?' she asked.

'September. The King must either acknowledge her as lawful consort before then or—'

'Has she asked him?'

'She has written to him on many occasions since he left her in January.'

January. Sweet God, so this dalliance was the real cause of Edward's delay in marching to his father's aid at Sandal. Were it not for the reckless passion of Beaufort blood in the son, the father might be yet alive... In a voice tightly controlled, Cecily asked: 'And has the King replied to the Lady Eleanor?'

'Once only,' Margaret Talbot sighed. 'From Stony Stratford at the end of last month, as he rode towards London. It was this letter which caused my daughter to break her obstinate silence. She wept, and talked of death, for herself and her infant. Because the King wrote coldly that he had no mind to mend his quarrel with her—'

'Quarrel?'

Margaret Talbot shrugged hopelessly. 'They – they disagreed about some trifle, Your Highness – as lovers will. My daughter is proud. She let him set out on his northward march without begging to be reconciled with him. They were equals in blood then and she would not kneel to him. But now—'

'Now he is the King,' Cecily said with slow-mounting anger, 'so John Talbot's daughter can at last humble herself before him, with hopes of being named his Queen. Is that the way of things, Madame? For, if it is, I know that the Lady Eleanor Butler has never loved my son for himself, without pride. She merely lusted for a young man's body and hid her sin under a cloak of meaningless ritual in Wigmore's chapel—'

'Not so, Your Highness,' Margaret Talbot cried sharply. 'It was the Earl of March who lusted after Eleanor Butler in her widow's garb. She had shut herself away from the world at Haughmond Abbey, meaning to take the veil there. But he laid siege to her heart and promised a marriage happier than her first had been. She went to him only after the priest's blessing. And she has kept her vow of silence to him ever since, expect to me her mother – even though tongues are beginning to wag at her pregnancy. Is this the action of a light and shallow-loving woman? *Or this?*' The Dowager-Countess thrust out a paper for Cecily to read.

She read slowly by the light of sinking candles...

*'I, Eleanor, daughter of John Talbot late Earl of Shrewsbury and widow of Thomas Lord Butler late Baron of Sudely, do hereby swear that the infant I carry, this year of Our Lord's Incarnation 1461, was sired by Edward, Earl of March, now Duke of York and sovereign King of England, after a form of marriage was pronounced over us by one Dr John Stillington in the chapel of Wigmore Castle. I*

*swear that I believed this marriage to be valid. But if it should be found to be invalid, by reason of witnesses lacking, and His Grace the King unwilling to make it lawful by full acknowledgement, I hereby undertake to give the King quittance of the contract he promised me on his word. Whatsoever form of Canon or secular law His Grace may call, to free him of obligation to me and to my child, I will neither question, defend nor struggle against in any manner. And if I be disowned, I will enter a nunnery, leaving my child to be fostered by others. To which pledge I, Eleanor Talbot Butler, put my hand this third day of June, in the first year of King Edward's reign.'*

Cecily read the document through twice. Then, unsteadily refolding it and putting it in her sleeve, she said gently to Margaret Talbot:

'Madame, I will speak privily to the King on this matter as soon as possible and will try to learn his intentions. God grant they may be to your noble daughter's most worthy honour.'

## 22

Edward had had a splendid morning in the city. He'd inspected the stands and decorations being put up for his Coronation. He'd welcomed home his two young brothers, George and Richard, from their six-month exile in the Low Countries. And he'd visited Shore's shop in Lombard Street to redeem the pledged jewellery of the House of York, and to approve the design of the new royal collar: a sequence of Suns and Roses on a broad double chain which was to take the place of the old Lancastrian 'S's... Everywhere he went, adoring multitudes followed him. And he'd never seen so many pretty girls and beautiful women in London before – they thronged windows and balconies – they jostled one another in the streets for a sight of him.

'Clearly Your Grace is the most eligible bachelor in Europe,' Sir William Hastings remarked as he strode along crowded Lombard Street by the King's side... Hastings had to shout above the excited cheering of the people who'd waited outside Shore's shop to follow Edward to Baynard's Castle.

The King gave his newly-created Chamberlain an odd sidelong look out of narrowed eyes. 'Would they love me so much, Will, if I were wedded?'

Hastings threw back his darkly handsome head to laugh aloud and to scan some upper balconies at the same time: the more luxurious and selective ladies kept themselves up there. ''Twould make no difference, Sire,' he answered, still glancing alertly upwards and from side to side. 'Your Grace is the hero of all men for your triumphs in battle. And women love what their eyes admire in the moment of seeing: they give no thought to their own, or others', wedlock... For instance, I doubt that old Shore's daughter-in-law even *remembered* she had a husband while you were on the premises.'

Edward bit his lip to stop a grin widening. 'I disremembered the fact also... Saints, Will, have you ever seen such a jewel among jewels? Pearl fair. And radiating a soft light in that dark room.'

The King's enthusiasm for Jane Shore startled William Hastings who had marked her for himself. He made haste to slant the conversation away from her. 'Your Grace prefers fair women to dark ones?'

'Aye. It is the white-gold kind that enliven my dreams! I imagine them, draped only in their own gilt tresses, waiting for me by an altar of black velvet.'

'That would be extravagant dreaming, Sire, for an ordinary man,' Hastings smiled. 'But for a king? – ah, surely not. For the luxuries of mere commoners are a king's necessities.'

'I rejoice that you understand that, Sir Chamberlain!' Edward shouted with laughter as he leapt to the horse his escort had trotted down Lombard Street to take him to Baynard's Castle.

CECILY HAD BEEN MUCH OCCUPIED by the return of her youngest sons, but nothing could put the matter of the King's marriage out of her mind. She must see Edward alone. Though that was not an easy thing, as she was beginning to discover: for he was always surrounded by courtiers, ambassadors, clerks, petitioners and hordes of unidentifiable hangers-on who followed his swift movements from place to place like a swarm of gnats. Also, he himself was restless and over-busy although Warwick was handling the main administration. And now the boys, returned startlingly grown-up from abroad, were longing for a private hour with the royal brother about whom all Europe was talking. Edward was coming to Baynard's Castle this midday specifically to see George and Dickon (whom he intended making Dukes of Clarence and Gloucester respectively) so that Cecily had scant hope of total privacy with her eldest son.

She had never known a man have such a talent for public living as Edward had displayed since his recent entry into London. Yesterday, he had eaten a meal by walking around the stalls of a market, picking up in his fingers whatever he wanted and talking to merchants and stall-holders at the same time! The common people adored him for this kind of behaviour; his guards and courtiers cursed him under their breaths; and his mother fretted for an opportunity to speak to him without having to broach a delicate matter abruptly.

The opportunity came that afternoon when she and George and Dickon went back to Westminster Palace with the royal party. In the drowsy heat, Edward took her to walk alone with him through the gardens to an arboured corner facing the river. There was a rustic seat and a table drawn up in the angle of a crumbling wall over which red and white roses cascaded; their shadows dark against the bleached stone; their perfume a quivering presence on the air... At the last moment, she almost drew back from intruding upon this idyll a subject which she knew must destroy it. But the subject had to be broached. As quietly as she could, she asked Edward his intentions concerning the Lady Eleanor Butler.

The sudden change in his manner was frightening. From the somnolent golden lion blinking in the sun, he sprang to enraged, hard-eyed attack: demanding to know what she had heard and from whom – the harsh choice of his words implying that he considered her guilty of spying upon him.

With careful calm, to keep her own lashing anger on leash, she told him of Margaret Talbot's visit. 'Is it true—' she concluded '—what the Dowager-Countess of Shrewsbury said?'

'Damn all Talbots,' Edward growled. 'And especially damned be the dark lady of Haughmond Abbey. Yes, I bedded her – she was willing enough. And if she bears me a child, she'll not be the first to do so. But I will not speak again with that proud and stiff-necked daughter of old Shrewsbury. Nor will I have her name mentioned in my presence.' They were standing facing one another now, royal mother and son: furious, passionate Nevilles with snapping blue eyes, and lips compressed into that obstinate straight line which young Dickon had made peculiarly his own.

'You will not order me, your mother, whose name to speak or be silent upon.' Cecily's voice was low – vibrant from the force of her breath.

'Madame, I am the King. Remember it.' He was

stretched menacingly towards her like the lion in his own coat of arms: the Lion of March.

'I do remember it, for that your noble sire had more right to the position than you have. Only when he looked for aid in his death-struggle, his son and heir was occupied with seduction.'

'God's blood, you shall not accuse me of letting my father die—'

'I do so accuse you.'

Their clenched hands met at the whitened knuckles along the back of the bench.

'Then, Madame—' Edward snarled '—I too accuse you: of infidelity to my sire. Why else am I so unlike all the other members of the family of York? Why else am I called "the archer's son"?'

She was shaking with rage and dismay for this destructive quarrel.

'Not for that,' she choked. 'I loved, but I disciplined myself. There was no dishonour, no infidelity. You were born of Richard Plantagenet's seed. You have grown up to resemble your Neville grandsire, Ralph, Earl of Westmorland. But you have the wild blood of Beaufort in you out of all proportion to the rest—'

She crumpled suddenly. 'Oh, Edward, Edward,' she cried, covering her face with her hands, 'I have a lifetime's knowledge of the power of physical love. For a man, no inner force is more intense – more unstoppable beyond a certain point: it has the strength of lunacy... For a woman, there is only one force greater: that of labour in childbirth which takes over her whole body – even her whole mind – to make her submit to its own conclusion... I am not censuring you for your love of the Lady Butler and your youthful impatience with restraint. But I am begging you to consider how a family must behave when it lays claim to great power and position as ours has done. The eyes of the world are upon it. It must harbour no guilty secrets for its own tormenting... I tell you that you were lawful born – that you may go in peace to your sacred anointing. But I implore that you take with you as Queen-consort the daughter of great John Talbot—'

'No.' His mouth closed like a trap.

'Then at least acknowledge that you formed a contract to wed her, so that that contract may be formally annulled. For, without annulment, any future marriage you make may be invalid and its offspring bastard-born. Edward, you are the King. You must have lawful issue.'

'I will give my Queen offspring enough in due course.' He linked his hands behind him and, with every appearance of restored calm, began to stroll back towards the Palace... Cecily watched him with a sense of rising panic: he was leaving her and nothing was resolved. Even the danger of the situation had not penetrated his consciousness— God, how complacent he was, how assured of his own power!

She swept after him. 'Edward—'

'Highness?' He waited for her. The casual expression on his set face had a streak of cruelty in it which she'd never noticed before; and she remembered, irrelevantly, that he'd put a Tower prisoner lately to an instrument called 'the brake' which had never been used since its invention early in King Henry's reign.

'Edward—' she drew alongside him but pretended not to notice his proffered arm '—about the Lady Butler's child: if it be a boy, and healthy, you would do well to acknowledge both him and his mother. Sons are not as light come by or reared as you appear to imagine. You know how many I have lost.'

'Oh yes, I've read old William Botoner's records...' He

quickened his step as he saw his Chamberlain and a group of his friends approaching from the Palace. 'But,' he went on, 'their litany of infant death does not alter my mind. I will not take Shrewsbury's daughter to wife. Nor will I have the Wigmore affair discussed by lawyer-priests. Stillington will hold his tongue. So will the Talbots. I'll see to it... And as for you, my mother, you shall remain first lady of the realm until I wed in good earnest. Be content with that – and silent on the other matter – and there will be peace between us.'

Exhausted, she admitted to herself that it was all she wanted: peace and friendship with her royal son. From henceforth, she would keep buried deep in her mind the reservations, the worries and regrets engendered by Edward's total rejection of Eleanor Butler.

No one could replant love where it had been torn out by pride. And yet – *and yet*— The letter of generous renunciation which a proud woman had written prickled inside her sleeve against the skin of her wrist... She had withheld knowledge of this letter from Edward until she knew she was finally beaten on the main issue. Now she took it out and pressed it into his hand: the document which told him how to gain complete freedom for only a little effort of admission before lawyers.

He was a grown man, soon to be crowned King of England. Surely he would act with responsibility towards the heirs of his splendid body...?

There was time for him to read the letter before the group of courtiers reached him but, after only an absent-minded glance at it, he thrust it into his gipsire. His whole attention was focused on the figure of a young woman among the courtiers.

As she drew nearer, Cecily recognised the Lady Elisabeth Lucy – a fair and slender girl with whom a betrothal to Edward had once been discussed; but, like many another such marriage project for the heir of York, this one had fallen through, though the young couple still remained very friendly. Seeing the lady's face now in brilliant sunshine, Cecily became aware of a peculiarly drawn look about the eyes which were fixed proprietorially upon Edward.

Sighing, she realised that the Lady Elisabeth Lucy's figure would not be slim for much longer. Another royal bastard was in the making. Blood of God, when would Edward learn that youthful squandering meant penury in old age?

Courtiers flocked around, chattering and laughing – the vivid colours of their clothing and the brilliance of their jewellery intensified by the sunshine on the white gravel path leading to the Palace.

Cecily was asking Sir William Hastings how his wife (one of her own Neville nieces) was when she became conscious of the swift, harsh-sounding footsteps on the gravel. She looked up. Warwick was coming – his tall lean figure seeming like a knife intent on cutting a straight path to the King.

'Sire,' Warwick said urgently – almost pushing the Lady Lucy from Edward's side '—news has come from the north: Margaret of Anjou has crossed the marches with a strong force and is threatening Carlisle.'

Indolence dropped from Edward like a cloak. He became at once the alert soldier, ready to ride out. But Warwick said: 'No. It would be unwise to postpone the Coronation. By your leave, I shall handle matters.'

Edward relaxed, and drew the Lady Lucy again close. 'Do so, cousin,' he smiled, 'by whatever means you consider best.'

'Aye. Your Grace be thanked…' Warwick's hard

humourless face remained close to the King's for a moment more – they were of equal height; though Warwick could seem taller when he wore the black-plumed war helm that had rubbed away the fringe of copper hair over his forehead – then the lord whom people called 'the Kingmaker' turned sharply on his heel and – sending up little spurts of gravel – strode back to Westminster Palace. From there, he would 'handle matters' without any further reference to Edward's authority.

The asking, Cecily knew, had been a mere formality. How long would it be before Edward realised that his cousin of Warwick was ruling England in his name? How long before he resented such Neville tutelage and took steps to free himself of it? It would be a mighty clash when it happened – more dangerous by far than her own quarrel with her son today. For Warwick would never compromise; would never accept that the apparently easy-going Lion of March could not be pushed.

Cecily shut her eyes against the splendour of the sun which Edward had adopted as his device with the white rose. Within her closed lids, the bright disc showed dark against a background of crimson.

THE CORONATION TOOK place on the 29<sup>th</sup> day of June... From the Tower where he had lodged for a while, Edward came to Westminster Abbey, escorted by 32 knights who wore pieces of white silk over their shoulders in memory of the great victory of Towton... A *Te Deum* was sung; then the new King was anointed by the Archbishops of Canterbury and of York before the High Altar. Afterwards, sitting in the chair of Saint Edward the Confessor and holding the royal sceptre, he received Saint Edward's Crown upon his head.

Under a canopy of cloth of gold carried by the Wardens of the Cinque Ports, the crowned King led the procession to Westminster Hall for the Coronation banquet.

Following close behind her son in this procession, Cecily was aware of having the highest place of any woman in the realm. Yet she would gladly have given it up to a Queen-consort of Edward's choosing.

Still, for this one glorious June day, the King's mother determined not to worry about anything. Either about the consequences of the Wigmore ceremony; or about Margaret of Anjou's ravagings in the north; or about Warwick's obvious intention to rule England. The shadow of all these things was as much in the future as was the maturity of young George and Dickon; walking behind their royal brother now – out of the shadowed Abbey – into the brilliant June sunshine that greeted the new reign. Two boys who were to be created this day Dukes of Clarence and Gloucester...

Cecily tucked her Book of Hours under her arm. In the moment of Edward's crowning she had opened it at the place where rested the white primrose which Richard had picked for her at Raby on their betrothal morning.

'See, beloved—' she had spoken to her dead husband in her mind '—the fulfilment of your dream of kingship.'

Tonight, she would go alone to Richard's memorial catafalque in St Paul's. And, in that aloneness, would count the bitter price of the dream – a dream which she feared was not yet fully paid, either in tears or in blood.

# BRIEF BIBLIOGRAPHY

*A History of Ireland*, E. Curtis, Methuen, 1936.

*A History of Medieval Ireland*, A. J. Otway-Ruthven, Ernest Benn, 1968.

*The Fifteenth Century*, E. F. Jacob, Clarendon Press, 1961.

*The Yorkist Age*, Paul Murray Kendall, Allen & Unwin, 1962.

*Lancastrians, Yorkists and Henry VI*, S. B. Chrimes, Macmillan, 1964.

*The End of the House of Lancaster*, R. L. Storey, Barrie & Rockcliffe, 1966.

*England in the Later Middle Ages*, A. R. Myers, Penguin Books, 1952-1965.

*Margaret of Anjou, Queen of England*, J. J. Bagley, Herbert Jenkins, 1948.

*Later Medieval Europe*, D. Waley, Longmans, 1964.

*Henry the Sixth*;=, John Blacman's memoir, Cambridge University Press, 1919.

*English Costume of the Later Middle Ages*, Iris Brooke, A. & C. Black, 1956.

*Life of Margaret Beaufort, Countess of Richmond & Derby*,

*Mother of Henry VII*, Caroline A. Halstead, Smith, Elder & Co., 1839.

*The Castles and Abbeys of Yorkshire*, William Grainge, Whittaker, 1855.

*Survey of London*, John Stow, Dent (Everyman's Library), 1945 edition.

*London*, Arthur Mee, Hodder & Stoughton in *The King's England* series, 1937.

*England Before Elizabeth*, Helen Cam, Hutchinson University Lib., 1967, 3rd.

*Some Ancient Interests of Fotheringhay*, R. A. Muntz, 1958 (booklet on sale in Fotheringhay Church, Northamptonshire).

*The College of King Richard III, Middleham*, J. M. Melhuish, booklet issued by The Richard III Society.

*Lord of London, The Story of Jack Cade*, Eric Simons, F. Muller, 1963.

*The Life and Reign of Edward the Fourth*, Cora L. Scofield, Longmans, 1923.

*The Reign of Edward VI*, Eric N. Simons, F. Muller, 1966.

*Richard III*, Caroline A. Halstead, Longmans, 1844.

# READ ON FOR MORE OF CECILY'S STORY IN 'THE ROSE AT HARVEST END'

*London, England, 1461*

The handsome young heir of the House of York has wrested power from Lancaster, and is finally crowned King Edward the Fourth. Yet, amongst this triumph, Edward secretly marries the beautiful and scheming Elizabeth Woodville: an impoverished widow – and a rumoured witch. In a sea of shifting alliances, the Wars of the Roses continue, more ferocious than ever.

*The Rose at Harvest End* is the third book in Fairburn's renowned Roses Quartet, and features Cecily Neville, powerful matriarch of the House of York, as she tries to settle the passionate family conflicts that will decide England's fate.

# THE ROSE AT HARVEST END

*June, 1461*

The interior of St Paul's church was quiet, this last Sunday evening in June of 1461 – doubly quiet by contrast with the city's tumult all about, where crowds were celebrating the coronation of King Edward the Fourth.

It had been a splendid summer's day, hot sunshine and blue skies. Now the light was fading so that only the high clerestory windows retained their outline. Lower down, there was a blurring of the Norman nave and choir and transept; a massing of shadows in the side chapels except where a pool of candlelight, yellow-gold in the greyness, lapped out from before the Lady Altar. Eighty pounds of wax burned there around a memorial catafalque whose draping cloths were powdered with the White Rose, emblem of York, and the Golden Sun that was the emblem of the new King.

The catafalque commemorated the King's father, Richard, Duke of York, slain six months ago near Wakefield by Lancastrian troops. It did not contain his body:

that was still in a temporary tomb at Pontefract – the severed head, recovered from a spike of Micklegate, sewn back onto the powerful neck. Richard of York might have worn the crown of England if only he'd outlived the Lancastrian Henry the Sixth.

Richard's widow, Cecily Neville, was kneeling by the catafalque. She wore a black silk mantle that curved like wings from her shoulders and covered her feet. The mantle had an upright collar, gold fastened, but no hood: hoods were quite out of fashion this summer of delicate, soaring headdresses with veils floating from their steeple-points.

Cecily, Duchess of York, had always been a leader of fashion. This morning, at her son's coronation, she'd been one of the most striking-looking women in Westminster Abbey – tall and slim, her hair fair silvering now but her eyes still intensely blue, her skin flawless; and that vital warmth and courage which had carried her through life's turbulence so far, still irradiating her personality. In her youth, her beauty had brought her the popular title of 'Rose of Raby'. Today, at forty-six, she was amusedly aware of being more often referred to as 'proud Cis'.

Certainly she was proud. Of her great Neville family background. Of her Plantagenet children. But, most of all, of her position as first lady of the realm and councillor to her eldest son, King Edward, who'd been proclaimed in March and this day crowned. Yes, let everyone see the swelling maternal pride! But not the fear – *never* the fear that lay like a lance-tip throbbing in a hidden wound. At no time must she speak to anyone, except to Edward himself, of that. Although the King turned, coldly angry from her, every time she broached the subject of his marriage. It was the one disruptive element between them. Yet the one she had to introduce again and again into their conversations, to make him do what was right by sheer frequency of talking.

'Edward, this matter must be settled one way or the other. Else it will destroy both you and your children.'

Cecily could hear her own voice, threatening, pleading with her obstinate son, through all the weeks since the disturbing news had reached her: that Edward had secretly wedded the Lady Eleanor Butler in Wigmore castle's chapel last Christmastime. There had been no witnesses to the ceremony. But it had been conducted by a priest, Dr Robert Stillington; and the lady was now carrying the child of the union. Yet Edward would not acknowledge her, not even for the purpose of seeking an annulment of his contract with her. He maintained that the Wigmore ceremony had been a mere charade, to get a stiff-necked young widow to his bed when he'd been only Earl of March, not King of England. Now that he *was* King, he'd be hanged if he'd parade this little dalliance before priests and lawyers, to beg them for his freedom.

Freedom was his already, he'd argued. It was only the lady's word against his that they'd ever stood together before a consecrated altar. Stillington wouldn't talk: the good doctor valued his position too highly as Dean of St Martin's-le-Grand. If he were discreet, he might be given a bishopric one day.

So there was no one else who would chatter. Except the lady's mother, of course. Although *she'd* only heard of events second-hand.

'As you have also, madame,' Edward had growled at Cecily. 'I tell you, there was no legal marriage between myself and Eleanor Butler. We quarrelled within a few days – she was an insufferable woman, demanding and proud – and we parted with no arrangement to meet again… Anyhow, the snow was lightening by then so I rode with the Welsh levies to join my father.'

'You joined him too late, Edward! Because of this reckless lust of yours, he died unaided – great Richard of York who never failed a friend nor broke his marriage vows to me.'

Edward had gone white to the lips while his mother spoke and a curious stillness had come over his body, like a lion's in the instant before the spring.

'Madame, were you as faithful to him?' he'd asked softly then. 'Remember, I've grown up with the label of "the archer's son" about my neck.'

Her hand clenched to strike him. Not for her own honour questioned but for the memory of a tall archer who'd gone to his death rather than take his commander's wife. A little of Cecily's innermost being had died with John Blaeburn in France all those years ago. She'd been carrying the heir of York at the time. Her body was Duke Richard's but her soul was John Blaeburn's. People had noticed how she'd favoured Blaeburn. They'd talked. And so had commenced the rumour that the handsome child, Edward, had been sired by a captain of archers.

Cecily said quietly now to her husband's empty memorial:

'Richard, you know that if Edward had been conceived in sin and born with nothing of Plantagenet royal claim in him, I would not have allowed him to take the crown of England from King Henry. I would have spoken out – denounced my own blood rather than let the holy oil be desecrated. But what now, if he weds anew by demand of the lords and commons, without first gaining quittance of his contract with the Lady Eleanor Butler? His Queen-consort will be but his harlot; their offspring unlawful born, never to inherit the crown.'

She stared intently at the candle flames, as though listening rather than looking. Then the pointed headdress bowed a little, as in a nod of acquiescence... 'So I shall speak,' she whispered, 'if he will not, before any such new marriage can take place.'

There would be time. Royal alliances were always a long while in the arranging and none had even been suggested yet for the new King. Cecily would use the intervening months or years to prevail upon Edward to set his affairs in order. And, if he still would not do it of himself, then she would override him by going to the lawyer-bishops. He would thank her in the end although the action would certainly cause a serious breach between them. This would wound Cecily because she loved Edward more than any of her other five surviving children. But a flawed marriage in the new royal line must be avoided at whatever cost. For the House of York had enemies aplenty, both in England and abroad, who would use any weakness of Edward's position for an attempted recovery of the throne by Henry of Lancaster. And Henry's Queen would never relax her baleful stare at Edward – would never miss one opportunity to attack him through Scotland, where she was now living in exile, or through France. Margaret of Anjou was an implacable enemy; a deposed Queen defending a weak consort and a younger son. Cecily understood Margaret very well. She'd known her for nearly twenty years and their ambitions were alike: to see their sons on England's throne. It was a contest which Cecily had won but in whose victory she could never relax while Margaret lived.

She stretched out her hands now to her husband's catafalque and laid her forehead on its White Rose emblems.

'Richard, when you come into Christ's Kingdom, pray

for Edward. He is young yet – careless, arrogant and reckless. He has too much belief in his luck and his popularity; too little understanding of human feelings. But I beg that your spirit may guide him to maturity. For my own part, I now make a vow of lifelong widowhood, so that no other love may distract me from the care of all our children. I hereby swear, in this House of God and before the altar of the Virgin Mary, never to remarry – for the children's sakes.'

There, it was done: the hot blood of her life dammed behind a wall of promise, never to seek the answering pulse of other blood outside the family of York... Many men had desired to wed her since Richard's death. Her sister, Katherine of Norfolk, had repeatedly urged her to accept one of the proposals. And she had passion enough yet inside herself to be kept sleepless by it in a lonely bed. But she believed that the magnitude of her sacrifice would somehow save Edward; and with him, his brothers George and Richard, and his sisters Anne, Elisabeth and Margaret, from the full exactions of life.

If she lived only for them, her maturity buttressing their youth, they might grow strong and wise. In them, too, she could forget herself; retreat into unaccustomed obscurity while they moved in the blaze of public life. She could become utterly absorbed in those other beings who were still a part of her; their minds understood; their responses anticipated; and their confidences often enough received to make it believable that she was their friend...

Crossing herself, she got up from her knees. Her black mantle fluttered open at the front to uncover the magnificent gown she'd worn at the coronation banquet in Westminster Hall this afternoon. She'd promised Edward to return there again this evening, for the festivities which would go on past midnight. But suddenly, the peace of her own home in Blackfriars seemed more attractive, and she realised how much the great day had drained her energy.

To look her best, she must rest for tomorrow, St Peter's feast, which was going to be another long morning of ceremonial. The King would wear his crown again in Westminster Abbey, and would then progress to the Bishop of London's palace at Lambeth, where he would bestow titles on many of his friends and kinsfolk. Sir William Hastings would become Lord Hastings. Wizened little William, Lord Fauconberg – one of Cecily's brothers – would become Earl of Kent. While Henry Bourchier, the King's cousin on his father's side, would be the new Earl of Essex.

But Cecily's greatest interest in tomorrow's affairs lay in the fact that her second surviving son, George, aged twelve, was to be endowed with the estates and Dukedom of Clarence... She'd hoped that her youngest boy, Dickon, would have received *his* promised Dukedom of Gloucester tomorrow also. But the King had decided at the last moment to withhold this gift for a few months, to avoid upsetting George who was always prone to fits of jealousy – indeed, he'd not been over-pleased on Friday last, at the Tower, when his small brother had been knighted alongside him in the royal chapel there. George's light blue eyes had bored into Dickon's grey ones all through the following meal at the King's table, with a hostility which had riveted Cecily's attention.

Clearly, this Dublin-born son of hers (big and softly handsome in the gold-fair Neville mould) had no affection for the thin dark boy who'd first seen daylight at Fotheringhay Castle eight and a half years ago. Perhaps it was as well, their mother had thought as she'd left the Tower with a great company of blue-clad knights bound for the Abbey, that young Richard was soon to travel north. He was to begin his training-in-arms at Middleham Castle in Yorkshire, in the household of his mighty kinsman, the Earl of Warwick, who had steered Edward to the throne... George would remain here in London as part of the royal entourage. Then he'd journey to Wales with the King later in the summer.

Two of Cecily's household ladies were waiting for her outside St Paul's church. There were also six men-at-arms in the splendid livery of York, and four litter-attendants.

'I wish to return to Baynard's Castle,' she said to the sergeant-at-arms. 'Tell the barge master that I shall not be going to Westminster again tonight.'

'Yes, Your Grace.' He held the litter door open while her ladies unpinned her hennin so that she could get inside.

The litter set off on the short homeward journey, through throngs of people drinking and dancing and shouting 'God save Edward' in the streets, around the leaping bonfires of this coronation evening.

The entrance-yard of Baynard's Castle seemed very quiet by contrast. For a moment, Cecily wished she'd gone on to Westminster after all. She had a sudden sense of isolation; of retreat from a life whose centre she'd been for so long. Dear Lord, it was hard to accept the physical limitations of middle age and the essential loneliness of widowhood! For the first time, she fully understood how lost her own mother had still been, long after Earl Ralph's death. Once, as a girl, she wondered idly and dispassionately what it felt like. Now she knew.

Abruptly dismissing her attendants and not enquiring what visitors might be in the Hall, she turned in at the little private door from the court that led to her solar in the southwest tower. At the top of the steep circular stair, she opened the door into the twilit room. It was a moment before she became aware of the slight figure sitting by the flower-filled hearth. Then—

'Beth!' she cried. 'No one told me you were here. I thought you were remaining at Westminster with Anne and Meg.'

Her daughter Elisabeth, Duchess of Suffolk, ran forward and kissed her. Even in the half-light, Cecily could see the shadows under the wide eyes; and her heart contracted with guilt for the unhappy marriage into which this girl had been forced ten months ago. Beth had become just one more sacrifice to Yorkist ambition. She'd been given to John de la Pole, the wild young Duke of Suffolk simply to keep him quiet. John was a restless, quarrelsome, unpredictable youth; son of the once-powerful Duke who'd been executed at sea, and of Alice Chaucer who was yet most troublesomely alive...

Elisabeth said, with her nervous stammer which was growing more pronounced lately: 'I c-came b-b-back alone. I wanted to s-spend a little t-t-time here again where I used to be s-so happy.'

Cecily busied herself with wine-cups and a flagon. She knew there was no advice she could give her daughter other than to accept God's Will in the persons of an impossible husband and an overbearing mother-in-law, both of whom hated the House of York because York had deposed their Lancastrian King and Queen...

While Beth talked in a halting monologue of her domestic troubles – not least of which was her inability to become pregnant – Cecily was thinking:

*This is the second of my daughters to make a miserable marriage.* Her eldest girl, Anne, had deserted the Duke of Exeter when he'd sided with Lancaster against York; then she'd wedded an obscure lover while her child's lawful father still lived in exile abroad. *Sweet God* – Cecily added to her thoughts now – *let us do better for Meg!* Margaret was her youngest and the most beautiful of the York girls. She usually lived with her mother here in Baynard's Castle, and Cecily adored her.

'I m-must g-g-go now.' Beth stood up abruptly. 'J-John will be angry if I d-do not return s-soon to Westminster.'

Arrogant young John de la Pole, great-grandson of a merchant, liked to display his Plantagenet-Neville wife in public. Her presence by his side proclaimed to everyone that his loyalty had had to be bought by the House of York for the price of one of its daughters; and that York was still nervous of former supporters of Lancaster. These facts amused John. His amusement did not endear him to his brother-in-law, King Edward.

Cecily went down to the water-gate with Beth, and remained there to watch the ornate Suffolk barge until it was out of sight among the jostle of other craft on the river, where thousands of lanterns had been lit and the bonfires reflected themselves in the dark water. She was suddenly conscious of her own ultimate helplessness to aid any of her children. Their destinies had been marked out too long ago by the strife which had rent England for years, York against Lancaster. Now all their lives would have to be spent buttressing the Yorkist victory. They would move further and further from their mother's influence as they grew older. But Cecily's concern would remain with each one of them on all their journeys.

## ALSO BY ELEANOR FAIRBURN

THE WARS OF THE ROSES QUARTET:
*White Rose, Dark Summer*
*The Rose at Harvest End*
*Winter's Rose*

OTHER HISTORICAL FICTION:
*The Green Popinjays*
*The White Seahorse*
*The Golden Hive*
*Crowned Ermine*

WRITING AS CATHERINE CARFAX:
*A Silence With Voices*
*The Semper Inheritance*
*The Sleeping Salamander*
*To Die A Little*

WRITING AS EMMA GAYLE:
*Cousin Caroline*
*Frenchman's Harvest*

WRITING AS ELENA LYONS:
*The Haunting of Abbotsgarth*
*A Scent of Lilacs*

WRITING AS ANNA NEVILLE:
*The House of the Chestnut Trees*

Printed in Great Britain
by Amazon